The Gr

by Michael J Holley

Copyright © 2013 by Michael J Holley

All rights reserved. This book or any portion thereof, in both printed or electronic form, may not be reproduced or used in any manner whatsoever without the express written permission of the publisher except for the use of brief quotations in a book review.

All characters, organisations and locations appearing in this work are fictitious. Any resemblance to real persons, living or dead, is purely coincidental.

ISBN 978-0-9575842-2-8
Ebook ISBN 978-0-9575842-1-1

Cover illustration by Simon Raine
(thesimonraine@gmail.com)

First published in the United Kingdom in 2013 (1)

Beach Hut Publishing
Cowes
Isle of Wight

www.michaeljholley.com

To Sophie and Dylan, for giving me the reason.
To Claire, for giving me the time.
And especially to Piers, for giving me the inspiration.

XXX

The following account is based upon a true story which never happened.

All of the characters are as fictional as any character, in any book, created in the mind of the author as a fusion of past experience.

Some of the conversations in this book have been translated from Corporate to English to enable the reader to comprehend the meaning.

Act One

The Trap

'Nowadays most people die of a sort of creeping common sense, and discover when it is too late that the only things one never regrets are one's mistakes.'

- Oscar Wilde - The Picture of Dorian Gray, 1890

Chapter 1

It was as if for a moment the world had stopped turning upon its ancient axis. The leaves that had once swayed in the nearby trees now stood motionless as if they were made of rock. The water of the lake resembled a sheet of ice, and the reflected woodland behind was detailed perfectly upon its surface. The birds had nested, and for an inexplicable reason, nature appeared to have sensed the impending drama that was about to unfold.

Every office in the building was quiet, their inhabitants locked, as if under a spell. The collective breathing was the only betrayal of an otherwise perfect poise. In. Out. In. Out. The walls were breathing in the same regular rhythm. Thousands of people connected at the same level of consciousness, each of us preparing quietly on our own... and waiting.

The note had been sent, by email, only an hour ago and the mood had shifted from confusion, to disbelief, then excitement, fear, and now finally to stillness. The minute hand on the clock had moved around its familiar face as if it were being chased. As time sped by, everyone's attention was drawn to their own preparations, and their own routines of readiness.

I had checked my shoelaces ten times at least, and others could be seen stretching out hamstrings, groins, and even shoulders. As the deadline drew nearer though, only minutes away, the preparations were finally over.

The note had been the climax of a lengthy period of gossip and speculation. The company needed to shed some employees quickly, and nobody could say exactly how they were going to do it. There had been some wild rumours, as there always would be in such circumstances, of sending people away to sea and never being found again, or perhaps poisoning people indiscriminately in the staff canteen. Counter balancing these extreme suggestions were the views of the conservative contingent, who thought it more likely that you would have to queue to hear your fate and be judged on a merit basis by a member of the board, but others knew this would take too long and the company needed quick results.

The attention that the subject had commanded over the preceding weeks, before the coming of the note, was at saturation point. I had been unable to concentrate on anything else.

When the reality of the plan was announced just an hour ago, people exploded with emotion. Some were questioning the ethics of the decision or complaining that it was unfair; some were dancing and others were crying. It resembled a jamboree from all aspects of life. It was a melting pot of personalities and characters, ironically displayed for the first time, in most cases, in this sterile environment.

Older colleagues, and those that struggled to walk, were allowed to go home if they so desired, in order to avoid the battle. They had formally chosen to waive any rights they had to receive the redundancy payment and stay with the company. For those that had already left, their future was unfortunately secure, and a lifetime in employment would greet them on Monday morning.

But for those of us who had stayed; for those that had committed to the fight; for those that had chosen to create their own fate, the time was nearly upon us. I had seen the D-Day landings in the movies, and noticed that moment of calm, mixed with adrenaline, that was always presented as the camera panned around the faces in the landing crafts. I thought to myself how I, now, was involved in my very own D-Day, knowing that this moment could transform my life.

The note, as I looked at it once again on my screen, was very clear about the guidelines. There were 3,500 employees on the site, and the company had announced 1,000 redundancies. These redundancy notices had been enclosed within their own individual gold envelopes and hidden somewhere on the site. A buzzer would sound over the public address system and this would be the signal for people to start searching. Anyone who was seen moving away from their desk before the buzzer was sounded would be given an offer of employment and forced to come back on Monday.

Once the employee had found a gold envelope they then had to return to the security lodge, at the gate, and register the notice with their company pass. The redundancy would then be formalised legally and you would be free to go on a full package immediately. Announcements would be made over the same public address system as the envelopes were returned; they would announce the returns in hundreds at first and then in multiples of ten for the last hundred.

I had ensured that my shoes were on correctly, I had taken my coat off in order to give me more flexibility, and physically I could think of nothing more that could prepare me for the off. So I sat in my own office, silently staring at the wall, and visualising the gold envelope in my hand. My mind began to wander, as it tends to do, and I started to think how the others would react when the buzzer sounded; would people be respectful and civilised, as if queuing at an airport; or would they react like a greedy child on an Easter egg hunt? The announcement had definitely said that there were no rules in the obtaining of the envelopes, and if people agreed to take part, then once again they would waive their right to press charges afterwards - did this mean that literally, anything goes? It could turn in to The Somme out there. Survival of the fittest would be key. I was not a gym addict and so certainly not one of the strongest there, but I was definitely younger than most and always fancied my turn of pace. Would this be required?

But the confusion of my thoughts disappeared while my eyes were distractedly studying the imperfect plasterwork in the corner of the ceiling, because as I was doing this... the buzzer sounded.

Initially I froze, out of fear maybe, but was then brought back to life by the noise that erupted from all areas of the building. I could hear the chairs above being pushed backwards as the tenants of the office upstairs, Human Resources, made a beeline for the turnstiles. The doors along my corridor opened simultaneously as people charged to the nearest exit.

The slight delay actually helped me, as I was able to realise that I would be at the back of the queue to get out. There were only two turnstile exits near my office;

each would only let one through at a time. I hastily turned around and noticed the window that opened on to the courtyard area of grass that I had looked out upon for twelve years. In the summer months, I used to open my window fully in a vain attempt to flood my stuffy office with a breeze, but at that moment I opened it to launch myself out of.

I landed on the grass, as others could be seen taking the window route from other sides of the square, and together we looked like a confused SWAT team. I had no plan formed in my mind of where to start searching for the golden envelopes and so, for the sake of a better idea, I turned on my heel and headed for the small opening in the courtyard that exposed the rest of the site.

People were rushing past me in all directions and immediately one of my previous questions was answered, as I witnessed a lady in her fifties being thrown to the ground by a middle-aged professor. It was a scene of complete and utter carnage that I would not have believed possible unless I had been stuck in the middle of it. I noticed that more people were moving to my left and this seemed logical given that eighty per cent of the site opened up to the left. I joined them and started sprinting at full speed, trampling over the fallen, shoving and nudging those alongside me, with absolutely no idea where I was heading. The charge had taken us up the main site road, with some woodland on one side and a car park on the other.

I kept looking for the gold envelopes but in the rush it was impossible to really be that observant. In the back of my mind I thought that if I could get ahead of everybody else then at least I could be running into unexplored territory. But as the run continued, and my lungs began to ache, I noticed a whole group of other people charging towards us. They must have come from the buildings at the other end of the site. In my exhaustion, and temporarily defeated, I suddenly moved sharply to the right and stopped just away from the main thoroughfare, in the woodland, doubled over and gasping for oxygen.

I lifted my head up and watched the chaos of people that were running in every direction. There was no discernible pattern in their behaviour, and instead of joining them again, I slumped down on a nearby log and just stared at them. There had to be a strategy for this game and following the crowds was not working. I had to branch off on my own and explore the parts of the site that were not being crowded.

Just as I had resolved to make it over to the football pitches on the far side of the site, I heard a rustling in the leaves behind me and then a small woman appeared from a bush clasping a gold envelope. Her face was cut quite badly, as if from thorns, but there was a maniacal smile etched on to it. She seemed to have a limp and as she drew nearer I noticed that her clothes were torn too.

Chapter 2

'Is that an envelope?' I asked the woman with the torn blouse as she came nearer.

'Piss off, what do you think it is?' said the woman, quickly stuffing the normal letter-sized, metallic gold envelope into her bra.

'Ok, ok,' I said, automatically putting my hands up. 'I just wanted to know what one looked like, that's all.'

'Well, you know now don't you?' she barked as she pushed past me.

'Where was it?' I shouted after her.

'Up a tree,' she replied. 'Ask that lot,' she shouted, as she pointed at some more people that were appearing through the same opening in the leaves behind me.

There were two men in their late fifties, even early sixties, and one girl in her twenties. They all had cuts and scratches over them and they were each holding a different part of their body in pain.

'What happened?' I asked.

'That woman's a fucking animal,' one of the men spurted out, pointing at my new friend who was, by now,

disappearing into the crowds.

'Look at her though. She doesn't care now, does she?' replied the other man.

'What on earth have you been up to?' I asked.

'She pushed us out of a fucking tree, that's what,' fired back the first man angrily.

'I told you Roger,' said the second man. 'It's each man for himself, you've just got to get in there.'

'I was in there,' said the man who was apparently called Roger, 'I had my bloody hand on the thing, and then she came along and ripped it out. Pushed me out of the fucking tree, about ten feet I fell, right on to my bloody hip. I had an operation on this.'

'Alright,' said the other man. 'We've heard. You haven't shut up about it. Besides you fell right on top of me. I should be the one complaining, not you.'

'Well, you could've stopped her, couldn't you,' said Roger.

'I couldn't because you were on top of me and I was stuck in a load of thorns.'

'You two shouldn't have been up the pissing tree in the first place,' said the young girl, in quite a timid, high-pitched voice. 'I was already there. That was my envelope, not yours or yours. You two started shouting and then before I knew it you were climbing up after me. Out of order. Like you two need the thing anyway. It

would've sorted me right out, you two are nearly dead. You're both sick, just stop following me.' The girl stormed off.

'ATTENTION, THIS IS THE SECURITY GATE. 200 HAVE NOW BEEN FOUND! MAY I REMIND PEOPLE TO PLEASE TAKE CARE,' the security voice announced through the loudspeakers that were positioned all over the site.

'200?' said Roger. 'Bloody hell. Come on Colin, we've got to find some,' and with this they both ran off and joined the throng. The announcement had visibly increased the panic amongst the crowds.

I stared after them for a while and then my attention was taken back to the hole in the leaves from where they had come. It was surely a better idea to move in the direction of the woodlands and make my way through the grounds undercover. As I stood up and walked off, crouching through the gap in the trees, it dawned on me how rough and competitive this was becoming. I obviously knew that an awful lot of people wanted to leave the company, but I was surprised to see how desperate they all seemed. In less than fifteen minutes the entire able workforce had been overwhelmed with a primal instinct to kill or be killed. I continued to walk through the trees and resolved that I too would have to become primal to compete with them. I consciously turned up my other senses, those that lie dormant most of the time, like my hearing and my smell, and I became like an animal searching through the woods for his prey.

Visions of Rambo were swimming through my thoughts, and I was unsure whether it was this image, or my increased concentration on hearing and smelling that caused it, but I completely missed a big, pointy out branch that jabbed directly into my bicep. It ripped through the sleeve of my work shirt, which had suddenly begun to turn red. Still in character, I did not hesitate to pull the entire shirtsleeve off, and tie it around the wound to keep the blood in. My vanity then took the better of me, so I pulled the other sleeve off so that it matched. I tied this one around my wrist in case I needed it later and set off again looking for the elusive envelopes.

I heard Security announcements while I was in the woods for 300, 400, 500, and 600 envelopes found. Panic was beginning to set in. I was trying to keep calm and reassure myself, but I knew that I could be walking around in these woods for hours. There was just nothing there. The woodland was so dense that it was a struggle to push through it and, for all of the searching, the only thing that shined in this light was an inside out Doritos packet.

Doubts were beginning to creep in as I noticed that I had been walking around for forty-eight minutes on my own. I had started to think about the people distributing the envelopes in the first place, I wondered who they were? But one thing was for sure, ghosts they were not, so they must have left a trail. I looked down around my knees and considered that no one had disturbed this bed of thorns, sticks and shrubs for years. I quickened my pace, beginning to hurdle over any obstacles, attempting to reach the other side of this undergrowth as soon as possible.

Eventually I was confronted with, what seemed like, a wall of holly and through the foliage I could just make out a path on the other side. I decided to climb up over the top of it to try my luck somewhere else and clumsily flopped down on to the gravel below. I found myself next to the lake at the edge of the site; the lake was big enough to have covered six football pitches. In the middle of the lake was an island that was normally a kingfisher sanctuary and, as I looked across, the sunlight bounced off of the water in that exact moment and highlighted a shiny rectangular object in a tree. The tree was right in the middle of the island.

In my excitement, I immediately kicked off my shoes and was emptying my pockets when from nowhere I felt a sharp pain in my shins. I looked down to see a man mostly submerged in the water, holding on to some reeds in one hand and a big branch in the other. He had a Geography teacher's jacket on, the type with patches on the elbows, and he was at least fifty years old.

'Oi,' I screamed, half out of pain and half surprise. 'What do you think you're doing?'

'It's mine,' he whispered back at me, 'don't even think about it. I found it first.' His desperate eyes shifting nervously about.

'Why aren't you getting it then?' I asked. 'Go on. Why are you holding on to the side?'

'Oh, yeah, you'd love that? You'd love it if I had a fear of open water? That would make your day, I bet. Yeah, take advantage of old Roy, he'll be alright, he'll be fine. Yeah, well, you just try. I'm watching you. You just move on.' I could sense the frustration in his voice.

'What are you going do about it?' I asked, considering it to be quite reasonable. 'How do you think you're going to get across?'

'That's my problem, not yours. Just leave me alone.' The man looked so distressed he even had tears in his eyes. At first I thought they were caused by the water from the lake but then I realised he was definitely crying.

For a split second I wrestled with my conscience,

but then I was alarmed by a noise coming from along the path that sounded like a gang of banshees. I looked over my shoulder to see about fifteen men running at me and then I looked back to see the man in the water had already struggled away from the edge. Without any more hesitation I dived in, making full use of the racing dive that I had been taught as a kid. I passed the sad little man and, using my under-fourteen's winning freestyle stroke, I made it to the island in no time. I pulled myself ashore, and climbed the tree in bare feet, tearing them to shreds on the branches. My hand reached out and finally grasped the golden ticket and, with the elation of knowing that I was on my way, I jumped straight down to the ground in celebration.

After all of this excitement, I sat down on the edge of an upturned wooden rowing boat that had been left on the island and watched as the group of men kept running around the lake for their next victim. As my eyes drifted back across the lake I noticed that my rival, the man that had attempted to make it across, had turned around and was now lying on his back on the shore. It looked as though he was crying and for a moment I pondered the emotional consequence of redundancy. There was also a noise that I could hear, but it was not the sound of crying, it was another sound. It could only be faintly heard from here on the island.

But then I realised what it was.

'ATTENTION, THIS IS THE SECURITY GATE. 700 HAVE NOW BEEN FOUND. PLEASE MAKE SURE THAT IF YOU HAVE RECOVERED AN ENVELOPE, COULD YOU PLEASE MAKE IT BACK TO THE SECURITY GATE AS QUICKLY AS POSSIBLE. WE HAVE HEARD OF GROUPS ATTACKING PEOPLE AS THEY RETURN. CAN ANY INJURED PEOPLE PLEASE MAKE THEMSELVES KNOWN TO SECURITY SO THAT HELP CAN BE DEPLOYED. - THERE WILL BE A TEST OF THE FIRE ALARMS AT TEN O'CLOCK, I REPEAT THERE WILL BE A TEST OF THE FIRE ALARMS AT TEN O'CLOCK, THIS IS ONLY A DRILL. THANK YOU.'

I opened my eyes in confusion and realised I was sitting in my office. The announcement of the fire alarms had just woken me up and I stared at the notice board in front of me, disorientated and depressed. I checked my right bicep but it was still intact and my heart sank. It was Monday morning... and nothing had changed.

***

My name is Ben Jenkins, I am thirty-four years old, I have worked for RC for twelve years, and I am a Gemini - the star sign is not important. I started work as a junior accountant not long after leaving university. I initially took the job to pay the rent and keep me in the manner that I was accustomed to, which being twenty-two largely meant going out, drinking and playing bass guitar. At that age it is no surprise for you to learn that my dream was to be a rock star touring the world, regularly returning to my pile in the country and its guitar-shaped swimming pool. This would appear in hindsight to have been a little naïve, but at the time it meant everything in the world to me and the job, well... the job was just a means to an end.

Since then I have gradually fallen completely in to the great corporate trap. I now wear the same badges as my fellow prisoners; I have a mortgage, a wife, I have two-year-old twins, and just recently I have acquired a big black hole where I used to keep my dreams.

Everyday has become the same monotonous slog. I cannot remember the last meeting I attended where I cared about what was being discussed. The claws of the corporate machine had finally taken hold and pulled me in to the soulless pit beneath.

On my first day at RC I had sensed an overwhelming blandness coming from the walls. I simply assumed at the time that this must be what grown up work felt like and, in my innocence, I ploughed on. I have often noticed though, that the beige walls seem to rub off on the employees that work here and before too long they all start becoming bland clones of one another. Unique expression is frowned upon. Repetition of what happened before is the mantra that keeps the machine turning.

RC, or Rannheiser Components, is a large multinational company specialising in batteries and operating in every country of the world. They do not save people's lives, they do not make a difference to the third world, and it is not even an interesting subject matter. It was just batteries, and if the company never existed then people would just buy their batteries from someone else, but through the decades it had actually built itself up into a corporate empire.

My primary objective since that first day was to make sure that I did not become one of them. I am not a particularly extreme person, I do not dress very differently to anyone else, I do not sound very different, and I do not think radically different, but I do value the ability to express myself. Up until a certain point I deliberately attempted to act in the most authentic way I could in order to keep hold of my identity.

However, despite these best intentions, I was

miserable. My working life had become just an exercise in existence. The twelve years had taken their toll and I had even begun to behave corporately when not at work. If I ever caught myself mentioning a phrase like "heads up", when I was socialising with friends then I would want to take myself outside and administer a single shot to the head. I was frustrated that I had succumbed to this but I felt completely powerless in preventing it. This was the viciousness of the corporate trap. It lulls you in to its illusion of comfort and, as it seduces you with the easy money and the bonus schemes, you never notice the bars coming down over your head. By the time you have looked up... it is too late.

I desperately needed to get out in order to save my soul but the trap had taken all of my energy and replaced it with this beige apathy. I assumed that this was just how being a grown up was meant to feel, my father did it before me and his father before him. You were not meant to be happy, you were meant to be at work. This was how it was meant to be, so stop whinging and get on with it.

Chapter 3

Beep. A new entrant has joined the conference.

'This is going to be difficult,' the voice at the end of the line announced, 'What I...'

Beep. A new entrant has joined the conference.

'...would like you all to do is put your phones...'

Beep. A new entrant has joined the conference. Beep. A new entrant has joined the conference.

'...on mute. There are approximately two hundred and fifty attendees... '

Beep. A new entrant has joined the conference.

'...on this call, and background noise...'

Beep. A new entrant has joined the conference.

Beep. A new entrant has joined the conference. Beep. A new entrant has joined the conference.

'...makes this format almost unworkable. We have no choice though, as this is the only option we have available.'

Beep. A new entrant has joined the conference. Beep. A new entrant has joined the conference.

'I would like to add,' said another voice, much older than the first, 'that if anyone does...'

Beep. A new entrant has joined the conference.

'...have a question, can you please type it in...'

Beep. A new entrant has joined the conference. Beep. A new entrant has joined the conference. Beep. A new entrant has joined the conference.

'...an email and send it to Winston Marks. That way we keep the noise off the line and hopefully answer as much as we can.'

'Ok,' continued the first voice, 'We shall endeavour

to ignore these interruptions as new entrants are joining. Eventually they will desist.'

Beep.... has left the conference

Beep. A new entrant has joined the conference.

Eventually, the mechanical voice stopped interrupting as all of the attendees that were to arrive in the virtual meeting had done so.

'Ok, I would like to begin with a quick introduction. I'm Winston Marks and my role is as the employees' representative in this matter. We also have Harvey Laithwaite who is an RC senior lawyer in legal, and we also have with us an independent advisor from the union, whose name is Mark Williams. So, I would like to thank these gentlemen for giving up their time today and offering to help our cause. First of all I would like to read out the statement that has been sent to me and a few other senior leaders by the Board.

'It is understood that a movement has been initiated by some employees of Rannheiser Components concerning the amendments to Pensionable Pay. It is the understanding of the Board that the intention of this movement is to encourage industrial action with regard

to the recent developments to the Pension benefit provision.

Although it is accepted that such involvement is not illegal and is a right of all employees, we would like to issue a reminder. It is to all of our benefit to ensure that Rannheiser Components thrive and compete at the very highest level. In order to do so, employees must continue to perform their roles and responsibilities with the same care and attention.

Those employees that participate in this proposed industrial action will be assessed, in the light of the previous statement regarding the performance of role and responsibility, and any such involvement will be seen as unfavourable when discussing future prospects.

We are sure that we will all continue to work towards a better future for Rannheiser Components.

Yours sincerely, blah, blah, blah...'

Winston Marks paused for dramatic effect before continuing to address the invisible crowd.

'We must respond to this statement, ladies and gentlemen,' he began again, his voice deepening as the wind from his own importance filled his sails. 'We are well within our rights to lodge a formal petition regarding this matter and we must not be scared off by leadership attempting to drive us off course. We are united as the workers. Those that have joined the union have taken action and, although it sounds very small, it will bring us greater power. We cannot allow ourselves to be swayed or bullied. We have rights and we should defend those rights. We have …'

'Bark. Bark, bark, bark. Ruff, ruff, ruff, ruff, ruff. Bark, bark, bark,' came the sound of a dog barking over the telephone lines.

'Excuse me. Could you all put your phones on mute,' ordered Winston, rather impatiently. 'I must insist.'

'Oh, eh, sorry, oops,' came a high-pitched, embarrassed, older lady's voice. *'Sit down. Can they hear me? Click,'* as she finally found the mute button.

'Stupid fucking woman,' whispered Winston Marks on the end of the line thinking that he too was on mute.

'Winston!' interrupted Harvey Laithwaite quickly, 'Winston. Thank you, Winston '

Winston Marks suddenly realised his error of assuming that he was on mute.

'Uh, hum,' he said clearing his throat, 'I'm terribly sorry for any language that you may have heard. Can I please remind everyone to keep their phones on mute. Thank you.'

The suppressed sniggering on the other end of the muted lines was deafening in its silence. Winston Marks's face turned a bright, crimson red as he bravely attempted to struggle on.

'I would... I would like to remind everyone to please join the union, so that we can raise an official spesition... an official petition... against this unlawful change in our working conditions. We cannot do anything, I say, without the union's support, and we cannot access this support until we have over fifty percent of you, the affected workforce that is, signing up.'

'Are there any questions that have come through, Winston?' interrupted Harvey Laithwaite, attempting to save any further damage.

'Ah, yes, we actually do have one,' answered Winston in surprise, due to his panic he had forgotten to keep an eye on his emails. 'For the purpose of this I will keep your name anonymous. That goes for anyone else that has a question on their minds, please do not feel as though we are naming and shaming anyone by...'

'What's the question, Winston?' interrupted Harvey Laithwaite again.

'Ah, yes, sorry, yes, so it reads, *"What's the point of all of this? The board will have paid top drawer lawyers to be all over it, and every action they make is measured and from a position of confidence?"*,' the panel paused for a moment.

'Thank you for your direct question,' replied Harvey

Laithwaite, who had now decided to take the lead. 'We would like to express our honest opinion that we think that we do have a case. The enforced change to our legal contract of work is not fair and this will make a considerable change to our compensation. On these grounds we have every right to appeal. Are there any other questions?'

'There aren't any more on here,' answered a quieter Winston Marks.

'Well, I suggest we end the call,' said Harvey Laithwaite, 'as this is not the most suitable format for such a meeting but, due to the number of attendees on various sites, this was the only option available to us. Thank you very much for dialling in and we will communicate how we are to respond to this latest message from the board in due course.'

Beep.... has left the conference. Beep.... has left the conference. Beep.... has left the conference. Beep.... has left the conference. Beep.... has left the conference. Beep.... has left the conference.

The phone was slammed down and, in the office that he was borrowing for the purpose of the teleconference, Dave Turner frantically looked at me and then for something to throw. If he had been in his own house listening in, clearly like the stupid woman with the dog, then he would have had innumerable objects to launch in the safe knowledge that no one would witness his outburst. But as he was sat in a private office which was only segregated from the rest of the open-plan office by three sides of glass, albeit with a frosted stripe about four feet off the floor, it was slightly more of a challenge to vent his anger.

I was sat quietly opposite unable to offer any advice or suggestions. He looked around for a target. After brief consideration he opted for the pad and biro that were sitting in front of him on the table. In a petulant, three year old's manner, he put his hand on the offending items and slid them off the desk making them land three feet away on the corporate, patterned carpet. He immediately felt self-conscious and quickly moved to pick them up before anyone could see. Unsurprisingly, this did not provide the desired effect of calming him down and allowing him to enter into the holy state of nirvana. Instead, he now felt a little embarrassed because as he was getting up the attractive girl in the office, had just walked past and smiled. He jumped to the conclusion that she had probably just seen the whole non-macho affair and now had less respect for him than she had already. Dave nodded his farewell to me and then stomped back to his desk, carefully placing the pad and pen next to his keyboard before entering a frustrated reverie.

Dave Turner was probably my best friend at work. He was certainly the person that I had shared the most lunches, drinks, jokes, late night stumblings, and generally time with, since I had been there. He was in his mid-forties, his grey hair had developed from his perpetual worrying and he was one of the most loyal people I had ever met. Dave came from a long line of 'salt of the earth' workers. His father before him had been employed by the council his whole life, and he would impress upon his young child the virtues of getting a good job and keeping your head down.

Dave was an honest chip that had been toiled from this hard and proud old block. He had worked for Rannheiser Components for twenty-five years, it was pretty much the first job he ever had, and he had worked his way up to an enviable position in the company where he was now comfortable with both; the work and the money he received for it. He had no desire to ever play the corporate game that was necessary in order to navigate through the political minefield that would achieve the higher positions. His father's voice would continue to echo in his thoughts, "get a good job and keep your head down."

He was never happy with this situation but, then again, he was not that entirely unhappy either. Due to this outlook on life he had decided a long time ago to just turn up for the next ten to fifteen years, tread water, and retire as early as possible receiving the final salary pension that was part of his contract.

The previous meeting, however, had been the beginning of the predictable demise of the RC Revolution Against Pensions group. A month or so ago the board announced that they would take away the final salary pension clause, for those that had been promised it in their contract, and freeze the pension based upon the employees' current salary. It did not affect me because I came to the company too late, I just wanted to listen to what they had to say but unfortunately, for those like poor Dave, it meant that fifteen years worth of inflation and promotions would not be considered. He was relying on this pension to give him the feeling in retirement that he had been slightly rewarded for the years of his life that he had wasted in the RC machine.

Unfortunately the anger that Dave was experiencing at that moment was only in part down to the promised pension being taken away. The rest of his frustration was down to himself. It was easy to stay at RC, he was comfortable and the years went by without very much ever changing. But it only took a sudden shift like this to be reminded of the flaky foundations to which his future was built on. If RC could change the pension then what else could they change?

He came to the conclusion that, for now, it would be better to keep his head down and hope it would turn out alright in the end.

Chapter 4

Recently an outsourcing company had taken responsibility for the safe housekeeping of the car park, and the maintenance contract still had some teething issues. A large amount of snow had fallen through the night, so by the next morning the UK was experiencing the usual interruptions that follow a few inches of snow. At RC, the main site road had been cleared by the gritters but the car park itself was still covered. In the old days this would have meant someone with a spade, being shouted at in a little shed, but now it required a great deal more. Firstly, there was the phone call to a national call-centre, which in turn would then be redirected to a local help desk who would aim to get back to your call within two working days. A representative would then be sent out to view the breach in contract personally and stand in the middle of a defrosted car park scratching his head at what exactly was the problem in the first place.

I considered turning around and going home but I had just spent an hour getting there, and even I would have had trouble justifying that. Perhaps, if I had only been faced with a normal day at work it would have been more tempting, but I was planning to meet a friend for lunch who had been diagnosed with cancer.

I really wanted to see him, and more importantly to see how he was doing, so I slowly turned on to the snow. I thought it safer to follow the existing tyre tracks and eventually they led me right up to the precipice of an invisible space. I knew it was there somewhere because it was the same space I parked in everyday. After a bit of wheel-spinning, and over-revving, I managed to abandon the car close enough to the space to be satisfied and headed off in the direction of the office building trying not to slip over.

I walked inside the nearest turnstile and was unsurprisingly met with a ghost town. Most people had cleverly stayed at home and I immediately decided to copy them the next day.

I sat through a slow morning, mostly alone in my office, staring out at the tree that was covered in snow outside the window. I was lucky enough to have my own office. This was no reflection of my position but merely of good fortune. Project Eagle, which was the name of the internal project in which I was employed, had claimed office space away from the oppressive open-plan sections of the building where most people were. My office was only big enough for a desk, two chairs, and very little else, but it was enough.

All morning I had been thinking a lot about James, the friend that I was to see later on, and hoping that he had heard some good news since the last time that I had seen him. Six months ago he was told that he had cancer of the kidneys but since then it had spread into his lungs. He was undergoing an aggressive treatment of chemotherapy in an attempt to kill it off but all it was achieving was weakening him further. He received the treatment on a three-week cycle and so we had chosen to meet up during his strongest recovery week.

James had worked alongside Dave and another of our friends, Mark Wilkinson, for years and the three of them had always been great friends. I had come along a few years later and really just tagged along with them. Wilks was a no nonsense Yorkshireman, he was a big guy and known for his straight talking. He was always looking to wind someone up and that someone was usually me, although he had a way about him that meant that you never really minded. He was much more senior than either Dave, or myself, and this meant we saw less of him than we used to, but when we were all together we often had a laugh. Sadly though, you would not have thought that when the two of them appeared in my office just before lunchtime. The lunch was going to be difficult and none of us were really looking forward to it.

Wilks had a Range Rover and given the huge amount of snow on the roads we thought it best if he drove. The journey itself was not as treacherous as I thought it would be, but inside the car was where the real danger lie. Wilks was the same age as Dave and his music taste reflected his years. We were subjected to Genesis for the best part of forty-five minutes and this audio torture was only interrupted, briefly, by a conversation that we had about the number of small spaces that you could fit Phil Collins in to.

When we arrived at the country pub where we were supposed to be meeting James, I jumped down from the car and carefully checked my ears in case they were bleeding. My attention was distracted during this brief medical, allowing Wilks to come up from behind and shove me in the back. My shiny black office shoes acted as the perfect skis and I careered off down the hill eventually landing on the pavement ten feet away. I looked up to see Dave and Wilks, heartily congratulating each other, and walking in through the door leaving me to pick myself up and brush my coat off. I followed after them through the door shaking my head to myself.

James was one of life's true gentlemen. He was the

type of person who would never have a bad word to say about anybody else. He would be able to have a joke, often at his own expense, but he would always stop well short of it ever getting personal or ever offending anyone. He was six foot four and usually had the most unfortunate spiky hair, although today when I finally noticed the figure that he cut, sitting delicately in the corner of the pub, this description would not have helped anybody to find him. It appeared as though he had lost a foot in height and his unfortunate spiky hair had all but gone. Dave and Wilks had already said hello and were both stood next to him smirking at me. I put on a brave face and pretended that everything was normal.

'Alright, mate,' I said, as I went up to him with my hand outstretched. He shook it and looked longer than usual in my eyes.

'Hello,' he said coughing slightly. 'How are you?'

'Well, apart from these jokers I'm alright, cheers,' I said, unconsciously patting down my coat again. 'Anyway, more importantly, how are *you*?'

'Oh, you know. So - so,' he replied. He looked at me as if to say, *'do you really want me to tell you the truth?'* but knowing that I did not want to know the specific details of his chemotherapy, or the emergency blood pressure situation that he had last week, or the way that his young children cry every time they speak to him, he decided to leave it at that. I nodded in a way that hopefully looked understanding rather than dismissive and we all sat down at the table.

'What have they been up to now then?' he asked me, suspiciously glancing his eyes at Dave and Wilks who were still grinning at each other.

'Just the usual hilarious, high jinks,' I answered. 'They thought it would be funny to push me over outside.'

'You should've seen it,' said Dave. 'He went arse over tit and skidded halfway down the pavement.'

'Brilliant,' agreed Wilks. James smiled.

'Very grown up,' I smiled back. 'I've just had to dust myself off outside.'

'I didn't think you were allowed to do that round here,' laughed Dave. 'You best be careful, James'll be getting the Neighbourhood Watch coming round his house.'

The three of them were all laughing and I joined in. 'It was these bloody shoes, James,' I smiled, 'that was the problem.' Given the tension of the situation I did not mind taking the hits, as long as it would help ease the atmosphere. James appreciated it as well, I think, and he started properly laughing but then the laugh turned into a cough, and then the cough turned into a choke, and then this resulted in him coughing up some blood into a handkerchief. Dave, Wilks and I just sat watching him, and after thirty-seconds he was back with us, only to raise his eyebrows as if to say, *'this is what it's like'*.

He still had a relatively good appetite, and during his gammon, egg and chips he explained to us about the three week cycles. He told us that he would have the treatment one week, then he would feel like shit for a week, and then he would gradually get better before going through it all again. We passed the time keeping him up-to-date with some of the gossip from work, and some of the usual in-jokes that would come out whenever we were together. We talked and talked about nothing in particular.

The three of us did a good job of keeping the conversation going with laughter and mickey-taking. I was aware that James was not involved as much as he would normally have been but he did seem to enjoy the fact that we were there. He was looking across the table at us, as a fond uncle would look at his young nephews, but a darkness and foreboding could be seen in his eyes. We had all noticed it and after we had entertained him for the best part of an hour, he then grew very tired and looked restless.

We told him that we probably should be getting back to work and I stood up to go to the toilet before we left.

When I came out the jokers were at it again. They were nowhere to be seen so I ended up having to walk right around the inside, and the outside, of the pub before I finally found them on the pavement giggling again like schoolboys. I looked around for James and could just make him out, shuffling slowly away up a hill in the icy grey, with his woolly hat pulled down and his scarf pulled up. I did not know at the time, but this would be the last glimpse I was ever to see of James.

Chapter 5

The situation that James was in had been playing on my mind for the remainder of the day. I decided to leave early and spend some time with the kids for a change before they went to bed. Seeing James had forced me to take a look at my own life and put things in to perspective. I spent a couple of hours playing on the floor with them and doing the kind of things that I could never remember my own Dad doing with me. Not that he was ever reluctant to do them but in those days you stayed at work until you were meant to go home. Maybe my lot in life was not so bad after all, at least I was able to work a bit flexibly when I needed to.

After the kids had gone to bed, I walked back downstairs and stood like a dummy in the middle of the kitchen. I sighed as if I had the weight of the world on my shoulders. My wife, Jane, was in the kitchen making a chicken pie that always cheered me up but tonight not even the thought of that worked. I had known Jane for fifteen years and apart from being my wife, she was my best friend too. I had never said that to her because it sounds pretty corny but if you spend most of your life with someone, telling them absolutely everything, then they soon assume that role.

She was a lot shorter than me, with dark brown hair and beautiful brown eyes. She had initially trained to be an artist at the Royal College of Art but, like so many other artists, she eventually had to rely on a normal job that would pay the bills. One unsatisfying job led to another until she was ultimately saved by motherhood which she embraced with open arms. She was now happier than she had been in years.

She looked up at me and noticed that I was uncharacteristically just stood in the middle of the kitchen staring.

'What's wrong with you?' she asked. 'Bad day?'

'I saw James,' I replied.

'Who?'

'You know, the guy that I work with who's got cancer.'

'Oh, yeah, I'd forgotten. How is he?'

'Not good,' I said, shaking my head. 'You know? He was coughing loads and his skin, oh my god, his skin is so pale. But the thing is I haven't stopped thinking about it since then.'

'What do you mean?'

'I don't know. He's in his forties, Jane. He's got four

kids for fucks sake. The youngest is only three. He doesn't smoke, he's not a heavy drinker, he's quite fit, and yet despite all of this, he then gets hit by cancer. It's not right. I mean, he's done everything that he's told to do. Life's a crock of shit. What's the point in it?' Jane just looked at me, not really prepared for a "meaning of life" discussion at tea time. 'Anything can happen to you at any time and you haven't got a clue when. No-one close to me has ever had anything like this before. I suppose I've just been lucky.'

'I think we've both been lucky, I guess we've just got to make the most of it while it's here,' she said and turned back to the pie.

I stayed silent for a while thinking. 'Do you think we *are* making the most of it?' I asked her eventually.

She stopped what she was doing again and looked at me, 'I think we've got a good family, we've got each other, and we're happy… well, I am anyway. They're the important things, aren't they? But, I suppose, come to think of it, only you know if you're making the most of it.' She looked at me and smiled.

'What if I'm not happy?' I said and Jane frowned. 'No, I don't mean with you or the kids, but I'm not happy with what I do day-in, day-out. I'm fed up with it. I'm really, really bored, Jane. It's just not me, or I don't think it is but what if this was all there was?'

'What else do you want to do?'

'I don't know, and that's the problem. It's so fucking frustrating.'

'Why don't you just leave then? You're only going to make yourself more miserable if you stay and I don't want a grumpy husband. Why don't you just give it up and do something else?'

'But what am I going to do, Jane?' the hopelessness of it was starting to dawn on me. 'I've got to earn money because one of us has to, and I can't just earn any money because we're used to spending what I earn now. I can't just watch football for a living. It's a catch 22. Oh, fucking bollocks to it.' And with that I stormed off upstairs with still no clear idea of what it all meant.

The next day was a struggle. I had hit the wine after my rant at Jane and finally fell asleep at gone midnight. I had crawled into work still half asleep and successfully avoided everybody on the way to my office. RC had existed on its current site for about sixty years. In this time it had built in the region of one hundred different buildings for specific purposes, ranging all the way from laboratories to normal office space. However, there were no batteries actually produced on the site, which meant that nearly every one of the three thousand inhabitants was distanced in someway from the main purpose of the company, and this created a bleak pointlessness to it all.

In amongst all of the buildings were splendidly manicured landscapes which had been created by the previous tenants, the Neville family, who had lived there for generations dating as far back as the fifteenth century. There still remained some remnants of the old estate; the substantial stables and coach house being the most well preserved, unfortunately however the majority of the buildings had been destroyed in a great fire that occurred two hundred years ago.

All of the modern buildings were built sympathetically around the remaining original structures in order to preserve their heritage. This had more to do with the listed buildings status of the originals rather than a history loving building strategy deployed by RC, but the end result at least produced a beautifully ornate backdrop for the day-to-day drudgery. There was a two hundred acre, working sheep farm which nestled between the main site buildings and an area of woodland, which in turn protected the site from the busy A-road beyond. There was also a large lake on the site, which I had dreamt of swimming across for the elusive gold envelope, and also a pond, which was still lined by the original conifers planted once as a memorial for a much-loved Neville.

When I eventually reached my office, I shut the door and sat quietly staring at the notice board for half an hour. It was only when I turned on the computer that I realised I had a meeting with my manager arranged in another half an hour's time. What made this realisation even worse was that it was regarding my objectives for the coming year. On that particular morning I could not even imagine myself working at RC in a week's time, let alone any longer, but while I was still there I suppose I had to play the game.

The other issue I had was that the internal project that I worked on, Project Eagle, was fundamentally flawed. The problem was that only I knew it. I had explained the reasons to my manager enough times that he had now stopped talking to me about it. All of the issues were out of my control and yet I had to somehow make sure that the way my objectives were worded could absolve me from any accountability over the ultimate success of it.

Project Eagle, in a nutshell, was an internal project that aimed to bring together all of the information systems that RC used across the globe. The benefit of completing this would be that the collection of information, and the comparison of it, across all sites and departments would be seamless and immediate. Idealistically this sounded fantastic and worth fighting for but I knew it was impossible. It had been called Eagle because of an optimistic intention for it to land at some point, but most of the employees at RC assumed that it was called after a bird of prey because, if successful, it would swoop down and take their jobs away.

I had been brought in to the project because of my experience in using a number of these systems in the past and, at the beginning, I was passionate about making a positive improvement to the way things were. It was not long, however, before I started to realise that the people that were on the project team had no idea about the way things were and I was a lone voice in many of the initial meetings. My manager, Rupert Savage, had washed his hands of me because I had become a constant thorn in his side and it had been like that for at least six months.

I had prepared my objectives earlier and I turned my attention to reading through them one last time. The idea in these sessions was never to over-commit. No prizes were ever given for not meeting your objectives. The skill was in making them look challenging whilst really aiming to keep fifty percent of your capacity free.

With a sigh, a headache and a bad feeling, I stood up and embarked upon the long journey to the office next door where my manager was gnawing busily on some raw meat.

Rupert Savage had the build of a prop forward and the looks of an anvil. His Napoleon complex came from his five foot six stature, and ever since he had worked at RC he had attempted to overcome his inability to look down on people by bringing them down to his own level, body part by body part. He was feared by most of my colleagues because of his bully-boy tactics but I was not as intimidated. This surprised me because I am not particularly that brave in real-life. I suppose I was just numb to his authority over me. He was in his early fifties and his face had formed in to a constant state of misery. He had a grown-up family and the other trappings that you would expect from the corporate life, but whereas normally you would expect to see a few photos around his desk, Rupert Savage had nothing. He was cold, heartless and, in my opinion, out of his depth in his current role.

'Are you ready?' I asked, as I poked my head around his door.

'Wait!' he shouted back with as much venom as if I was part of the Taliban. I did as I was told and waited in the corridor as if I was waiting for the headmaster. 'Right, come in,' he shouted a couple of seconds later. 'What do you want?'

'It's our meeting Rupert? You know? The one about

the objectives? Is now a good time?' I asked hovering above the chair opposite his desk.

'It's never a good time. Go on then, sit down, let's get it over with,' he fixed me with an icy stare, it was the type of stare that if we were outside of work could be followed by a head-butt.

'Do you want me to just start then?'

'You might as well,' he said incredulously as if there was any other way of proceeding. 'You've done this sort of thing before, so what have you written down this time that I'm going to shoot holes in?'

I ignored the previous remark and began reading out the objectives which I had prepared earlier. After each one I looked up at Rupert Savage to gauge some kind of reaction but instead he just stared right through me. I finished the list and braced myself for the onslaught.

'That's it, is it?' he said with a cynical laugh. 'What about the rest of your job? You know the one you get paid for?' He paused and enjoyed my wounded animal expression for a moment. 'What about the project deliverables? You can't be serious in leaving out anything that makes you accountable for delivering any part of this project?'

'But I'm not responsible for delivering any part of this project,' I challenged.

'Yes, you are,' he answered back. 'If you're not, then

who is? Your role is to manage your areas of the project. They have to be delivered when we say they will.'

'I've told you enough times that...'

'Excuse me, you don't tell me anything,' he interrupted.

'Ok, I didn't mean I've told you but I've *raised* my points before regarding the project's feasibility and I don't see what else I can do.'

'You've raised those points and I don't agree with you, so all you can do now is go about delivering what I've told you to deliver. If you can't do that then you need to tell me that you're not able to deliver what we've promised to our stakeholders and sponsors, and I'll have to look for someone else that can.' I sat looking at his big, ugly face which was goading me in to saying something that I would regret.

I reached for the nearest thing that I could find, which happened to be the stapler on the edge of his desk, and stapled 'Fuck Off' across his forehead. He screamed in pain and I was worried that the noise would travel along the corridor so I had to silence him. I reached out for the stress ball on the edge of his desk and shoved it in to his mouth then, with laser quick reactions, I grabbed the Sellotape dispenser and wrapped the tape around his head. After checking that he could still breathe through his nose, I then left his office and disappeared without a trace.

I did not say anything for a while and eventually he spoke again. 'Right, so you need to add a few more objectives with some accountability then.' I made up my mind that I would have to seek some other counsel regarding what I could do about these objectives. It was obvious that I was not going to get anywhere with Savage. 'What about your development plan?'

This was a corporate idea that the Human Resources department had implemented to ensure that RC cared for their employees' futures. It was a long-term plan that was meant to include your aspirations and long-term goals. This was great if your ambitions stretched as far as RC but slightly more risky if not. I had complied with it many years ago and had not changed it since. It was a work of total fiction but it was the type of nonsense that was enjoyed by senior management. I had included the aspiration to one-day move up in the company but, in the short term, I wanted challenging and developing roles that could give me a breadth of experience. I read it out to Savage who, after processing the potential challenges, gave up the thought of arguing and simply nodded his head.

'Is this ok then?' I checked.

'It might as well be. To be honest I don't really care. All I have to do is make sure that you've got one and it's reasonably sensible. I'm not going to be managing you any longer than I have to and you'll be someone else's problem then. If you want my opinion, you're not up to this and you need to start delivering soon.'

'Thank you. I do enjoy these little chats of ours Rupert,' I said with a sarcastic smile.

'Ok, are we done then?' he asked and I shrugged. 'Thank god for that. Right, close the door on the way out.'

I stood up and almost ran towards the door. As I resurfaced in the corridor, I took in a big breath of oxygen and then noticed Dave stood in the doorway of my office laughing to himself.

Chapter 6

'What's up with you?' I said quietly as I ushered him into my office and shut the door.

'I just heard the end of that,' Dave joked. 'He doesn't get any happier, does he?'

'He's a nightmare mate. This is why I try to avoid him most of the time.'

'Oh well, don't worry about it now because tonight's the night that we're going to P-A-R-T-Y.' My face lit up. He was right. Tonight was the night of the Christmas party.

'Oh yes, I can't wait,' I said but then my face dropped. 'It's going to be bloody fun for me with Ebeneezer Savage, next door, there. Once he's had a couple of drinks inside him who knows what's going to happen.'

'You'll be alright mate. We're all going. Just stick with us, it's going to be a right laugh. Mind you, it's going to be shit in the canteen though.'

'I know. Whatever happened to the good old days of corporate expenditure?' I asked. 'The days when no expense was spared and we could all get happily out of our faces and wake up in the woods of some strange hotel.'

'Ah, good times,' Dave glazed over and then snapped back to life. 'Are you bringing Jane?'

'Yeah, I think so. As long as we've managed to sort out a babysitter. You know how it is?'

'I do. We've not managed to get one.'

'You're kidding.'

'No, I'm not. Anyway, what's the drill for tonight? I'm leaving here at about three-ish, I need time to get myself ready.'

'Ready? What's that going to be? Throw on your good shirt and put on a bit of High Karate?'

'Oh yeah,' he said sarcastically, 'in terms of getting dressed I won't be taking long but I'm meeting Stretch in The Barleycorn first.'

'How are you getting from there?'

'Kate's going to be picking us both up and taking us. I've got it sorted mate.'

'Righty-o. Well, I'll have to meet you there because I'm stuck at work until five.'

'You what? No one's going to be here that late.'

'The people in my meeting will be. Can you believe that? A week before Christmas, the night of the Christmas party and I'm stuck in a four o'clock meeting talking about a finance process. Ridiculous.'

'You'll have to get away swift after that.'

'I know. I bet most of them won't even turn up anyway.'

Unfortunately they did and it was nearly five when I finally did get away. It was going to be close because I had to be back in the canteen at work with Jane, all dressed up, by seven. I lived at least half an hour away but it was usually more like three quarters of an hour. The rush that I was in, made what happened next even more unbelievable.

For all of the nights that I would drive home without any delays, why would there be a large queue of traffic waiting to get through the gates and out of the site that night? I was already running late and I could not afford to spend any more time "not" leaving work. The site road was a two way road and the righthand side was empty. It was only about two hundred yards to the gates and the whole queue seemed to be turning left, I wanted to turn right. There was an automatic metal barrier at the gate on both sides of the road, but the other side was up at the time and I could easily pass through without any resistance. It took me a matter of seconds to decide what to do. I pulled out of the queue of traffic and sped towards the gates on the wrong side of the road, out through the 'In' gate, to freedom.

When Jane and I pulled up again in the work car park it was just before seven o'clock. There had been no more delays and when I arrived home I was greeted by a babysitter and a made-up, dressed-up, Jane. It only took me about ten minutes to get ready and then we were on our way again.

When I saw the looming shadow of work towering over me for the second time that day a sense of dread came over me. Every year Jane hated the Christmas party anyway because she always felt as though she was left at the table on her own while I was busy getting drunk somewhere else. Although this was only partly true I had to promise to stay with her all night this time so that she would drive us home. Neither of us were looking forward to it so we reluctantly dragged ourselves towards the building, hoping that an alien attack was perhaps imminent. Jane was looking stunning in a dress that she had bought for a wedding the year before and I was rattling around in the faithful tuxedo that was having its annual outing.

Like a primary school that becomes a Polling Station, your place of work seems strange when it is being used for a different purpose. We felt as though we were trespassing as we crept through the deserted corridors that would normally be full of people. The silence was eerie and the glow from the printer lights filled the empty offices in a strange, science-fiction type green light. I sensed that we were disturbing it in some way and we walked silently through the long corridor that ran the length of the main building. When we finally arrived at the canteen, my desire to come across as comfortable had turned into a sense that I had become Jane's tour guide. I had begun to point out interesting facts like where I often sat to eat my lunch and how it was redecorated last year.

'Sssshhhh,' she said sharply, after I had pointed out that the photographer at the door was not usually there. She then began politely smiling at no one in particular, a charming trait that Jane always had whenever she felt uncomfortable. We queued to hang our coats up and, deftly avoiding the photographer, we entered the 'grand hall'.

'Oh, look, they've covered up the food counter,' I said pointing, and stating the obvious, 'and they've taken the trays away. That's nice. Now it doesn't feel like I'm at work at all.' In truth they had made an effort to transform the place from the usual busy lunch canteen into a nice function room, fully equipped with large round tables and a stage at one end. But, there was no getting away from the fact that the ceiling, and the walls, and the corporate flooring, and the corporate RC logo's stamped on everything, and the corporate pictures, and the corporate air, and the corporate people, shouted back at you, 'YOU'RE AT WORK ON A NIGHT OUT, YOU LOSER!!!'

At the far end there was a champagne reception where everyone else was mingling. I was disappointed to see that we were not actually that late. I would always like to turn up near the end of these things so that I could grab a glass of champagne, drain it, and then be ready to be seated at the tables. If, instead, you arrived early you would have to stand around holding your glass of champagne, nursing it so that you were always holding something. Then you would have to make excruciatingly polite conversation with people that you hated between the hours of nine and five, so why on earth would you want to spend any more time with them socialising. Also, you were showing your wife to them, as if she was a window into your real life. What if she would unknowingly say something that contradicted a harmless story that you had exaggerated at work? What if she really liked talking to someone that you considered to be a wanker? It was much safer to protect her from these sharks and get her to the tables as quickly as possible.

'I hate everyone here, I think,' I whispered to Jane, as I handed her an orange juice with an apologetic smile.

'Don't say it too loud, your voice carries,' said Jane with her polite smile still firmly attached.

As I looked around at the people gathering in the small end room, I could see quite a few people that I knew but polite nods were sufficient for most of them. I then saw Dave, and our other friend Stretch, stood at the far side away from most of the others. I smiled back and then rushed over to them as fast as I was able to without physically dragging Jane behind me.

We all said hello and both of them cordially pecked Jane on the cheek just to prove that they had manners. I could tell that they had been deep in conversation about something and our appearance in front of them had thus prevented this conversation from developing. I assumed they were looking around at all the girls, both employees and wives, and commenting on how well they scrubbed up. I had been involved in enough of these conversations through the years to understand why it was probably best to keep quiet.

Eventually Dave broke the awkward silence. 'Eh, Ben, your boss is here. Old Savage. We saw him earlier with his wife. It was funny though, he must have been stood in a hole because she looked taller than him.' We all smiled at each other but then noticed that they were stood about ten metres away looking right at us. We all froze and looked back quickly.

Chapter 7

After my heart had temporarily stopped for a moment, it appeared that Rupert Savage had not heard Stretch implying that he was stood in a hole. After this catastrophe had been avoided we all breathed a sigh of relief and waited for the seating tactics to begin. At these functions it was paramount that you stayed alert when everyone moved into the dining area. You could never be too sure about who was going to be sat at your table and one hesitation could ruin your entire evening. Thankfully when we had all stopped moving, it was just the four of us on one side of a round table and another party of four on the other who had no intention of making friends either. The night was beginning to look up and we were just about to take our seats when I instantly felt an urge to say hello to Savage, who was sat on the table behind. I had already finished a couple of glasses of complimentary champagne by then and the Dutch Courage was taking effect.

'I'm just going to say hello to Rupert, you'll be alright for a minute, won't you?' I said to Jane.

'Which one is he?' she asked quietly.

'You see the one over there who looks like a Bulldog that's just stepped in some dog shit,' I said gesturing with a nod of the head and a raise of the eyebrows. 'I won't be long.'

I walked around the table which was directly behind us until I was standing right by his side. He had been looking in the other direction and was unaware of my approach.

'Hello Rupert, Happy Christmas,' I warmly announced, as he had just raised a glass of red wine to his lips. He responded by jolting forwards, spilling most of the contents into his lap and then choking. He looked threateningly at me while his wife started dabbing at his groin area with a serviette until he was so irritated that he brushed her away. I waited a moment until he had recovered, trying not to smile and then continued. 'Sorry, I thought you had seen me. Have you had a good evening so far?'

He stared back at me but for some reason he could not find the words he was looking for.

'It's quite strange coming back to work in the evening, isn't it?' I asked, still waiting for a response. He was looking straight at me but now the stare was beginning to look homicidal.

'Is this your wife?' I asked. She leaned over him to

say hello and actually seemed very pleasant, I suppose Eva Braun was probably pleasant too, but still Savage said nothing.

'Well, Happy Christmas, nice to speak with you, and have a good evening,' and with this I walked back to my table smiling like the Cheshire Cat.

Jane looked at me with a curious expression when I returned and she must have known that something had happened but before she had a chance to ask, Stretch had put his hand on my shoulder. Stretch was a bit older than everyone else, more experienced as he would call it, and we had known each other for years. His nickname had derived from the sentence, 'he could always *stretch* a joke just a little bit too far,' and he was always the one that you could rely on to make an inappropriate remark at the wrong time. The reason that Stretch, as a name, stuck though was the unintentional irony of it - as he was only five foot three.

Stretch had once been in the Police Force when, in the eighties there had been a national shortage of officers and they were forced to temporarily relax their height restriction. Stretch had applied and been initiated within the week. He had revelled in his role in authority and had just begun to get used to the inflated power that such an officer of the law enjoys, when unfortunately the number of officers that were being recruited increased. Stretch was sadly pushed back into an office role and his dreams of being in the front line, fighting crime, disappeared. He only lasted another six months and since then the world of accountancy had claimed him. He never took himself, or any situation, seriously and in all the time I had known him it was hard to remember a normal conversation.

'We've got a game,' he said as he leaned towards me and shouted into my ear.

'What sort of a game?'

'Having said game, it probably isn't one actually. We've got a thing that we're going to do. Dave's just gone to the bar to prepare the first round.' My eyes looked up to the ceiling in dread. When Dave returned he was carrying three glasses of Sambuka. 'Right we all have to make a choice from the bar. This is the first round.'

'It has to be something different though, and special,' added Dave.

'What's so special about Sambuka?' I asked.

'Watch this,' said Dave and then grabbed the candle from the middle of the table and set all three alight. 'Voila! Enjoy. 1, 2, 3, go.' We all downed the drinks and put the glasses back on the table with varying facial expressions.

'Your turn now Ben,' said Stretch.

'You don't have to show off,' said Jane. 'You know what you get like at Christmas parties. Every year you say the same thing and then a year later it all goes out the window again.' She then gave me the look that only a wife can give their husband when he has regressed to his childlike state.

'I'll be alright,' I said laughing it off.

'You don't have to show off,' mocked Stretch, 'you know what you get like. If you'd rather just get a normal drink then that'll be fine.' Well, if encouragement was what I needed then this did the job. I went to the bar and came back with a single shot of tequila and three beer bottle caps. Jane took one look and started shaking her head.

'What's all this about?' asked Dave.

'We each fill our bottle top with tequila, like this, and then we lift it up gently to eye level, like this, and then we pull down our eye lid, like this, and... aaarrgghhh.' I shook my head and closed my left eye that was now stinging. Dave and Stretch started laughing and then it was their turn to start shaking their heads.

'Oh come on, that's not a drink,' said Stretch.

'Rules is rules,' I smiled while I dabbed at my leaking eye with the serviette.

'Ok then,' said Dave and grabbed the tequila. Thirty-seconds later his eye was bright red and he was thumping the side of the table. Everyone started to notice us so Stretch quickly grabbed Dave's hands and I passed him his serviette. Now faced with two of us completing the task, Stretch had no choice but to follow suit. A minute later we all looked as though we had been poked in the eye.

'This was meant to be fun,' said Stretch holding his eye as if it was going to fall out.

'I'm laughing,' I said.

'Right, your turn then Stretch,' said Dave.

'Hang on a minute, I can't see.'

'Use your other eye then.'

'Oh yeah, that's better.' Stretch walked off to the bar and returned with three whiskies. 'There's no way I can top tequila in the eye unless we inject rum into our foreskins, so I've opted for a straight whisky. At least I'm going to enjoy this one.'

Thankfully the three of us did enjoy Stretch's choice and Jane entered the conversation once more. All of us tucked in to the food when it came but the initial game did set a tone for the remainder of the time we were sat at the table. We were talking, having fun and for the first time since I had been at RC I was actually enjoying a Christmas party, but we were finishing the table wine rather quickly. When the bottles on your table are empty this usually acts as a natural indicator for you to slow down, but Stretch turned around and asked a lady that he knew behind him if it was alright if he could take one of their bottles. Jane gave up reminding me about my annual promise and we continued to sit at the table drinking.

After the meal had been cleared away, a young girl stood up on the stage and started to sing. I turned around to listen as she belted out a couple of Sinatra standards. I was relieved for the pause in drinking but as my imagination began to wander, I started to lose focus in the girl.

I sat in the hotel bar in Monte Carlo and watched the lady perform. She looked as though she was born to be on that stage, and maybe in another life she would be, but the necklace was identical to the one that I had seen on the yacht only that afternoon. She had to be involved in it somehow and I needed to get closer to her in order to get the information about Goldfeld. When she finished singing, she stepped down from the stage and walked directly towards me. Her face shone with a beauty that could only be found in Monte Carlo, her olive skin glowing against the low-level electric candlelight. This woman could have been anything she wanted to be, so how did she get wrapped up in this sordid affair? After she had finished singing she meandered through the tables, not taking her eyes off me, and as she approached I waited for her to sit down but she then continued on her way towards the casino. I knew I was required to follow, so I calmly finished my Martini and waited another thirty-seconds before doing so.

The casino was busy and it took longer than I expected to pass through the general gaming tables on my way to the VIP room. The security staff moved aside as I drew nearer and, once I was within the smaller confines of the room, I immediately saw her stood under the lights of the Roulette table. I needed to join the game to make contact and after that I would be able to get closer.

Jane was stood at the roulette table but the movement involved between our table and the casino had not been good for me. A tsunami of drunkenness washed over me as I approached her and unfortunately, as I leant on the table to steady the room, a number of chips went cascading to the floor. The man who was throwing a ball into a wheel became very angry with me and started pointing towards the door. Jane, who was of course sober, managed to translate the man's strange dialect and it transpired that he wished me to leave.

The rest of the evening was unfortunately a blur in my memory. I do not remember getting into the car, which in hindsight Jane did very well to find all on her own, and I do not remember having to stop the car to be sick before we had even reached the main road. I only know this last part because I was told the story, by an angry Jane, the next day. She had apparently not stopped the car in time and I had reached for the only receptacle which I could find, which happened to be Jane's handbag. This would have been bad enough but when we arrived home she had to roll her dress sleeve up to fish out the front door keys. The night, it could be said, had ended on a particularly low point.

Chapter 8

Gradually the memories began to materialise as I lay in bed the next morning, discovering that a towel had been laid over me and a bowl placed by my side. My head had the sensation of a very large man squeezing it from both sides, inside my stomach it felt as though a Russian circus act were performing inside it, my mouth tasted like a crematorium, and my eyes seared as though someone had spent the last hour putting cigarettes out in them. With every memory that was recalled it was acknowledged by another thump from within.

I pulled myself out of bed and made my way downstairs, hoping desperately that some dry toast and a glass of orange juice would begin the recovery. Jane had already left with the kids and a note on the kitchen side simply saying, 'Thanks!' confirmed exactly where I stood. This did not help the way I was feeling at all but, out of an instinct for survival, I put it to the back of my mind knowing that I was not in an adequate state to concentrate on anything at this juncture. After an hour, the toast and orange juice (and the Paracetamol) had done surprisingly well, and it then occurred to me that I still had to get to work. Savage had obviously been there last night and I hoped he had forgotten about the wine incident. I also wondered what the probability was that he had personally witnessed any of my other behaviour. Depressingly I knew that even if not, then he certainly would have been briefed about it this morning by some do-gooder. I thought it best to make an appearance so that I could gauge the atmosphere and at least be on hand if a defence was required.

I changed into my suit, whilst trying to move as little as possible, and although it took longer than usual I eventually made it outside. The glaring, wintery sun was low in the sky and it seemed to bounce off a million different surfaces directly towards me as if I was inside a massive mirror-ball. This did not help my headache or indeed the problem that my eyes were having trying to focus. I took the drive slowly and silently, a policeman would have thrown the book at me if I *had* been stopped, but fortunately I made it all the way without any drama developing and walked to the turnstile.

RC had turnstiles at every entrance to the buildings as a form of security. The site itself was in parkland, and therefore almost impossible to secure, so each door had a floor to ceiling turnstile installed. Each employee had a credit card sized ID badge that would unlock the turnstile and grant access to the treasures within. However, the turnstile would not unlock that day when presented with my rite of passage. Due to being in quite a numb state, it took me a while to realise this. I must have pushed against the unforgiving bars thirty times before finally concluding that it was not working. The old turnstiles were not totally infallible and, they had been known to break in the past, so I wandered slowly around to the next entrance and tried to gain access there. That did not work either and, nor did any of the remaining five turnstiles, so left with no alternative I walked in to the shiny corporate reception at the front of the building.

'Hi,' I grunted to the receptionist that I knew vaguely. A couple of years ago I had once helped her to change the tyre on her car.

'Good morning, or is it afternoon?' she replied with a glint in her eye.

'Hmmm,' I muttered shaking my head knowing that this was the universal sign for, *'I have a hangover'*.

'Not another one who was at the ball last night?' I nodded. 'Oh, dear,' she looked at me sympathetically, 'at least you've made it in. I don't think many have.'

'Good for them,' I said. 'Listen, I don't know what's wrong with my card, I've tried it in all of the doors and it just won't work.'

'Here you go then,' she smiled and pressed a button that made the glass gate next to her desk open automatically.

'Thanks very much,' I said trudging through it into the bowels of the building.

'No problem, have as good a day as you can,' she shouted after me.

I walked through the carpeted corridors, past the offices full of people and activity, and remembered the different mood they all had last night. The smell and the sounds comforted my hangover, as I kept walking through to the back of the building on the ground floor where my little office was situated. Once again I thanked the gods of office space for giving me my own office.

The amount of corporate bullshit that is applied to the virtues of the open plan office is a great example of how this world works. I have never met anyone that enjoys an open plan office although it is true that some tolerate them better than others. In the old days people had their own offices, people knew where they stood in the world. If you were more senior you gained a bigger office and then the further it moved down the scale the more people would be sat in your room. This was the way that it worked; people knew this situation well and were comfortable within it. It kept the managers separated from the workers, which in my experience is always a good thing, not because I don't like senior managers but it destroys the natural environment in an office. The energy and communication between people can flow more freely, and less formally, if people do not feel as though they are being watched continuously.

But thanks to the changing culture which we are now influenced by, in almost all things we do, we are conditioned in to thinking that having everyone sat in one big room is truly the best thing since sliced bread. We are taught that the incessant noise level which distracts, and results in the residential population getting headaches, is actually, "good communication happening between employees in a dynamic way". It is more productive because you spend less time having to move between offices, or rely on office memos or emails, because you can just swing your chair around, shout across an expanse of office and have your question answered immediately. Forget the people who are trying to concentrate in between these two dynamic employees. Also, as most work in the modern day is performed on the telephone, a call centre vibe quickly develops where the noise levels increase and the person with the loudest voice suddenly is perceived as the next in line to Beelzebub's throne. Lastly, it is supposedly better at promoting a sense of 'Team' even though as mentioned before, with a manager sitting right next to their direct reports, this can be tested. I wonder how many people actually feel comfortable on a Monday morning, informally discussing what happened at the weekend with their workmates, when their manager is three feet away writing their performance review.

In my experience, the funniest part to any open plan office is the planning stage, when it is decided where people sit. You will often have the management sat at one end of the large room, with slightly bigger desks; maybe better views and maybe individual printers' etcetera. The rest of the workers are then wedged in to the remaining office space closer together, with one printer between twenty people - printer queues and gossip around the printer surely contradicting that productivity claim. Everyone then spends the first week trying to position desk dividers, files and plants in such strategic positions that they can block out everyone surrounding them. The light and airy 'open plan office' then takes on the form of a Brazilian favela. Meeting rooms are then cleverly provided for the encouragement of more formal discussions but there are never enough of them to house the demand.

The new trend is to not even provide a *desk* for every employee and instead they now have 'hot desks' in which you can just plug in your laptop and work. This means that you are not sat near your team, no one else is able to find you and nobody has any sense of ever belonging anywhere. Like a building full of professional gypsies that are free to travel across the plains of the office. I wonder how long it will be before people start micro industries of selling lucky staplers to people nearby or bare-knuckle printing for money.

I finally reached my own office and sat quietly at the desk, still delicate from the hangover and now extremely anxious about why my ID card would not work in any of the turnstiles. Had someone seen my behaviour last night and terminated my employment immediately? Had I broken a cardinal sin and been punished? I sat there contemplating all of the possible corporate crimes that I had committed, if only I could remember them in detail then I might have been able to think of an excuse.

The phone began to ring, making me jump and suddenly I was aware of how nervous and sick I felt. I picked it up.

'Hello,' I said tentatively.

'Hello, is that Ben Jenkins?' said an officious voice on the other end of the phone.

'Yes, that's right,' I answered, not really sure if a small lie might have been more suitable at this moment. More like, *'No, but I've been instructed to take any messages for him.'*

'My name is Darren Heavyside, I'm the Head of Security at RC,' he said in a military manner, my heart had actually stopped and the only thing still working was my ear. 'Did you have any trouble getting into the building this morning?'

'Y...Y...Yes, something does seem to be wrong with my card though,' I sounded guilty before I even knew the reason.

'Do you know why that could be?' continued Mr Heavyside, showing his experience of doing this before, probably in Guantanamo Bay. What do I say now? No – and then make out that I've done loads of things wrong, or Yes – and then fail to produce any more detail when he asks for it. I was in a bind.

'I'm not sure, really,' I plumped for.

'Well, you should, shouldn't you?' he upped his gear on this question and I remembered the scene in Casino Royale when James Bond was strapped to a chair. A mere noise emitted from my mouth, one that I considered at the time to be a noise that would show that I was intelligently thinking over his question but probably sounded like I was just about to be punched in the face.

'In your car?' he suggested as if that would help. Surely he could not know that I was over the limit when

I drove in this morning.

'Last night?' he went on, gaining no reaction from me. I must admit that I was getting slightly bored of the game by now but to tell him to hurry up would surely count against me. I could not think about last night, the whole evening had been placed in to a part of my brain that was inaccessible at that moment.

'Well, I'll tell you, shall I?' he liked to ask questions, there was no doubt about it, I could not help but think how generous he was in his conversational manner.

'Could you please?' I asked politely but with an ounce of irritation creeping into my voice.

'You drove your vehicle... around the wrong side... of the traffic calming device... on leaving the site perimeter gates... at seventeen hundred hours yesterday evening,' he announced.

'What????!!!!!!!', I thought to myself. Of all the things that were going through my mind this was not even on my reserve list. I could barely remember even doing it, let alone worry about it.

'Oh, well, I am very sorry about that,' I replied facetiously.

'Dangerous driving is not acceptable on the site premises,' Heavyside continued, 'An incident may have developed as cars can enter the site at speed from that corner and we cannot allow such a blatant disregard for the rules as this.'

I was getting quite worried again now, it sounded as though he was going to send a swat team in through the window and take me off to some mountainous torture chamber.

'I'm very sorry,' I repeated, 'there was a traffic jam turning left, and after all I didn't appreciate that I was being dangerous.'

'Yes, well I know why you did it. That does not make it right though. I have watched it back on CCTV and it looks like something that would feature on one of those police programmes,' his tone started to soften now and he even allowed himself a celebratory snort of humour. I could not help but think though that he was getting slightly carried away with such a trivial act and the whole discussion was becoming surreal.

'Will I ever have my pass re-instated, please?' I asked hoping to bring the conversation to an end.

'Yes, you may, but only when you have received *suitable* punishment,' he emphasised the word 'suitable' and it sounded like this was the bit that he was looking forward to. I ran through all of the possible punishments that someone in such a dead end job could bestow upon me with absolutely no authority. The only real sentence that I would have been scared of, is if he had said that him and the boys were standing outside my office door at that very moment tooled up. Instead he came up with, 'So, I will be emailing your manager and alerting him of this incident. I will then re-instate your pass.'

'Thank you very much,' I was not really sure why I was thanking him, but it seemed the best thing to say to get him off the phone quicker.

'Never do anything like this again otherwise the penalty will be severe,' he threatened with a sinister undertone. I was perplexed as to what exactly this could be when he continued, 'Your manager is Mark Wilkinson. Correct?'

'Oh, um, yes. Yes, definitely, that's right,' I confirmed. It had taken me a while to agree, because I suddenly had to think, Mark Wilkinson had been my manager five years ago but then I realised that it was probably then when I had registered my car on site and I had never updated it. Mr Heavyside thankfully seemed satisfied with this and said goodbye. I sat back on my chair and breathed a huge sigh of relief.

Darren Heavyside put the phone back on the receiver and moved his attentions back to the white cat which was sat on his lap. An evil smile crept on to his face and he reached across his desk and pressed one of the red buttons on the console in front of him. The shutters folded back and revealed the top secret operation centre which he was building inside the hollowed out volcano.

Every time an employee broke the rules it meant that they would be silently abducted and initiated into the brainwashing programme. Once the target had been passed through this system they would emerge on the other side with no recollection of their former life. Training would then be issued and, once completed, they would be reinstated at RC as a security guard.

Up until now Heavyside had only collected forty-eight of his recruits but the army was becoming stronger day by day. Soon it would be The Calling and RC would fall.

Wilks had only been my manager for a brief six-month period and I had absolutely no problem with Heavyside passing on the bad news to him. But as I sat there thinking about how fortunate I had been, I started to get an idea. Perhaps there was scope for something here, I made up my mind to walk around to Wilks' office and see how he was doing.

'Alright, Wilks?' I said two minutes later standing in his office. It was slightly bigger than mine and even had an extra table at one end. I explained the conversation I had just endured and the idea which had come from it.

'I don't *know* if you've *actually* done anything

wrong, have you?' said Wilks.

'I was hoping you were going to say that,' I said smiling.

'It's not a public road, and there aren't any markings to say you can't do it,' he paused, as if to think through all possible counter arguments. 'No. Bollocks to him,' as Wilks said this a faint ping could be heard behind him. Sure enough it was an email from Heavyside. 'Ah, here we go,' he said turning back to the computer. 'Leave this with me, Ben, I'll straighten him out.'

Wilks came in to my office five minutes later and explained that he had disagreed with Heavyside's email, which caused Wilks to then receive an immediate phone call. Heavyside apparently explained that RC have a policy that all site roads will reflect the highway code, Wilks had argued that this was not clear and what I had done the night before was not dangerous in his opinion. Heavyside respectfully disagreed and the conversation hit upon an awkward lull. Wilks then pressed Heavyside to reinstate my pass, to which he agreed to on the condition that Wilks would have a word with me. Wilks ended the conversation by saying that he was too busy with such trivial issues and suggested that the Head of Security should get on with proper security work instead of wasting everybody's time.

'One for the people,' I thought to myself after Wilks

had left. I was still smiling and it dawned on me that it was the first time that I had remembered smiling on my own at work for a very long time. I started to think about all of the things which had irritated me for so long and I considered that maybe I should do something about them in the future. Perhaps it was time for someone to stand up to these ridiculous episodes that occurred in the corporate world. A folk hero, a man from the people, one of their own standing up against the tyranny of corporate bullshit, an assassin of administration. I would have to be careful but at least it would be exciting. I would be the talk of the corridors; the mystery man that questioned The Man.

Chapter 9

A few weeks passed by and Christmas came and went. My mood had lifted since I had been away and I was able to forget about the mind-numbing boredom which I was usually faced with. I began to realise that I could actually be happy as long as nobody forced me to travel in to work each day. Unfortunately this triggered a number of other questions to which I had no answers.

On the eve of returning to work I had tried to solve the great mystery of what to do instead and, because I had no idea, it sent me into an even greater depression. The first week of January had slipped by and it was as if I was in hibernation. It seemed to be raining continuously outside and the damp atmosphere added to my general mood. I sat in my office watching raindrops chasing each other down the window.

Project Eagle was still flightless and over the last month it had actually gone backwards. The team togetherness was beginning to separate as each member started to protect themselves. I found it easier to cope if I just stayed in my office and avoided as many people as possible. As Rupert Savage started to panic about delivery, he brought more and more new faces in to the team and the project started to become a mess. Every meeting was divided in to those who realised it was impossible and the others who were desperately trying to find a way to impress. The constant strain was tiring and I had given up even trying to explain why the project was unachievable. I was just existing in my role, providing the bare minimum to get by and actively avoiding as many of these fresh-faced irritants as possible.

I was largely successful in getting out of their way but there was one meeting that could not be avoided. It was a staff meeting that was arranged to talk about a personnel initiative called the Mirror Survey. It had nothing to do with Project Eagle; it was all about the employees well-being. I was obviously in the perfect state to be discussing such a subject with my fellow colleagues.

The Mirror Survey was a study that collected data on a number of different areas that affected an employee's enjoyment, motivation, and development at work. Every year the results would say the same thing; people had too much work to do, for not enough pay, and their work-life balance was not satisfactory. There would also be obligatory questions on health and safety, questions relating to the confidence in the Board, and whether the employees felt as though they could challenge people more senior to themselves. I did not care about any of this. I knew what my opinions were on all of these and I also knew that I would not be listened to either. It was another example of how corporate life worked. It was never important to actually *make* changes to someone's working environment but as long as you were seen to be discussing it then this would be sufficient. The only thing I had in common with Rupert Savage was our shared hatred of such time-wasting activities. I had managed to avoid him since before Christmas and thankfully the wine incident was now at the back of our minds.

There were approximately twenty of us crammed into a meeting room that was designed to only hold ten people. The rain could be seen running down the windowpanes and the gloomy outlook transferred inside. It was refreshing to see how most people shared my enthusiasm for such events and the general level of whinge before we began was pleasing. Savage was looking restless at the front and kept checking his watch, eventually a grey-haired lady walked in looking apologetic and stood near the door.

'At last,' he said standing. 'Right this is the Mirror Survey. I don't want to spend any longer than I have to in this room, so let's get on with it.' He put the first slide up on the white screen. 'Same old nonsense. We've got four different areas to cover and I need someone to make a note of it all on that flip chart. Who's going to scribe?' he stopped talking and stared at us all menacingly. "Scribe" is one of those corporate words that is never heard elsewhere, it refers to the act of writing on to a flip chart, and it was the last thing I wanted to do.

Thankfully, while the rest of us looked out of the window, a chap in his forties stood up and agreed to do it. Every team has someone like Kevin. He still lived with his Mum, his job was the only purpose to his life and he was in constant denial about his well-developed bald spot.

'Kevin, stand there and write down what people say,' said Savage pointing to the flip chart again.

'Can I make suggestions too?' asked Kevin.

'Of course you bloody can,' said Savage shaking his head. 'Right, the first one we've got to talk about is Pay and Reward, the scores for our department showed that the overall number of people that were happy with their salary has come down from last year. Surprise, surprise. Anyone got anything to say?'

'Can we have more money?' I asked impatiently.

'No,' answered Savage.

'I'm good then, thanks,' I said. He looked at me as if to say, *'don't start.'*

'Right, next area is Work-Life Balance? Write that at the top Kevin. So we can all read it, please. This scored lower than last year even though the management team made attempts to improve it so what's not working?' He looked at us all hoping that someone would say something. I think most of us were trying to remember what improvements had been attempted. He started to look at me, 'Jenkins, what do you think?'

'I'm not sure how it's changed.'

'Well it has. When I was younger you had to stay in your office for eight hours a day, five days a week, and when you went home for the weekend that was your balance. Heaven forbid that work would get in the way of your kid's nativity play. Nowadays I don't know where half of you are at any given time and I'm not allowed to even ask you. Sounds good to me. How's that getting worse? Anyone?' The whole room stayed quiet. 'Ok, good, it must be the other teams that have given it that score.'

In my opinion the work/life balance should be 90/10 in favour of life but I knew this would be too revolutionary for this particular forum.

'I feel,' began Kevin from the flip chart, 'that I'm working extremely hard at the moment and I'm still being expected to pick more and more up.' Savage looked like he was going to lunge at him. 'I'm working miles more hours to get through it all, and if anything, it's getting worse rather than better for me.'

'Oh well, what a pity. It'll get better once the project's been delivered,' said Savage and flicked to the next slide. Kevin spun back round to face the flip chart and turned red. 'Next item up is Leadership. Specifically, on this one, the bad score relates to direct line management support,' he turned around to look at the screen and I detected a slight vulnerability in his manner.

Savage was exposed like a wounded animal. The entire crowd sensed it and the jeers began almost immediately. He looked as though he was going to cry and the angry mob began chanting 'Sav-age out, Sav-age out, Sav-age out.' His mouth opened, perhaps he was going to explain or even apologise, but just as he was about to talk, someone near the back threw a pen at him. It bounced harmlessly off the top of his head and landed safely near the window but it had visibly rocked Savage. The angry mob, still chanting, saw this as their moment to attack. The front row piled in first like a well-marshalled offensive manoeuvre and then it was the turn of everybody else. Soon there were a combination of bodies in either a state of launching themselves in full attack or retreating for their next effort. Somewhere at the bottom of the pile was Savage, curled up in a ball, protecting himself as best he could.

I stood at the edge and watched as the master plan which I had created was executed perfectly. After that moment there would be no more Savage, instead we would have a democracy, a harmony amongst the team that would listen to reason rather than fear. That day would mark the beginning of the new way. I would be elected as the democratic leader of the people because they would still need direction, but firstly there was business to be taken care of. Savage's lifeless body was dragged from the room and pulled outside into the pouring rain. In the middle of the courtyard stood a large tree, the same tree that I had looked out upon from my office in darker times, but it was now needed for another purpose. The mob lifted the body up into the tree and then hung it as a warning for all of the other senior management of RC. The revolution was here.

The audience waited for Savage to choose his words as we all looked at the text on the screen. Only 60% of employees thought that their direct manager gave them an adequate level of support. I considered that even this was generous but I kept my opinions to myself. 'Now,' said Savage, 'I appreciate that some of you may find it difficult to speak your mind whilst I'm in the room, so if you would like me to leave for a moment then I suppose I could.' We all looked around at each other and, due to a lack of desire from anyone to tell him to leave the room, we all silently shook our heads and he remained. 'Has anyone got anything to say about this?' he asked threateningly. We all stayed quiet and there was an awkward silence before Kevin started fidgeting at the front.

'I'd like to think,' began Kevin, 'that you're always there if I need support in anything, and I feel confident that I could raise any concerns directly to you.' Everyone agreed whole heartedly to this and there was an abundance of nods from everyone.

'Do you?' questioned Savage.

Obviously nobody was going to say anything to the contrary because we knew it would not get us anywhere. I was under no false impression that Savage would change his ways if I complained about his manner, I doubt he was even capable of changing anyway, so we all happily nodded.

'Oh god,' said Rupert Savage sighing as he saw the next slide. 'Last up then, Health and Safety. Apparently we've scored lower than last year on this, so what do people think? Do you even care?'

Everyone shrugged and shook their heads, that was everyone but Kevin. Instead, he stood at the front and visibly calculated how many potential death traps there were lying around the office. 'What does it relate to exactly, Rupert?' asked Kevin, as if this was going to help him eliminate some from his list.

'Apparently,' replied Savage impatiently, 'people feel as though the office, and by this I understand it to mean the open plan offices more, are untidy and that there are lots of files piled up against the walls.'

'That is true,' nodded Kevin wisely. 'I've often thought that could be dangerous.'

'Don't be so stupid, Kevin,' shouted Savage. 'It might be dangerous to a blind employee that walks around the offices with one hand on the wall but as we don't have any of those then we don't have any accidents. The figures speak for themselves; there's been no recorded injury that has occurred in any office since records began.'

'But still, maybe we should tidy up our offices a bit, just in case,' suggested Kevin.

'In case of what?' shouted Savage.

'I just think it might be an idea,' replied Kevin who was now starting to lose the confidence in his voice. A few women near the front, who liked Kevin, began to agree with him and one of them even said that she had once tripped over a file.

'How about this?' suggested Kevin, buoyed by this unexpected endorsement. 'We're all so busy and the problem that I find is that I simply do not have the time to organise my paperwork properly. I have meetings all day long and there's just no time available. So, how about we put some time aside once every couple of weeks to have a filing session.' His supporters jumped at the idea and the excitement then took hold across the whole room. Savage shook his head in disbelief but then started to realise that at least the meeting would have provided a positive action, even if it was ridiculous. I sat at the back watching my colleagues convince themselves that this was a major problem in their lives and I started to realise that these were not my people.

'I'll put a recurring meeting in all of our schedules for every other Thursday, shall we say for two hours?' asked Kevin, eager to press his victory home. It seemed as though the entire audience, apart from me, thought this was a brilliant idea. I am still not really sure if they were all keen to agree to this because it would block out time which they could use for themselves, or just because they genuinely thought that it would be a good idea, but they were definitely happy that they had agreed.

So it was, that for the rest of my time at RC I had

every other Thursday afternoon blocked out for filing imaginary paperwork, and this was the only improvement that came about from the Mirror Survey that year.

After the meeting I sat back down in my own office, watching the raindrops, and noticed that I was beginning to get more and more frustrated at work. I was actually feeling angry that the project was pointless and it was never going to end. The idea of just leaving, throwing the towel in, entered my head but then left again immediately. What would Jane say? While I was simmering away in my office, I thought back to the rest of the team gleefully looking forward to cleaning up their desks next Thursday. That did not help.

Chapter 10

Lunchtime was a welcome distraction when it came. My mood had not improved and, although I had talked myself out of doing anything rash, I was still frustrated about work.

The rain was still coming down as I walked miserably across the car park to the lunch canteen. I would always have lunch with the same group of people and it was the only part of the day that made me feel remotely normal. Dave was already there, along with Wilks and Stretch, and that day happened to be one of the days where Emily had joined us as well.

Emily Sanderson tried her best not to sit with us all of the time in case people started to associate her with us. She was younger than me, about twenty-eight, and quite attractive in a quirky sort of way. She had short, blonde hair that was always well-styled, her blue eyes were hidden under a deliberately long fringe, and her designer clothes always made her look good. She was still on the right side of the age-line. I always believed that there was a point, probably at around thirty, when you would shift in your consciousness to nearer forty rather than just older than twenty. Emily was definitely still nearer twenty. She was not married, she had no kids, her boyfriend did something which sounded cool and, although she had been at RC for about seven years, she did not seem affected.

I let out a weary sigh as I flopped down at the table in the seat next to Dave. The canteen was busy and I was glad they had saved me a space. On every table were the same dull, monotonous conversations; colleagues talking about work, a team all trying to impress their new manager, two senior executives talking in a hushed tone about a top secret strategy. It was the same every day and that was why I was so glad to have my gang. We would never talk about work - that was the rule - although we were obviously allowed to discuss the people.

'Did anyone else have to get in that lasagne queue?' I asked, as I removed the plates from my tray. They all shook their heads and a quick look at their meals would have told me, that apart from Emily who had a salad, everyone else was eating homemade sandwiches. 'It took ages,' I muttered to myself.

'Don't worry about that,' said Stretch smiling. 'What about "The News" last night then?' He was referring to a TV programme which had started on a channel way down the list called Naked News. The idea being that the normal news was delivered by women who simply had no clothes on. It was a strange concept which looked as though two old men had dreamed it up in a pub one night, but Stretch was obsessed with it. He was looking right at Dave and I because we were the ones he had mentioned it to the day before.

'Yeah,' smiled Dave. 'I saw it. Good one, Stretch.'

'Did you see the one with the dark hair?' asked Stretch, and Dave nodded. 'She didn't have dark hair anywhere else, did she?'

'Aw, come on Stretch,' said Dave painfully, acutely aware of Emily's presence, but Stretch just smiled. Emily was used to this level of conversation, secretly I think that was the reason why she wanted to sit with us, but also it was the reason why she probably wanted to sit with others as well.

'I haven't seen it, but… what I don't understand,' said Wilks looking puzzled, 'is why they bother reading out the news.'

'Because it's the news,' said Stretch.

'But it's not though,' insisted Wilks. 'It's a weird fetish show for perverts like you that have a thing for newsreaders. They don't do anything seductively. They literally just read the news, and unlike BBC they sound as thick as pig shit.'

'But they don't take their clothes off on the BBC,' said Stretch not understanding the point. Wilks gave up and returned to his sandwich.

'I watched it last night as well,' I said. 'I'm afraid to say Stretch but I'm with Wilks too. It seemed almost medical to me.'

'I don't know what's wrong with you all,' said Stretch. 'They're reading the news and they've got no clothes on. It's brilliant.' He looked around at our unconvinced expressions and then said, 'oh well, suit yourselves.' We all secretly smirked at each other while Stretch sulked.

'Hey,' said Dave suddenly remembering something. 'Have you heard who's leaving now?'

'Who?' asked Emily, desperately lunging on the change of subject.

'Lee Marvin,' stated Dave.

'No way,' replied Emily, 'You're joking. Why's he going?'

'He's probably just had enough,' said Dave. 'He's been here for forty odd years. He's off on the old CR.'

CR stood for Compulsory Redundancy as opposed to VR which stood for Voluntary Redundancy. They had become more and more common as RC continued to reorganise and restructure.

'They can't be getting rid of his job,' said Emily.

'No, probably not,' said Dave, 'but he's shit, so they'll use CR as the excuse. They'll probably get someone else in straight away who can do the job, rather than someone who just sits there thinking about the next drink.'

'Jammy sod,' said Stretch.

'Yeah,' I nodded, half daydreaming, 'imagine that.'

'Just think,' said Stretch, 'you get all your shares tax free and three times your salary paid in a lump sum.'

'Get in,' I exclaimed. 'That'll be very nice. I'll just be really shit from now on then.'

'From now on?' said Wilks.

'Very funny,' I said. 'What do you think the chances are for me to get that?'

'None,' said Wilks, 'they'd sack you.'

'That's the ticket though, isn't it?' I said. 'I mean, if you wanted to get out then that would be it.'

'Oh yeah,' agreed Dave. 'You wouldn't want to leave any other way. Not with all those years behind you.'

'They're giving them out like Smarties in marketing at the moment,' said Wilks. 'Have you not heard? There's about a hundred of them going. They're all getting paid a year's notice on top as well.'

'What?' I said shaking my head in disbelief. 'I used to work in there as well. Fuck it.'

'You heard the funny bit about that?' said Dave, we

all shook our heads. 'You know HR have a counselling service, well they've had to recruit twice as many counsellors to talk to the marketing people that are staying.'

'Brilliant,' laughed Stretch.

'Honest to god, you couldn't make it up,' smiled Dave. 'We're actually having to counsel the ones that are staying. Have you ever heard of anything so crazy?'

As Dave was shaking his head, I was trying to prise my lasagne from its oval serving dish and get it on to my plate of chips. It was one of those square portions that had been cut out of a larger pan at the counter. I had it delicately balanced on the end of my fork, which was the method of transfer that I usually favoured, and I was just about to switch it across when all of a sudden I suffered from what I can only define as a spasm. The shiver started in my right ear and travelled all the way down my right side thus making my right hand flick uncontrollably. The innocent fork took on the role of a trebuchet and it sent the lasagne flying up through the air. The sturdy block of hot mince climbed about two feet and disappeared over my right shoulder.

The next sequence of events all happened in slow motion. The entire table looked stunned while I glanced down at my empty fork. Any hopes I had of a safe landing were short-lived when I noticed their expressions of shock turn to horror as they all stared past me. In fact the whole canteen seemed to go silent. The tables were tightly packed in and I knew there would be someone who was sat close behind. As soon as I looked around my heart sank.

The offending lasagne was perched on the top of a man's shaven head. Judging by the size of his neck, and the bit of head that I could still see, he was a big man too. The sauce had started to run all the way through his stubbled hair and on to the collar of his jacket. I leaned across and tried to scoop it back into the oval-shaped bowl, which I still held in my left hand, but this coincided with the victim turning around to see what had just hit him. The result of these two opposing actions produced an unfortunate outcome where the lasagne, that was now in my fingertips, was smeared across the man's very large face. He looked at me with murderous eyes for the whole time that I struggled to get the hot lasagne away from his forehead.

I was unable to speak because of the shock. I just sat there holding the dish that was now reunited with the flattened lasagne. Without averting his stare, he gradually turned around and stood up, his full height only then becoming apparent. He was about six foot four, built like a gladiator and his shaved head showed off a varied collection of scars.

'What do you think you're doing?' he said in a sinister, gravelly voice. I wanted desperately to say sorry but I was still stuck for words. I was slightly relieved to notice that he looked around the canteen first before leaning a little nearer to me and whispering, 'do you know who I am?' I shook my head silently. I was so glad that I was in a public place because this guy looked like he was just about to rip my head off.

'Sorry,' I finally said, breaking the spell. 'I don't know what happened. One second it was on my fork and then…'

He continued to fix me with his icy stare and I could tell he was thinking about what he could do to me, 'what's your name?'

'Um, ah, why?'

'What's your name?' he repeated.

'Um, Jenkins,' I said tentatively.

'Ben… Jenkins?' he asked and a look of recognition could be seen in his eyes. It was very hard to keep concentrating because he had a white sauce spread across his scarred features. 'I know who you are.'

'Do you?' I said in a slightly higher pitch than I would have liked.

'Yeah I do,' and he then leant even closer to me so that only I could hear. 'I'm going to keep a very close eye on you. If you even scratch your bollocks I'm going to know about it, alright?' I was not quite sure what he meant but this was definitely not a time for clarification. I raised my eyebrows to agree because that was the only part of my body which wanted to move.

He then stood up again to his full height and towered over me. He took one last, sustained stare and then moved off slowly between the tables with his knuckles dragging on the floor. The two people he was sat with immediately followed suit and for a couple of seconds afterwards I stayed where I was until I suddenly realised that I had been holding my breath. I turned back round to my table and took a big gulp of air.

'Who the hell was that?' I asked once I had recovered. Dave, Stretch and Emily were all still stunned but thankfully Wilks answered me.

'That was Darren Heavyside,' he said.

'Head of Security, Darren Heavyside?'

'The one and only.'

'Oh bollocks.'

The rest of the lunch passed very quickly and, after the threat of immediate violence had past, we even managed to begin laughing about it by the time we had all finished.

'Anyone up for a walk?' I asked. 'I think I need some air before I go back.'

This was one of the benefits to working within

parkland and we would usually make the most of it before we returned to our dreary jobs. Everyone else nodded and we soon made our way out of the canteen. I was half expecting to see Big Darren waiting for us but thankfully the coast was clear.

While we were walking along a gravel path under some trees, I suddenly noticed a wooden sign stuck in the ground that had not been there the day before. I moved closer and noticed that it was a warning sign.

CLEVER SPARKS remember to look out for WET LEAVES.

13 accidents were reported last year concerning wet leaves.
1 serious accident reported.
It is impossible to maintain clear paths completely.

CLEVER SPARKS remember to look out for WET LEAVES.

I froze again while the world revolved around me. Was this for real?

Chapter 11

During the next two weeks more of these helpful posters popped up. They were divided in to four quadrants - red, blue, green and yellow - and the text was stamped over the top. There were six-foot canvasses adorning the stairwells reminding you to hold on to the bannister, they also appeared in the canteen teaching us the dangers of salt, and they were even locked in frames above the urinals commanding you to wash your hands. They were absolutely everywhere and you could travel no more than twenty yards before being reminded of some inane fact of life.

I was convinced that I was one of these Clever Sparks because I already knew the dangers they alluded to. In fact I was sure that I had already learnt most of these lessons when I was five or six years old.

Was it the tone of the message, the colours or the sentiment that made me so angry? I was under the impression that usually an employee would go through an interview process initially to gain employment. If, during this interview, he behaved like Mr Bean then the candidate's chances would be seriously hampered. To imply that not only was I normal to have learnt these skills so early on in my existence but also that my spark was higher than the average, was quite frankly offensive. I would hate to have been the person that these posters were aimed at. I felt an urge to do something about it.

I was still keeping my head down in relation to work and by deliberately keeping a low profile I seemed to be missing out on most of the dishing out of activities. Although in one way this was fantastic because it meant I was not wasting my time discussing pointless things with stupid people, it did mean that I spent much more time staring out of the window. This is the excuse I give for the idea of sabotaging the Clever Sparks Campaign being allowed to germinate.

Human Resources were to blame. There was no doubt about this because their corporate logo was stamped on every poster and I could even guess how it originated. There would have been three objectives at the beginning of the year; keep a record of how many accidents there were on site, promote accident avoidance, and raise the profile of the group. A clever spark would have come up with this gem of an idea in a blue sky session. The manager of the group, who was hardly making waves to be the next CEO, had seen an opportunity to tick off three of his objectives in one fell swoop and rubber stamped the atrocious experiment. It was then left to a school leaver, who was trying their best but missed the point by a country mile, to come up with the posters. Things happen in the corporate world because there are people there to do them but if those people were not there, then those things would not happen and nobody would notice their absence.

The driving incident was still fresh in my mind and especially how Wilks had won by gently pushing back against the authority.

A small group of men gathered in the heart of the forest, hidden between the oak trees and the undergrowth. They were sitting in a circle, collaboratively hunched forwards with their heads not more than a foot apart. The dampness of the ground seeped into their clothes but this was the way in which they had been forced to live. The founder of this group had been exiled and made to give up the responsibility which he had for the surrounding villages. In a desperate attempt to win back his rightful place and bring down the new rulers of the land, he had formed this small group of outlaws each with their own reasons to fight.

'They're everywhere Robin,' said Little John. 'You

can't go anywhere near the castle without seeing one.'

'They've even been put up in the outlying villages,' said Will Scarlet.

'We have to do something about it,' said Alan-a-Dale.

Robin thought carefully and then said, 'we'll break into the castle at night and put up our own signs.'

'How?' asked Friar Tuck.

'The same way we've always done,' smiled Robin.

'I meant how are we going to make our own?' asked Friar Tuck.

'We'll just copy theirs.'

'Why don't we just take theirs down?' said Little John.

'Because there's too many of them. It'll be too hard to carry them all back here and hide them. We've got to travel light.'

'I don't see the point in any of this,' said Marian. 'King John won't be bothered by it and he'll still expect the villagers to do as he says.'

'Ah, but he'll be undermined,' said Robin with a twinkling in his eye. 'It'll cause confusion and ridicule. Besides, it'll let the villagers know that there's someone out there fighting for them. It'll give them hope.'

'Maybe but there's a big risk that one of us is going to get caught.'

'Yeah, there is,' nodded Robin. 'But we're here to protect the people and that's something we have to keep on doing.'

'What about the Sheriff?' asked Will Scarlet. 'It was a close thing last time with that Lasagne.'

'We'll just have to be extra careful,' said Robin. 'We have to do this and we have to do it now. We need to start making the signs.'

The band of brothers, and Marian, set to work creating the signs that would be put up around the county as decoys. After an hour they had finished and Robin stood back and admired their handiwork. One of them read:

CLEVER SPARKS remember to BREATHE.

100% of deaths are caused by not breathing. Breathe every 2-3 seconds whilst walking around offices.
DO NOT breathe whilst swallowing.

CLEVER SPARKS remember to BREATHE.

Other examples were; Clever Sparks Open Their Eyes, Clever Sparks Avoid Walls, and Clever Sparks Are Careful With Scissors.

Robin smiled as he collected them all together and hid them from view. 'We'll go out tonight,' he said. 'They won't be expecting us.'

Just as I had placed the last of the posters in my top drawer the door suddenly opened. It made me jump in my chair so forcefully that my legs banged against the desk. I looked up as innocently as I could and noticed Savage stood in the doorway.

'What are you doing?' he said.

'Nothing, nothing - well, working obviously.'

'Hmmm,' he looked less than convinced. 'What are you doing generally at the moment?'

'Oh, you know, this and that. Very busy actually.'

'Something's come up and you're going to have to find time to do it.'

'Ok, what is it?'

'I need you to go to a conference for me. You need to represent Project Eagle, god help us.'

'Sure. When is it?'

'Four weeks time in New York.'

'Cool. I think that should be okay. What's it about?'

'Nothing much, some finance thing, that's why I'm not going. I just want you to make sure that nothing is said about our project. If it is then I just want you to make a note of it. Whatever you do, make sure you don't talk about Eagle. That's all we need.'

'Oh right, ok. How am I going to know where to go?'

'By the email I'm going to send obviously.' Savage tutted, mumbled something under his breath and walked out leaving the door open.

That was another one of these rules that you were expected to obey. It was called the open door policy. The idea being if the door was open then the person was available. It never made any difference to me though, people would walk in to my office if the door was open or closed, so I kept it closed at all times.

I finally left my office at seven that evening. It had been a trial of concentration to stay that long but I knew I had to wait until the corridors were completely deserted. I collected up the posters, already prepared with Blu-Tac, and hid them in a folder.

I crept around the corridors hoping I was not going to run in to Big Darren. It dawned on me that I had not seen him since Lasagne-gate and he had probably dreamed of meeting me in a dark corridor ever since. I did not waste any time in sticking the posters up all over the building. I put them up in stair wells, vending machines, both sets of toilets, and even the central café. At each designated point I would quickly glance around and then suddenly attack the wall with a poster.

I had just put up the last one when I heard a noise in

the adjacent corridor. I was in no-man's land, I could not retreat and there were no rooms to jump into. I decided to tackle it head on and walked confidently towards it. The noise came around the corner before me and it turned out to be one of Heavyside's henchmen. Thankfully he did not recognise me and I was able to walk right past him. I walked on for about ten more yards before he shouted back along the corridor, 'STOP!'

'Shit,' I thought. 'Yes?'

'Are you staying any later?'

'No, I'm just about to go.'

'Ok. Didn't you know you had to tell us if you were working late?'

'No, I try not to do it too much. I knew I had to tell my wife but…'

'Next time, don't forget to tell us,' he carried on walking and so did I.

'Another rule,' I thought.

That night I went home satisfied. I had become the Robin Hood of RC. Ben Jenkins – Folk Hero. I liked the sound of that.

Chapter 12

'Hey, Jane, look what I've got here,' I said as soon as I opened the front door. I had happily driven home from work and could not wait to show her the Clever Sparks posters.

'Aren't you going to kiss the kids first?' she said almost immediately.

I disappeared upstairs and came back down within a minute. They were both tucked up in bed by the time I had returned from work but for once I knew they would understand. If your Daddy's a folk hero then some kind of sacrifice is inevitable.

'Anyway I want to show you these,' I said fumbling with my bag.

'Hello,' said Jane.

'Oh yeah, hello by the way. Sorry but for once I'm proud of something that I've done at work and I can't wait to show you.' She looked at me and waited. 'You know the signs that I was talking about at the weekend. The ones that have come up at work telling you how not to have an accident. Well, I don't know what happened today but I kind of snapped. I was sat in my office, thinking about how patronising they were and I just thought to myself, *'why don't I do something about it?'* So I did.'

'Oh god, what have you done?'

'These.' I took out copies of the posters and gave them to her. She looked at them for a while and then looked perplexed.

'You mean you've just made up some posters with stupid messages on?'

'Not just that, babe. I've only gone and put them up on the walls as well.' My enormous smile was not met with the same expression from Jane.

'What a dick,' she said. 'Did anyone see you?'

'No, you see, I was clever. I waited until everyone had left and then I quickly went and did it.'

'They'll know it's you.'

'How?'

'Because you're the only knob that would. Everybody else is a boring nerd, or according to you they are.'

'True. But it's a big place and I'm anonymous.' She shook her head and walked off into the other room. 'You should have seen me though, babe,' I said following her. 'I was like a ninja, the way I was darting around. I couldn't stop laughing to myself. I still can't. Do you not think they're funny?'

'I think they're weird. I think you're weird. Did you not have any proper work to do?'

'This is better though. I'd rather do stupid things like this than waste my time on a dead horse of a project.'

'Is it still no better?'

'You're kidding. Nothing's changed on it since before Christmas. I don't know how they're getting away with it. Seriously, there's millions of dollars getting spent on it, every single week that goes by. I can't be bothered even telling you about it anymore, it's amazing.'

'Why don't they just stop it then?'

'The people who should be stopping it don't even know about it. It's all hushed up.'

'Why don't you tell them then?'

'That's not the way it works. It's not my money, I'm just trying to get out of the way of the firing line. I tell you, when this thing blows up they'll be looking around for scapegoats. I'm trying to distance myself as much as possible and just keep my head down.'

'It seems like it,' she said and looked down at the posters that I was still holding.

'Oh, by the way, I have to go to the US in about a month's time.'

'Do you?'

'Yeah, some conference or other. Get this, I have to

turn up just to make a note if they mention our project. That's it. I'm not even allowed to say anything about it.'

'You should tell people it's shit and it's a waste of money.'

'That's why you're not working for a corporate company Jane. You can't just say that to people. I'm best just staying out of it.'

The next morning was still cold. It had rained the night before and the pavements had all frozen. I shuffled across the car park with my slippery work shoes doubling up as ice skates and walked in through the turnstile. A couple of girls near the water machine started whispering and looking over at me. They were joined by two others, a man and a woman, who also began to look over and the woman started pointing. Eventually the man started to clap and all of the women followed him. I was unsure at first how to react so I just stared back but eventually I waved at them, hoping that this would make them stop.

By this stage other people had come out of their offices and had started to clap too. Then the corridor was filled with clapping employees and I was still stood up against the turnstile. I milked the applause for a few minutes, what else could I do, and then a couple of big chaps came over to me and lifted me up on their shoulders. I was then carried around the corridors whilst still being followed by an ever growing crowd of appreciators. There were shouts of encouragement, people holding up the posters aloft and even a few groupies seemed to be shouting for more than just a high-five. The revolution had come and I was the figurehead. No longer would the workers be subjected to such absurd rules.

The office was freezing when I arrived the next morning. I had been thinking about the posters on the way in and a part of me was still excited about the stir that they would have caused. I knew that the change would not be too extreme but I wondered if at least someone had noticed them. But I was disappointed to see that nothing seemed to have changed at all. I had walked casually around to the cafe where I had put up two of the beauties on the noticeboard but no one had seemed to spot them. There was a queue of people all lined up waiting for coffee and looking almost directly at them, still there was not even as much as a snigger. I sulked for the rest of the morning.

The canteen was quiet when I arrived but at least my regulars were there. I sat down and almost immediately started teasing out whether they had noticed the posters. I decided the night before with Jane that it was probably best not to tell anyone that I was involved just in case the wrong person found out.

'Anyone seen those new posters which have turned up?' I asked. Most of them, to my dismay, looked blank.

'Which ones?' asked Stretch.

'The Clever Sparks ones.'

Stretch shook his head, Emily shook her head and Wilks shook his head.

'Oh, I know what you mean,' said Dave. 'I saw one of them this morning I think. Someone's put up some joke ones. What was it? The one I saw said, 'Clever Sparks know the way to Amarillo'. Is that what you mean?' he asked.

'Yeah, they're the ones,' I smiled. 'What do you think?'

'Ok, I suppose. It made a nice change to see something different.'

'It's not that funny though, is it?' said Stretch. 'If it was me I would've put something like, Clever Sparks don't shit themselves.'

'Very grown up,' said Emily.

'Or, what about, Clever Sparks don't get caught perving at the secretary on the third floor,' said Stretch again.

'Aw, she is fit though,' said Dave.

'Which one?' said Wilks.

'The tall one with the dark hair,' said Stretch.

'I don't know her,' said Wilks.

'I'll show you this afternoon,' promised Dave.

'Good, I'm glad you've got that sorted out,' said Emily. 'To change the subject, I've been told that I'm going to the US next month. Has anyone been there before?'

'Yep, I have,' said Wilks.

'And did you go Business Class when you went?' she asked.

'Yeah of course,' he answered.

'I only ask because I'm going economy.'

'Gutted,' said Dave.

'You shouldn't be,' said Wilks.

'I am,' she said. 'I've been told that I can go to the finance conference but I'm only allowed to travel economy. It's something to do with cost cutting.'

'Ouch,' said Wilks.

'I'm going to that conference too,' I said. 'I'd better be travelling business class.'

'I doubt it, unless you can wangle it,' Emily said. 'I was told that anyone going to the conference has to go economy because there's so many going from the UK.'

'Twats,' I said. 'No wonder he's giving it to me, the bastard.'

'Who's that?' smiled Dave.

'Savage, who else. He told me yesterday that I had to go.' The table all laughed at my misfortune once again and I sank down into my chair. It would do me no good to complain to Savage about it but the change of rules had really wound me up. It was always expected that long haul flights would be business class, it was a given, so to send us economy was a real sickener. Here was an example of RC saving a few hundred quid on my plane ticket but on the other hand they were throwing millions away on my project.

The reaction to the posters left me underwhelmed too. Obviously to be a folk hero these days you needed to be a little less subtle. Perhaps my protest was too discreet. Robin Hood, I thought to myself, would not have stooped so low to win over the villagers. Surely there was a place for a slightly middle of the road revolutionary in a corporate world. But I considered that a middle of the road revolution would be a roundabout, and you cannot get anywhere by following one of them. I sat back dejectedly wondering why I bothered in the first place.

Chapter 13

The rest of January, and the beginning of February, flew by in a whirlwind of nothingness. The project had remained stagnant throughout this period and the only progress seemed to be that the costs figure was rapidly increasing. My dream of becoming a folk-hero had disintegrated once again and, much to my disappointment, all of my posters had been taken down. In a way, the US trip was the only thing I had to look forward to. I had come to accept the economy ticket fiasco but it still rankled if someone mentioned it.

I went through the motions at work and ticked off the days dreaming about New York City. I had seen Emily a few times at lunch, not every day but enough to arrange to meet each other at the airport.

It was around ten in the morning when I arrived and I could see Emily stood at the checking-in gates, right at the back of a very long queue.

'Hi ya,' I said, as I tried my best to look like a seasoned traveller even though I was carrying a case, a laptop bag, and a suit bag. I had actually travelled to

Germany quite a bit over the last five years and was relatively experienced on European flights. I knew enough to know that going through check-in with three bags was going to make me a laughing stock amongst the serious long haulers. Luckily, I noticed that Emily also had three bags and her case was much bigger than mine. As I approached I knew I would have to take on the role of her protector and guide her through the confusing world of an airport check-in.

'Hi there,' she said with a pleasant smile. Her short blonde hair looked perfect with a pair of sunglasses resting on the top of her head. She had a pair of tight blue jeans on that really showed off her long legs and a white blouse that was tucked in with just the right amount of cleavage showing. I suddenly felt good knowing that we would be travelling together.

'How long have you been here?' I asked as I put my bags down next to hers.

'Only about ten minutes,' she said looking up at the ridiculously large plastic clock that was hanging from the aluminium roof.

'Is the queue moving quickly?' I asked, 'mind you, come to think of it, we should have plenty of time to get through. These things are always slow. Look at that desk next to ours - empty. You know what that is, that's the business class check-in. We'd be sat having a beer by now if we were going through there.'

'It's only ten in the morning, Ben,' said Emily, 'it's not as if we're going to Benidorm.'

'Yeah, that's true, fair enough.' I felt a bit boyish with that last remark and tried to rein it back. 'Maybe instead we could be having a pleasant Danish and an Arabica Coffee by now.' What was I talking about? 'Look there's someone going up to that desk now,' I said looking at a small man in a cheap suit that looked more like a car salesman than a businessman. 'Unbelievable, and we're stood here behind Dumb and Dumber and The Clampetts,' I hinted at the small, inbred collective in front of us in the queue. I must have been a bit loud though and Dumber looked around forcing me to quickly study an advertisement for American Express behind his head. When he turned back I began staring in envy at the other desk again. 'Look, he's gone through already. How quick was that? I can't believe we're going economy.'

'I think that desk is going to Copenhagen, Ben,' Emily whispered.

'Oh, er, yeah, of course it is. I should have seen that,' that was twice within thirty-seconds that she had corrected me. I reminded myself to calm down and stop talking rubbish. I also became aware of how much I sounded like a pretentious prick to the other people in the queue.

'I had a look at all of the films that are on,' I said trying to be optimistic about the flight.

'On where?' asked Emily.

'On the plane. Do you know that we get five less films in economy?' I was at it again and this time I was showing how sad I was as well. I was probably the only person travelling on US Airways that year that had spent an hour trying to find out which films were being shown in February. Emily just nodded and raised her eyebrows, struggling to find anything to say.

We stood in silence after that and waited, and waited, and waited, until eventually The Clampetts were at the desk with their five children. Unsurprisingly it turned out that they had too much baggage, so we had to wait even longer for them to pay their additional allowance. Then the Dumbers went through and finally it was our turn. I already had everything out and I reckon, if there was a stopwatch going, I would have broken the record for the quickest ever economy check-in.

Part of the airport was under construction and I was struggling to work out where we needed to go next. Disappointingly Emily seemed to know exactly where she was going and in the end I just followed her. That was until she abruptly stopped and two men in suits who were walking past stopped as well.

'Hello,' said Emily in her friendly work tone.

'Emily Sanderson, well, well, well,' said the taller of the two men. 'The future of RC. What are you doing here? Wait, you're not getting a plane, are you? How very clever. Where are you going, is it Hamburg or the US? Come on let's walk. It must be the US because the Hamburg flight's just left. What are you going for? Not the finance conference? Who would've thought it, that's where we're going. Are you staying at The Sheraton? Well, there's nowhere else is there? What are you doing for dinner tonight? You'll have to come with us to the basketball at Madison Square Garden. Do you like basketball? In fact do you even like sport? That's one thing that I don't know about you, young Emily. I would have thought you look like you do. What is it? Love it or hate it? The marmite question.' He rested for a second to laugh at his own joke, long enough for Emily to answer that she liked it, and then he was off again. 'Ah, I knew you would. Listen, are you going this way? Of course you are. We're all going to the same place. Come on then, we haven't got all day. Who's your friend? Is he coming to the conference as well? He looks very smart.'

'This is Ben Jenkins,' Emily said quickly.

'Pleased to meet you, Ben Jenkins,' he carried on at the same pace, 'I'm Stuart, Stuart Hamilton. For my sins,

I'm the manager of R&D Finance. Haven't come across you before. Where do you work? Is it Central Finance? It must be if you're involved with this lot. Ah, perhaps your part of Eagle, no? Is it all it's cracked up to be? Are we going to have our prayers answered? I'm on the Steering Group and I hear that progress seems steady. We usually fall down at this stage though. What do you think the chances are of success?'

He finally stopped and I knew why. I had known senior managers before that would act like this. They would talk nonsense, draw you in, act friendly and then suddenly hit you with the money question. What made me additionally aware was that I had heard of Stuart Hamilton before. Dave had once worked with him and told me that he was a pompous, loathsome character that would sell his own Grandmother in order to get ahead.

'I think the project is progressing exactly as Rupert Savage has told you,' I said. 'I can't see any reason why it won't deliver.' If I had a choice of being stuck in a room with an angry Stuart Hamilton or an angry Savage, I would pick Hamilton any day of the week.

'Really,' he replied slowly, clearly thinking, 'what about the costs?'

'They should be in line,' I said hoping that lightning would not be able to strike me down in an airport. We had been walking all the while that Hamilton had been talking and we were coming up to the passport control area.

'That's not what I heard. Anyway I'm sure we'll get to know more very soon.' He stopped and then suddenly changing his voice, he was off again. 'We have to get through this bloody line first. Through here,' and he darted down an alley between The Sunglasses Shop and Boots. 'Fast Track. It's the only way to get through this thing.'

We all followed him and emerged in front of a private gate directly in front of the security conveyor belts. We could see every other passenger on every other flight staring at us from the long, snaking line ten feet away. There must have been at least a hundred people there. In their eyes was a mixture of envy and curiosity.

Stood behind us at our private gate were a pilot and his flight crew. I have no idea how we managed to get through. I was half expecting the guard to check my boarding pass and humiliatingly send me to the back of the long, snaking line. I was already rehearsing the walk of shame in my head. I do not know what Hamilton said as he went through but we all followed like school children on a field trip.

On the other side, as we were still putting our shoes and coats back on, he simply walked off knowing that the top secret fast track was even cooler if you ignored it afterwards. A pompous manager probably showed it to him once and did exactly the same on the other side. Nobody else spoke as we quickly caught up with him, 'I take it you're going in to the lounge?' he said to Emily.

'No, we've got economy tickets,' said Emily, a little embarrassed.

Hamilton stopped where he was and thought for a moment. I stood next to Emily feeling younger than I had felt in years. I wish I could have grasped the situation and walked off to make my own way through the airport but I knew what he was just about to say and, although I am not proud of selling out, I waited. 'We could both sign you in on our 'frequent flyers,' said Hamilton. 'Steve, have you got yours with you?' The man who had learnt to keep quiet, nodded. 'Of course you have. Good man. Right, you two, follow us.'

We followed them up the stairs and on to the executive floor. There were three different lounges that I could see and we walked up to the middle one. Again we stood behind the grown ups like children in an extremely weird looking family unit and eventually I gained access to the business class lounge.

Chapter 14

I expected the business class lounges to be filled with plush sofas, class A drugs, and fluffers but I suppose one out of three would do. It was better than being stuck in the cattle market of the departure lounge watching stag do's preparing for their weekends in Prague. The lounge was bigger than I thought, it had forty or so small round tables evenly spread. There was a self-service bar in the middle and a television corner at one end. There was a restrained reverence in the room that you usually only find in libraries and churches. As soon as we sat down they announced that our flight to New York had been delayed by two hours. There was a flurry of activity as people all around us, dressed in suits, pulled out their mobile phones and made frantic looking calls. Then, calm again.

Everyone had their laptops open and looked busy. Emily pulled hers out of her bag and opened it up. I watched her without comment and then decided to walk up to the bar and see what was on offer. There were all types of hot and cold drinks available and a small collection of snacks. As it was only half ten I opted for a cup of coffee and a blueberry muffin then made my way back to the table.

'Do you want me to get you anything?' I asked Emily. She said she wanted an orange juice so I went to fetch it.

I then sat at the table for an hour eating, people watching and finishing my coffee. I spent a lot of time watching the top of Emily's head as she concentrated on her laptop. After an hour I was bored. I looked around at the bar and while it was empty I thought I would go and get myself a proper drink. I returned with a gin and tonic trying to hide it as I walked back through the tables. Emily looked up and shook her head. It was like having Jane here I thought to myself.

'Are you going to be working all the way there?' I asked eventually.

'No way,' she said. 'I just want to get this finished that's all. I should have done it last week but didn't.'

'Thank god for that. I was getting worried that I'd have to do some work in a minute just to join in. People are starting to look at me funny.' She smiled and put her head back down again and carried on working.

Another hour later and finally our flight was called. I then realised that I had no idea where we were in the airport. I could not see Hamilton, he was probably sat next to the pilot by now, so we followed a bunch of people that looked like they knew where they were going. We walked through various fire doors and hidden corridors before appearing directly in front of the correct gate. There were a bunch of other RC employees at the gate who must have been going to the conference but when we all walked on to the plane only Emily and I turned right. The rest of the RC contingent were travelling business class. Fortunately I had drunk three gin and tonics by this stage and felt much calmer about it.

We settled in to our seats and watched as those around us tried to squeeze rucksacks, and duty-free bags, into the overhead lockers. I had a family next to me who were desperately trying to keep their three-year-old son entertained with a puzzle book. The air-hostess came along with a travel pack for the little brat and this at least appeared to subdue him temporarily. I sat staring in front of me imagining what it would be like in the other section, how many three year olds would be in there?

'A red wine, please' I ordered, as soon as the seatbelt sign had switched off and the air-hostess had pulled her trolley up next to us. Emily politely asked for an orange juice and then smiled with a subtle shake of her head at my wine.

'That'll be five pounds, Sir,' smiled the air-hostess.

'Oh, will it? Do you take cards?'

'Yes Sir.'

'Jolly good then. Here you go.'

'I'm claiming this back,' I said to Emily after the air-hostess had gone. 'How much have they saved on our tickets? They can at least pay for my sustenance.' I poured the little bottle of cold red wine into my plastic glass, took a sip and started playing around with the TV remote control. Emily took her laptop out. 'You're not going to carry on working, are you?'

'I just have to finish this,' she said as if someone was holding her at gunpoint.

'I've got no time for work, I've got a whole schedule of films to get through,' I said still slightly embarrassed about looking them up beforehand. 'An American Gangster's first up, of course if the films weren't here then I'd be working away like an ant.'

'Of course you would.'

I put my headphones on and Emily turned back to her PC. After the film had finished I went to the toilet and when Emily had to stand up to let me back in she used the interruption as a suitable point to put her laptop away.

'At last,' I said.

'That's enough,' she said looking proud of herself.

'Time to get a proper drink.' To my surprise she then reached up to press her hostess light and I saw more than I was bargaining for. The angle of her unbuttoned blouse put me within a foot of a firm, ample right breast. I stared for a moment before remembering where I was and quickly looked up. I think she was unaware of how much I had seen and continued to surprise me even more by ordering a double scotch.

'Wow,' I said, 'you're not playing games.'

'Surely you didn't think I was going to drink orange juice the whole way?' she said laughing. 'I think I've had enough orange juice and I've done enough work. What was the film like?'

'It was alright but I missed the middle part, I think I dozed off for a bit.'

'You didn't miss much. I've seen it before. Russell Crowe's not my cup of tea,' she said turning her nose up. There was a pause while we both looked at our little screens, a foot away from our eyes.

'What is your type?' I asked.

'Let me think,' she smiled. 'Athletic, good with his hands, good teeth, nice eyes, not too soft. Preferably not smelly but I don't know if that's even possible. Oh and funny as well. Someone that can make me laugh.'

'That's a fair shopping list but you've just described Stretch.'

'Urgh, no. He's old enough to be my Dad.'

'He might well be.' We both laughed and looked back at the screens.

'What do you think of Stretch?' she asked.

'Legend.'

'But seriously?'

'Honestly the guy's a diamond. You can tell him anything and he's as safe as houses. There's never been a dull moment when he's around.'

'He's a bit of a dirty old man though, isn't he?' she turned her nose up again and this time I noticed the little wrinkle that appeared at the top.

'No, I don't think so, it's all an act. I bet he's as quiet as a lamb at home. He just does what he has to do at work to get through the day, like all of us really. His sense of humour's just a bit more edgy than others, or maybe he's just got the balls to come out with it. Mind you, I've seen him scare off a few in the past. He can be a bit too much sometimes. Do you remember that girl, I can't remember her name, but she came to lunch with us once on her first day. Stretch was on one and she never came back. I think after a week she left RC altogether.'

'Oh yeah, I remember that girl, um, Rebecca Armstrong.'

'That's it,' I said. 'Quite tall, with dark hair. She literally only came to lunch with us once. The tipping point was when he started going on about the, 'would you rather' questions. I think that was the time when he went around the table asking us, if we had a teenage daughter who was a lesbian, would you hide in a cupboard when she had her friends round?'

'Uh, yeah, exactly, I can't believe anyone would be put off by that.'

'That is funny though.' I started smiling as I remembered it. 'Without him it would feel like a prison sentence sometimes, I mean it.'

'I don't know what all of this says about me. I've been having lunch with you guys for years.'

'We all know you love it Em, otherwise you wouldn't keep coming back.'

'I think, like you said, I keep coming back to escape the day job.'

'Noooo, you love that as well. You must do. You're always so conscientious at work. Now look at me, I hate my job but I act like I hate it as well. You keep getting promoted because you're doing well at it. That's a good thing right.'

'Little do you know,' she looked at her screen and sighed.

'I take it you don't then?'

She took a deep breath. 'No. I fucking hate it.'

'Oh,' I said taken a back.

'I've always hated it but we needed the money. My boyfriend was trying to be an artist which pretty much meant that he laid on the sofa all day and played computer games. I had no choice but to stay at RC and get as much money as I could.'

'What's he doing now then?'

'He still a shitty, wannabe artist but he's laying on someone else's sofa now.' I stayed quiet. I never really knew what to say to girls when they started talking about relationships. 'Anyway I don't have to worry about him anymore.'

'When did that happen?'

'A couple of months ago.'

'You didn't say anything?'

'Well, I'm hardly going to broadcast it at lunch in front of you lot.'

'I suppose not but even Stretch can be sensitive when he wants to be. I saw it once, I thought he was ill, he goes all red behind the ears.'

'Hmmm, but anyway I don't have to keep working at RC anymore.'

'What? Are you leaving?'

'I don't want to be there and it's not making me happy so stuff it.'

'Just like that?'

'I'm only twenty-eight. I'll just get another job. One

that I enjoy.'

'Like what?'

'I don't know yet, something creative though. It would be cool to work for a small tech company. I don't know what I'd do but it might be worth having a look.'

'I'm impressed. If you just up and leave then I'll be incredibly jealous.'

'Why don't you do it too?'

'Oh, I don't know. I've got little mouths to feed, mortgages to pay, I can't just leave it all behind and chase the dream.'

'Why not?'

'I can't afford to. I'd never forgive myself if we all started living under a bridge. It just can't be done. When you're at my stage of life you have to be a bit more measured.'

'Jesus, you sound like you're sixty. What do you mean, 'your stage of life?' You're only a few years older than me.'

'Yeah, I don't feel like it though.'

'That's because you hang around with Dave and Stretch, they're both more than ten years older than you.'

'It doesn't feel like ten years though.'

'That's because you're all in the same zone but your decisions are influenced by theirs and they're at a completely different stage of life to you.'

'I suppose so but what can you do?'

'You need to start taking control again.'

'Yeah maybe you're right but I don't know if I could be as relaxed as you are about what's coming next.'

'It'll always turn out for the best, it always does, you're never going to be living under a bridge. You've got too much going on for that to happen, so instead of thinking like it's the end of the world, start thinking like it's the beginning of a new world.'

'I don't know, and besides,' I took a deep breath in, 'I haven't got a bloody clue what I want to do instead.'

'Start thinking about it then, you don't want to find out when you're sixty.'

'Yeah, right. Oh well, what will be will be and now I must get back to my movie schedule.'

'Sad.'

'Yep, Juno's next.'

'I haven't seen that.'

'Well, saddle up then and turn the channel on to seven. Seize the day.'

I did not concentrate too much on Juno. The same thoughts that had depressed me for months had all just been turned over. If only I knew what I wanted to do then it would be easier to start working it out. It was alright for Emily to give me the rallying cry but she was on her own and had nothing to lose. I had everything to lose.

By the time the plane had landed I was in a real slump. The red wine had worked through the system and accompanied with the gin, I was now feeling almost suicidal. All I wanted to do was get to the hotel and go to sleep.

I had been to New York several times before and while the yellow cab drove us from JFK to our hotel on 52nd Street I just watched the life go by the window. I always loved New York because it seemed to have a feeling of eternal hope about the place. Anything was possible and as you watched people going about their lives each of them looked like they had a purpose. On the inside of the car, on the wrong side of the glass, I could only look on and imagine what that must feel like. Emily was talking continuously about the buildings, about the people, about the shops, I think the several whiskies had kicked in and I just nodded as she kept going.

A group of college kids came running up to the taxi. They were dressed like typical American college kids and it felt like we were in the middle of a Tommy Hilfiger advert. One of them had a beat box playing some kind of hip hop and they started pushing flyers up against the window advertising a club night they were obviously organising. Our driver wound his window down and shouted at them like Danny DeVito. Emily and I sat in the back seat smiling at each other. It was the most stereotypical New York situation that I could imagine. The kids ran off to harass the next set of innocent bystanders and suddenly the taxi pulled up outside our hotel.

The Sheraton was a huge, towering skyscraper which had at least fifty floors. It looked so impressive as we climbed out of the cab and looked up at the daunting entrance. While I was stood on the sidewalk, that familiar wave of excitement took hold when you're just about to walk into a hotel which you have not been to before. The lobby was a vast expanse of carpet, with plants lining the edges, and as we walked in we were met by at least a hundred other residents that were either coming or going. The entire attack on the senses made me forget about my own problems and when Emily suggested that we meet back downstairs at the bar, it seemed like the obvious thing to do.

I checked in and found my room on the eighteenth floor. It was always exciting when you put the card in the door and turned the handle. You never knew what to expect but The Sheraton delivered. All of the usual facilities were present but they looked new and clean and there was a good amount of space around the bed. I threw my bags down on the floor and was going to head straight back to the bar when I suddenly remembered about ringing Jane. I had promised I would ring to let her know I was safe.

A text came through when I had been on the phone for five minutes. It was from Emily. *'I'm in Lounge Bar on 44th floor. Got you a pint.'* I told Jane I was feeling tired and needed to get my head down, then left for the bar.

Chapter 15

The Lounge Bar was unbelievable. When you walked in you were met with a panoramic vista of New York from the forty-fourth floor. You could see Central Park, Times Square, the Hudson and New Jersey beyond. I stopped for a moment and took it in before noticing Emily sat at the end of a counter which ran in front of the window. The counter was empty given that it was only three in the afternoon but it felt a lot later to us. Emily had another whisky in front of her and next to her was my untouched pint of lager.

'Right then,' I said sitting down. 'Thanks. Just what I need.'

'No worries, thought it would be.'

'What an amazing view,' I said.

'Yeah, I've been soaking it in. I don't think I would ever get bored of this.'

'No. It's pretty cool.'

'I need to go to the loo. I've been waiting until you got here.' Emily stood up and started walking off towards where I had come in.

'Fair enough.' I looked around at the empty bar. 'I guess I'll save your seat in case anyone else wants it.'

She had left me to look out on the whole of New York. I started to think about my future. It seemed to me that the one thing I needed to find desperately was something else I could do that would earn me the sort of money I had already been used to earning. I looked at the millions of people that were running around below and wondered about all of the different jobs there were in the world and yet I was struggling to think of just one.

I was hungry and looked around, luckily finding a bowl of peanuts on the table behind. I reached out and moved them in front of me. I was staring at them and then it suddenly dawned on me that you hardly ever saw them in British pubs anymore. The lack of hygiene involved with multiple piss-stained fingers foraging in to the same bowl was probably the reason but the American's were not bothered and neither was I. I was looking at them individually and imagining that every nut was a different job. I took the metaphor one step further and realised that I had settled for the one on the top because it was the easiest to obtain. But career selection based on what is easiest to obtain is like reaching for the piss-stained nut on the top. Perhaps if you were to spend a bit of time, maybe working out what you wanted most in a nut, and then searched through the bowl for the ideal candidate then you might find a lovely untouched perfect nut for you near the bottom. This nut may make the rest of your life wonderful. If I was a giant monkey and I reached into the bowl would I be able to find the right one? Perhaps I would end up with my hand covered in piss anyway while I rooted through the rest of them. Is there even such a thing as the perfect nut?

Suddenly I noticed a presence next to me. I looked around like a scared rabbit, with my hand still shaped like a monkey claw, and saw Emily looking strangely at me.

'Oh alright? I was miles away,' I said. 'You gave me a fright.' I returned my hand to a normal hand shape so that she would not notice, but her eyes were looking at me like I was weird.

'Deep in thought?' she said after a brief pause.

'Deep in the shit,' I sighed. 'No, no, no, I didn't mean that. It's just that you've interrupted me comparing myself to a giant monkey selecting nuts for jobs. You know how it is.'

'Yeah,' she said.

'Yeah.'

Emily and I spent the rest of the afternoon and early evening looking out over New York gradually drinking more and more. I had a lot of fun with her which surprised me because I had not really spent that much time alone with her before. We talked a bit more about her ex-boyfriend and how he was a waste of space, we talked about how much of a saint Jane must be to put up with my grumpiness and how cool she must be to let me find something that would make me happy. The time flew by until the jet lag started to creep up on us and then we called it a day. As we said goodbye to each other by the elevator she gave me a little kiss on the cheek. It was nothing really, just a friendly way of saying goodbye but it was nice. I smiled at her, she smiled back, in our eyes there seemed to be a deeper understanding and then the elevator turned up and she was gone.

What with the jet lag, the alcohol, and the thoughts going on in my mind I slept like a disturbed log. I slept for about twelve hours and most of my dreams were filled with monkeys throwing nuts at my life that had taken the form of an ample right breast. The mysterious Lefty was another life, maybe a better life and at least the monkeys were not attacking that one. I made the decision to change my life, I defeated the monkey and I was just about to see the left breast when the alarm went off. I was wrapped up in a sheet, on the floor and my full-length window bathed the room in February sunlight.

The rest of the day was bearable. There were no requests to be involved in any of the sessions, nobody knew who I was and apart from Project Eagle being mentioned as the great white hope, the day was relatively painless. It seemed that the global finance organisation was relying on my project to deliver every efficiency they had targeted for the next five years. That would be a blow for them when they found out. All I had to do was make notes though, and this was what I did. In fact I wrote enough notes to fill a whole side of A4. My wrist was starting to hurt.

Eventually the work sessions finished and everyone disappeared to their rooms to get ready for the evening event. It was almost a military operation to get all of the delegates collected in the lobby and then marched the four blocks over to Park Avenue and The Waldorf Astoria. It made me suspicious. There was something about the organisation that felt familiar and then I saw him, at the very front directing the affair was, my dearest friend Darren Heavyside. I kept my head down and nudged Emily who was stood next to me. She cottoned on immediately and when we were filing out of the door we turned our faces the other way. He would not have been expecting me to be in New York anyway and after all, lasagne-gate must have been a month ago by now.

The group of about two hundred and fifty delegates walked the four blocks along 52nd Street like a huge coach party. We suddenly saw the famous Waldorf Astoria as we were nearly on top of it. A ripple of excitement went through the crowd as we walked through the familiar doors. We were all ushered in to the Grand Ballroom, catching our breath at the ornate splendour that surrounded us. There were diamond chandeliers, decorative gold cornicing, paintings on the wall in heavy gold leaf frames, and an overall sense of majesty. It was the authentic nineteenth century splendour that initially took our breath away. However, as soon as we were seated around large round tables with white tablecloths, we started to become accustomed to it. I sat there thinking to myself that it was not all that different to the works canteen really. This was before I had a drink.

Emily and I tucked into the table wine almost before we even sat down. We were on a table with ten other people we did not know and who had no intention of wanting to know us. So we talked to each other for the entire meal and started up where we left off the night before.

After we had finished eating, the waiter dropped a

few pieces of paper on the table.

'What's this?' I said, picking one up.

'It looks like a song sheet,' she said, 'oh no, you're joking.'

My heart sank too. I looked around at the room full of intoxicated corporate-ites that did not get out much. A sing-song was exactly what was going to happen.

'I'm not doing it,' said Emily. I smiled not really thinking hard enough about how I could get out of it.

The DJ, who had been playing a mixture of classic rock and europop in the background, stopped the music and introduced a 'Professional Singer' to the stage. This 'Professional Singer' then sang a couple of opera style songs and an African styled, Paul Simon-type number. But, if this musical entertainment seemed a little eclectic to us then the next bit took it to a whole new level.

We were instructed to pick up one of the song sheets that had been distributed around all of the tables and if we could not find one then we should share with someone else. Emily suddenly stood up and walked out of the room leaving me sitting there on my own with a song sheet in my hand. Next we were encouraged to stand alongside someone we did not know. The rest of the people stood around my table all looked at me and I looked at them. Within two seconds all of them had partners apart from a lady in her sixties, who looked Swedish and also looked as though she had enjoyed the wine a little too much.

'Ok. Yeah,' shouted the 'Professional Singer' over the microphone, as if she was addressing the Live Aid crowd. 'Ok. Who wants to have some fun?' There were a few murmurs from the crowd, and I was trying to pick out her Eastern European accent. 'I said who wants to have some fun?' This time there was much more of a response as the audience easily succumbed to her efforts of participation. 'That's better. Ok. Yeah. Right, everyone reach your arms up into the sky. Reach 'em up until you can't reach no more.' This was awkward. I did not really want to comply but this over-energetic Swede next to me was looking at me with a big smile on her face, arms already raised above her head. I had to look at least like I was trying, so I put my arms half-heartedly above my head. 'Yeah,' she kept saying. 'Put your heads back and close your eyes. Imagine that you're floating high, high, high above the clouds.' Someone fell over just in front of me, as if the simple task of putting your arms up and closing your eyes needed zen-like balance. I put my head back but kept my eyes open. I imagined that this was what a scene from a cult gathering would start like and I wanted to keep my eyes open in case anyone tried to inject me with something. I did notice that Agneta, (I assume this was my Swedish partner's name) had complied hook line and sinker with the request and was floating somewhere above the clouds, vulnerable and exposed to any suggestion.

'Ok. Yeah,' the jumped up singer continued. 'Now, I want you to put your hands on your partner's shoulders. Alriiight. Niiiice.' This was getting worse; I stayed where I was, but Agneta pounced on me with both hands and put them on my shoulders. I felt like I had to reciprocate, so gingerly, I moved my arms up and rested my hands as gently as I could on the elderly ladies bony shoulders. As our faces were only a foot apart I forced a smile and then desperately tried to look around. I looked for Emily and spotted her, stood by the door half hidden behind a curtain, killing herself with laughter.

'Now, yeah, now,' the singer continued. I was rapidly thinking of what my bail out line would be. 'Now I want you to twist yourselves down. Like if you were doing Chubby Checker's twist. But keep your hands on. Do it together. Yeah. Twist all the way down. Then twist all the way back up. I'm lovin' it.'

I was not loving it. Agneta was enthusiastically throwing herself in to the task at hand and was pushing me down. I was hoping she would have had a bad hip but these Scandinavians always seemed to look after themselves too well. I was about two foot taller and as we were both going down and up, every now and again, her head was in an unfortunate position. As she pushed me down I had no choice but to push her back down. It was one of the most awkward and uncomfortable experiences that I have ever endured and it seemed to last forever. 'Down... and then back up,' kept being relayed over the speakers. 'Down... and then back up.' After a while I began to have an out of body experience. It was so uncomfortable that I literally became numb and hovered above.

Eventually the repetition ended and the trance-like dance, that most of the room had been locked into, stopped and I separated from Agneta like a coiled spring. There were still some, when I looked around, that were holding each other much tighter than necessary and performing a version of the Lambada. Thankfully I had only been bending down in a weightlifter's style with dear old Agneta.

'Ok,' the torturer continued. I wondered if this was the sort of behaviour that happened in work camps during the war. 'Now, how good was that?' There was a ripple of agreement. 'Yeah. Let's go. Ok. Right, now, yeah, we're gonna go for a song. Let's sing. Yeah. Everyone look at their song sheets. Now, this side of the room,' she said, with her arm out stretched in front of her looking to her left. 'I want this side of the room to sing the odd numbered lines, and I want this side,' looking to the right, 'to sing the even numbered lines. And I want you all to sing the chorus, right? Ok, yeah, ok, let's do it. Yeah.'

The music started and I glanced to the words on the paper that Agneta was now holding. I recognised the music to be Queen's One Vision and the title on the bit of paper read, 'One Team'.

The song, which needless to say I did not join in with, was sure enough a cover of Queen's One Vision but the words had been changed to apply to a corporate environment. Out of the room of two hundred and fifty people I would estimate that there were probably two hundred people singing along. They were stood in the direction of the stage, some even had their arms aloft and they were looking at each other whilst singing and nodding their heads as if they believed every word. I had never witnessed such an incredibly awful scene as the one that had gradually unfolded in front of me. Agneta had thankfully found some other elderly Swedish people to latch on to so I took the opportunity and ran for the door. I reached Emily who had tears in her eyes and I stared back over the room in disbelief. This was the loudest message I could have ever heard to tell me that these were not my type of people. I was not like these people. I was not one of them. I needed to escape.

Chapter 16

Emily and I ran out of The Waldorf laughing to each other. I was so relieved to be getting out of there that I had completely forgotten that we were in the middle of New York City. Is there possibly anywhere better in the world to fall out into when the night is still young? As soon as the door opened and my feet landed on the sidewalk there was only one sensible decision to make.

'Let's find a bar,' I said.

We walked south along Park Avenue towards The Helmsley Building and then took a right along 47th Street.

'I can't believe what I've just done,' I said.

'It looked funny from where I was standing.'

'Yeah it would have done, thanks for deserting me.'

'I could tell how it was going to pan out and I didn't fancy any of that.'

'I can't believe it, she was like Skeletor.'

'Who?'

'That woman, she was like Skeletor from He-Man.

All bones and teeth. It was horrible.'

'You looked good though. I didn't know you could move like that.'

'Old snake hips, that's what they used to call me. Oh no wait, it wasn't that it was something else. What was it? Oh yeah, that was it, I remember now, they just used to say I was shit. '

'You were good, especially that clean and jerk action that you had going. I've never seen anyone dance up and down like that before. New York has seen something special there.'

'Whatever, stop taking the piss. It was horrible. Is that a bar?'

'Looks like it.'

'Connolly's.'

'It looks like a Wetherspoon's.'

'This is what we need. A good old Irish Bar. I bet there's more Irish bars in New York than in the whole of Dublin.'

'To be sure,' Emily tried an Irish accent.

'That's terrible. What was that? Pakistani?'

The two of us walked in and were greeted with the universal stare. Whenever you walk in to an empty bar or restaurant the people in there will always stop and look. If you are not local then they stare a little longer and, if you are dressed like you have just come from

The Waldorf Astoria then they stare even longer still. It was only then that I noticed how stunning Emily looked that night. In the grandeur of The Waldorf she blended in with her environment but now we were in a pub, and five other blokes at the bar were wearing jeans and hoodies, she suddenly looked amazing. Her skirt was just above the knee and her legs looked incredible. Her top was strapless but she had a small cardigan over the top of that because of the February chill. All of the men then stared even longer but not at me. She went to sit down at a table knowing that she had attracted some attention and I went to the bar to get some drinks. The five blokes all turned back round casually and returned to their conversation about baseball.

'I've got us some whiskies,' I said holding a couple of triples.

'Are you trying to get me drunk, Mr Jenkins?'

'After what I've just been through I need one of these and I didn't want you to feel left out. I saw how much you put back yesterday.'

'Cheers,' she said chinking my glass.

'Cheers.'

We stayed in Connolly's for a couple of hours talking about people at work, talking about New York, talking about whisky, talking to the guys at the bar about policemen - I think one of them might have been one - and generally getting drunk. We were certainly not the first couple who had staggered out of Connolly's at midnight and we would not be the last. The great thing with New York is that it is almost impossible to get lost.

We stumbled down 49th Street until we saw 7th Avenue and then we found The Sheraton where it had always been. On walking into the hotel lobby we saw a hotel bar just off to the right which still had some drinkers in.

'A night cap, m'lady,' I said bending over and bowing.

'Oh Sir, you do spoil me.'

We walked in and ordered our usual tipple, and then chose to rest at a table in the corner. You could see the hotel lobby from where we were sitting but it would have been very hard for anyone there to have seen us. To my surprise something then happened that put the icing on the night. A disturbance could be heard coming from the main doors to the hotel and as the noise began to grow, the culprits came into view. There was a big chap being supported on both sides by a New York City cop. He looked incredibly drunk and Emily and I glanced at each other as if to say, *'I thought we were bad.'*

There was a fair bit of shouting by the man in the middle and eventually the hotel porter came out to meet them. The police had to speak loudly to be heard over the man who was beginning to get aggressive.

'Calm down, Sir,' said the cop on the left. 'I am trying to help you and this man here is going to help you too. Do not make it hard for yourself, I do not want to take you in Sir. Yeah, we found him outside,' the cop said to the porter. 'He was urinating on the sidewalk. I believe he is one of your residents. Can you make sure he gets to his room?' The porter nodded and beckoned the junior porter to come to his assistance as well. 'Ok, Sir, you must now go with these gentlemen who will see that you get some rest.'

The big man was passed over to the hotel staff and the police walked off. The porters had a job trying to support him and in the struggle he was turned to face our direction. Both Emily and I looked at each other, then looked back at the man. It was definitely, without any degree of uncertainty, Darren Heavyside. I smiled and took another sip of my drink.

'It looks like he's been enjoying himself,' I said to Emily.

'That's horrible if he was pissing on the street. He's an animal.'

'Don't tell me you've never done that?' I asked. My eyes were beginning to lose focus by this stage and I had to sit on the front of my seat to make sure I stayed awake.

'When I've been very desperate I have occasionally been forced to,' she said after some thought. 'Ok then, where's the worst place you've wee'd in public?'

'I once went off the top of a cross-channel ferry. I've got a feeling that it blew back on to the deck though because my trousers were soaking. What about you?'

'I'm obviously a lady so I don't have a full catalogue of events but there was one time when I had to go in the middle of a Radiohead concert.'

'Urgh, in the middle of everyone?' She smiled and then our eyes stayed locked on each other. We were looking deep into each other's souls for what seemed like hours and then all of a sudden I started to feel the room spinning. I looked away and took a gulp of air. I stared into the lobby trying to concentrate on my breathing, it would not be cool to end the night vomiting over a table.

'Do you want to have a look at my room?' Emily said quietly. 'Just to see if it's different from yours.'

'Huh,' I said suddenly feeling really drunk. 'Yeah, alright.'

I do not think we spoke all the way from the bar to her room. There was another man in the elevator who looked as though he was staring at me and I could not look him in the eye. When we walked into her room I sat on the edge of the bed and Emily went to the bathroom. I do not think either of us had still said anything. I sat looking at my reflection in the mirror, analysing the state that my eyes were in. I am sure they looked worse than normal. Then I suddenly realised where I was and I looked around at the strange bags lined up against the side of the room. There were some hair straighteners discarded next to the television and they were not my wife's. Some clothes were abandoned on the floor and a book on the bedside cabinet, the cover of which I did not recognise. Everything started to look unfamiliar. I was in the enemy camp. What was I doing?

The lock on the bathroom door clicked and the bright light stretched in to the room. Emily stood in the doorway wearing nothing but a pair of knickers and a bra. She looked incredible. Everything was still where it was meant to be. She reminded me of the girls I used to know at college and that felt strange too. I was transfixed by her and could not move from the edge of the bed. My mind flashed back to the glimpse of Righty that I had sneaked the day before. I started wondering what it all looked like underneath. She began to move closer and when she was only about three feet away she reached round to her back and undid the clasp.

The bra fell into her hands and finally exposed, for the first time, was Lefty. He looked much the same as his brother but just on the other side. I stared for probably too long, it felt like she was a lap dancer and I was waiting for the song to begin. She moved closer and then closer again. She bent down so that her face was getting nearer and nearer. I noticed that she was also a fan of the bend at the knee, clean and jerk style. Lefty and Righty passed by my eyes and just before our lips met, I suddenly had the moment of clarity that I probably should have had about ten minutes beforehand.

'Sorry, Emily,' I spluttered as I stood bolt upright. 'This isn't right. I can't do it. Sorry.' I made my way to the door and without even looking back, I opened it and fell into the sanctuary of the brightly lit corridor.

My room was a few floors above and while I stood in the elevator my own reflection was intimidating me. I could not look myself in the eye, I knew I had let it go on too long and I just hoped it would end there. My room looked very similar to Emily's but instead of hair straighteners next to the television there was a set of keys and to my relief they were my keys. The familiarity of my own possessions made me realise how close I had come to throwing everything away. The only part of my life that was okay could very nearly have been lost. I held my head in my hands sitting on exactly the same edge of the bed that I had been perched on not ten minutes before, but a few floors down. I had two pert breasts looking down at me then, but instead those had been replaced with the cold, stark reality of my own miserable life. I had no idea what I was doing anymore.

My phone started ringing in my pocket. I had forgotten that I even had it on me. That would have been interesting if I had not decided to leave. I fumbled to get it out of my pocket and attempted to focus on the display.

'Yep,' I said.

'Ben? Is that you? It's Wilks.'

'Alright mate, what you doing? I'm in New York.'

'Oh sorry. What time is it?'

'Don't know. Late I think.'

There was a pause on the other end of the line.

'Hello, hello, are you still there?' I said.

'Yeah, I'm here.'

'Are you alright, mate?'

'Yeah,' he replied distantly, *'listen I've got some bad news, mate.'* He paused, and in that silence I knew immediately what was coming next. *'James died last night.'*

Chapter 17

I was speechless for a moment, and I suppose there was nothing to say, but you do have to say something on the phone.

'How? I mean do you know any... you know... details or... or... anything?'

'I don't know much,' Wilks said. *'I've just had a call from his wife, that's all. He passed away last night,'* there was a pause, as neither of us could think of anything to say. I was trying to get my head around it. *'Anyway,'* he continued, *'I just thought I'd call you, you know, let you know.'*

'Cheers mate for doing that, appreciate it,' I took a deep breath in, 'I can't believe it. James. I guess we knew it was coming, you know, one day. What can you say?' I thought of his kids and the tragedy that had suddenly hit their family. I was going to mention it to Wilks but then I felt a lump coming up in my throat and thought it best not to let it out. 'Blimey,' was all I managed and then regretted it instantly.

'Yeah, bit of a shocker, eh?' said Wilks.

'Have you told Dave yet?' I asked.

'I've tried him but you know what he's like with his phone. He won't have it switched on.'

'Typical. Do you reckon he knows it's got a charger?'

'Bet he doesn't. He's probably still looking for the handle to wind it up with,' we both laughed, glad of the distraction, the respite that we needed from the horrible reality.

'Do you want me to keep trying him?' I asked.

'It's alright, I've left a message to get him to ring me back, I've text him as well. I don't really want to tell him in a message so I'll wait for him to call.'

'Fair enough,' I was devastated. 'Alright mate, well, thanks for letting me know, appreciate that, see ya later, yeah?'

'No worries, see ya later.'

I stared at a sock on the carpet. What was I meant to feel? It was nothingness. Numb. Empty. I laid back on the bed and the room started spinning. Fuck it. I sat back up and sighed. I decided the best thing for it was to go for a walk.

New York at half one in the morning is still relatively busy. The shops are all shut and the roads are emptier but there's still a steady stream of cars and people passing by. I turned right out of the hotel and walked up towards Central Park. What I needed was a bench. After six blocks I finally found a row of them backing on to the park. I sat down and made myself look as big as I could, after all I was in New York in the early hours.

What a mess. My head was so scrambled that I could only keep coming back to the same three themes. James was no more, I nearly blew my marriage and Emily's boobs were fantastic. I kept going round and round. In the end I needed to hear Jane's voice.

'Hello?' she said.

'Hi ya, it's me.'

'Oh hello, I wondered if you were going to be bothered to ring. What time is it?'

'Um, don't know, um, two-ish.'

'What're you still doing up? Haven't you got to be up early in the morning?'

'Yeah yeah, ssh a minute. I'm sat on a bench on the edge of Central Park. I had to get out to think.'

'Why? What's wrong? Be careful. God, you're on your own in the park. I was watching this thing on the telly...'

'Ssh, James is dead.'

'Oh no, really?'

'Yeah. Last night apparently.'

'Ah, that's a real shame. It might be for the best though, you know how it can be sometimes?'

'Yeah, yeah, maybe. He's got four kids, Jane. Can you imagine what they're going through? It's devastating.'

'It is, Ben.'

'What's it all about? This life game, eh Jane? It's fucking hard.'

'Why don't you go back to the hotel now and get to bed, you're coming home tomorrow.'

'Yeah, ok.'

'What's the conference been like?'

'Yeah.'

'How about that girl you know? Is she still there?'

'Yeah.'

'Alright, well go back to the hotel now and get some sleep. I love you.'

'Love you too.'

On the way back to the hotel I started to cry. It was unlike me. I usually bottled things up. Walking through New York at night was not a good time to start showing public displays of emotion. I kept my head down and walked as fast as I could. Even amongst all of these people, in one of the busiest cities in the world, I felt completely on my own. I had no idea how I was going to get out of this trap that I found myself in. Perhaps the trap was life itself. Maybe I just had a problem with life. Whatever it was, some part of me knew that I was losing control. I was empty, drained of any spark, there was nothing left that I could use. I made it back to the hotel room and laid down on the bed fully clothed to finally pass out.

At breakfast the next morning, it would be an understatement to say that things were a little strained. I came in to the restaurant at The Sheraton which was laid out for the normal breakfast fare and noticed Emily sat at a table near the entrance. I was hoping to avoid her if possible, but as luck would have it, she looked up just as I was looking at her. I had no choice but to go over. I had already decided in the shower that morning that if I saw her I would just pretend that nothing had happened between us the night before. In an ideal world everyone would act like boys in these situations and just happily go on forgetting that anything happened, but girls always wanted to talk about it.

I sat down and politely smiled at her. I suppose I must have looked embarrassed otherwise she would have started in some other way.

'You don't have to feel weird at all,' she said. 'It was just one of those things.'

'Yeah, it was pretty crazy,' I said.

'I was really drunk.'

'Same here.'

'I threw up after you left,' she said.

Even after this bit of information, which I did not really need to know, I still found myself looking at her chest and really wanting to see the boys again. Maybe I could touch them this time, right here in the restaurant. Would she mind? Would *that* make things weird between us?

'I went for a walk after I left.'

'Where?'

'Actually I had some bad news just as I got back to my room.'

'Oh no, what?'

'You know James?'

'Yeah.'

'Well he's dead.'

Emily took hold of my hand on the table and said she was sorry.

'It's alright but all in all it was a bit of a night. Know what I mean?'

'I do. Where did you go?'

'Central Park.'

'Was it not dodgy?'

'I don't know, I couldn't really see.'

'I want to talk about what happened in my room.'

'We don't have to,' I said.

'No, I want to.' *Terrific.* 'It was all my fault and I'm

really sorry. I should never have asked you up and, well I must have been drunk to have stripped off like that.' She laughed and I laughed back, somehow hoping that if we could laugh together about it then maybe it was alright. 'I don't usually do things like that. Honest. I feel like some kind of cougar.'

'I think they're older. You're younger so that would make you a… a… gold-digger.'

'Ha, that must be it then.'

'Sorry to disappoint you again,' I said, 'but I don't have any money either.'

'Oh well, that one over there looks like he's got a few bob. I'll sit next to him on the way back.' We both laughed again and maybe this was going to be alright.

'You have nice boobs by the way,' I said it with a smile on my face but as soon as I did I realised that it was probably the wrong thing to say.

'Let's not talk about that, eh?' She looked embarrassed and there was no way of taking that back.

'I guess I'm still a bit drunk. I'm going to go and get some breakfast now, do you want anything?'

'I'm fine.'

I walked off swearing at myself.

The rest of breakfast went okay and I had a lot of respect for the way that Emily dealt with it. If we followed my approach then it would have been at least five years before we could have sat at the same table again. After this crisis was averted it freed up space to properly mourn the loss of James.

It was hard for me to understand why I was so choked about it. He was slightly more than a work colleague but not as much as a really close friend. We were mates and he was the first mate I ever had who died. I think that was what brought it home to me more than anything else. It could have been me and if it had, what would I have achieved?

As I travelled back to the UK later that day the one over-riding theme that I kept dwelling on was the briefness of it all. I was already in my mid-thirties and I had done nothing. I had a family, who I was truly grateful for, but even a sixteen year old could have one of them. I wanted more. For the first time in my life I was scared that nothing else would ever happen. I had been on the ride; university, job, marriage, mortgage, kids, I had stopped at them all but now what. Where was the next stop? Retirement? That was the fear that began to consume me.

Emily was asleep in the seat next to me on the return plane trip. I glanced across and could not resist looking at Lefty and Righty moving gently up and down. I had been so close the night before to creating some kind of nightmare. It would not have made my life any better, in fact it could have torn the only shreds of goodness away. I looked at her lips, slightly apart, dry from the post-drinking dehydration and I smiled. Right at that moment I felt something hit me. It was enlightenment.

I knew immediately that I was different. A surge of confidence washed over me while I sat there watching her. If I had the strength to get a grip of myself the night before and stop the unthinkable from happening, even though I was hammered, then surely I could sort the rest of it out.

From that moment on, everything changed, even the economy seats became slightly more bearable.

Act Two

The Escape

'That was a memorable day to me, for it made great changes in me. But, it is the same with any life. Imagine one selected day struck out of it, and think how different its course would have been. Pause you who read this, and think for a moment of the long chain of iron or gold, of thorns or flowers, that would never have bound you, but for the formation of the first link on one memorable day.'

- Charles Dickens - Great Expectations, 1861

Chapter 18

When I returned to the UK the world looked different to me. Colours seemed more vibrant, sounds came across as symphonies and something had definitely changed within. It was as if I had swallowed a tab of LSD at JFK airport, and if this was true then at least I would have been able to understand the response better. I was expecting to feel worse than ever before when I touched down again in good Old Blighty, but instead the effects of the epiphany were still there.

The initial seed that was planted on the plane, while I was looking at Emily's blouse, had grown as I thought about it more. Suddenly the fear that was crippling my decisions had started to push me on to different ideas. I knew I had to do something because if I waited then nothing would happen and then I would probably die of boredom instead. I thought of everyone else around me and could finally see what Emily had seen. I was hanging around with people that had already given up. I knew that if I was going to make a change then I would have to do it on my own and this perversely made me feel stronger. There was no one else to rely on, or even blame, and so I suddenly knew what I had to do.

But I had to be given permission first.

I walked in the front door but it was too late to see the kids because they were already asleep. Jane was sat watching the telly when I walked in to the lounge. She turned and looked at me, instantly recognising that something was different.

'Hi ya,' she said. 'How was it?'

'Not too bad. No delays at least.'

'What's up?'

'What do you mean?'

'You look different.' She looked at me suspiciously. 'How much wine did you have on the plane?'

'Not much. How different?'

'You're smiling for one.'

'Oh that. Well, you'll be happy to know that I've worked it out.'

'Worked what out?'

'*IT.* Anyway how've things been here?'

'Normal. The kids have missed you though. Ruby was crying at dinner.'

'Ah, bless her. Is she alright now?'

'She's fine. In fact she was fine as soon as I brought out some more pasta.'

'I've got them a present each from the airport so that

should cheer them up tomorrow.'

'What about me?' she said.

'What about you?'

'Um, your wife who looks after your children day and night.'

'Yeah, I've got you something too. As if I'd forget that.'

'Ok then I'll let you off. Now what have you worked out?'

'Life.' She looked confused. 'When I was on the plane back today, I was kind of mid-Atlantic when something suddenly struck me. I've got to make a change.'

'Finally.'

'What do you mean?'

'I've been telling you that for about a year.'

'It wasn't that easy before.'

'Why is it now then?'

'I don't know.' I thought for a moment, she had a good point. 'Because I came up with it myself this time.' Jane looked at the ceiling. 'Anyway, I want to do something else.'

'What?'

'I don't know yet.'

'Wow, Professor Brian Cox is going to be shitting himself.'

'All in good time. I definitely know what I don't want, and that's doing what I do at the moment and life's too short. So, I'm getting out.'

'How?'

'Redundancy.'

'But you've not been made redundant.'

'I know, but that's the beauty of it. Wilks said at lunch the other day that they're giving them away like smarties, all I've got to do is get one for myself.'

'How are you going to do that?'

'I don't know yet but that's what I'm after.'

'Right,' she looked less than convinced. 'So you haven't really worked anything out then.'

'Yes, I have. I now know what I want. I want to be made redundant from RC.'

'What are you going to do after that?'

'I don't know but I don't need to know at the moment. The redundancy payout will be more than enough to give me some time to work it out. I'll keep thinking about it but the most important thing is that I can see a way out. '

'I'm happy for you.'

'At last, I can see a way out.'

I needed help though. I knew that Savage would not take kindly to me walking in the next morning and sharing with him my desire to leave, so I had to think of another way. I needed to talk to someone that I could trust who would not mention my plans to anybody else, and someone that I respected enough to believe. My thoughts turned to the only person that I knew who fitted this brief - Wilks. I knew he had been involved in this sort of thing in the past and he was also pretty shrewd when it came to playing the corporate game.

The Miller's Pond was always quiet at lunchtimes, only employees of RC would ever be there between the hours of eleven and two. It was one of those old pubs that had that old pub smell of polished wood, open fires and damp carpets. To keep up with the newer chain pubs in town they had started serving food but few people would eat there twice, so the smell of food never really took over. The bar itself was quite small in relation to how many tables there were and you would normally have to wait a while to get served. Luckily for me there was no one else in there on that day. I was sitting at one of the old stools by the bar waiting for Wilks, when he walked in.

'Alright mate,' I said. 'What do you want?'

'What ales are on?' he looked along the pumps behind the bar. 'IPA, cheers mate.'

'A pint of IPA then as well please,' I said to Rod, the Landlord, who had been stood waiting to be called into action. 'Cheers for coming Wilks. I just want to talk to you about something and I didn't want to do it at work.'

'Curious. You're not gay, are you?'

'No, why?'

'You wouldn't want to say that at work, would you?'

'I suppose not but then again I probably wouldn't want to tell *you* that at work either. Why would I make such a big deal of coming out to you anyway? Why would I tell you? Why would you care? What if I was?'

'Fucking hell mate, I was only joking.'

'Cool. Shall we sit down somewhere?'

'Good idea,' said Wilks relieved, and he followed as I walked all the way over to the furthest table from the bar. 'Shitter about James, isn't it?' he said as we sat down.

'It's terrible. A tragedy. Have you heard anything more?'

'The funeral's next Monday. Are you coming?'

'Yeah, definitely. It's the least I can do.'

'Good lad,' said Wilks.

'You just have to, don't you? If there's other stuff on, then it'll just have to wait. I still can't believe it's happened, you know? I know we've been expecting it but when it happens it's still a shock.' Wilks nodded. 'To be honest it's what's given me a wakeup call. It's why I want to talk to you actually. When you rang me I was in

New York.'

'Yeah, you said.'

'I realised when I was there that I was about as unhappy as I could get. Your phone call nearly tipped me over.'

'Sorry about that.'

'No, no, I'm glad you did but it just got me thinking, I've got to do something about it.'

'Jesus, if you want me to give you relationship advice then you're probably better off talking to Rod over there. I'm three divorces down and now The Samaritans won't even talk to me.'

'If that was the problem then you can be safe in the knowledge that I would've even gone to Dave before coming to you. So, don't worry, it's not anything that's going to be out of your comfort zone. It's about work and, I suppose, more specifically it's about leaving work.'

'You mean the turnstiles,' he said joking.

I took a deep breath. 'No, between you and me, I want to be made redundant.'

I stopped and waited for his reaction.

'Well, I wasn't expecting that. How come?'

'I'm fed up mate and it's not going to get any better if I stay. I need a fresh start, I need to do something different. I've just got to get out. I don't belong here.'

'Right, ok. Well, we'll miss you.'

'But I can't stay just for that. You know what I mean?'

'True. What are you going to do instead?'

'I don't know but it's going have to be better than this.'

'So, what do you want me to do about it?'

'I've been here for twelve years so I can't just hand my notice in.'

'No, definitely not,' agreed Wilks, adamantly, 'you want to make sure that you get the full package.'

'Exactly, and I don't know which is the best way about it.'

'I haven't got a clue what you do at the moment. Where do you work?'

'Unbelievable. I've been in Project Eagle for about two years.'

'Ha ha, brilliant,' he started laughing. 'All you're going to have to do is sit tight and that thing's going to crash and burn anyway.'

'Are you sure?'

'All projects end one way or another.'

'I don't know about this one,' I said, 'it's so bad that they may keep us there forever, like some kind of endless Chinese torture.'

'Maybe with Project Eagle,' he said smiling, 'but

seriously it should end. That gives you the perfect opportunity to bail out. I'll let you in on a secret, but don't tell anyone where you heard it. We're going to be getting rid of loads of business accountants soon.'

'But I'm not one of those anymore. That's what I used to do.'

'Yeah but at the end of the project you'll have to be put somewhere. All you need to do is tell old Savage that you've made a mistake and that you want to get back in to what you were doing before. Easy.'

'But what if I end up getting a job?'

'Trust me, you won't. Not because you're not good enough but it's a question of simple maths. There are currently two hundred people in the system at the moment, all more senior than you, who are wanting to be moved into those roles. There's only about seventy roles to move into. It's a big, big problem that isn't common knowledge yet but there's going to be a whole lot of people that are unhappy by the end of it.'

'You're joking. So you reckon I just put down that I want a business accountant role and it's a done deal.'

'In the bag.'

'But how long's this bloody project going to take?' I asked.

'From what I've heard, the writing's on the wall.'

'But what if it doesn't end?'

'It will,' he assured me, 'they all do.'

'What do I have to do now then?' I asked.

'Have you got a development plan?' I nodded that I did. 'You have to make sure that you've written on it that you want to move back in to being a business accountant. Us managers are bound by what's written on those forms. Savage'll have to stick to it if you can get it signed off.'

'And then just sit tight?'

'Yep, there's nothing else you can do really. These things take time but there's no doubt that eventually you'll get what you want. Just don't get impatient. Whatever you do, don't get impatient.'

'Ok, I won't. Cheers mate. I appreciate that.'

'Not at all. Thank fuck it wasn't to do with your marriage.'

'It nearly was.'

'What do you mean?'

'Nothing.'

It seemed like a straight-forward thing to do. When I arrived back at the office, after another pint, I set to work on changing the development plan. I had never given it a second's notice in about five years. How ironic it would be if this were my ticket out of here. I deleted the bit that was about "challenging roles" and typed in that I wanted to return to being a business accountant. I backed this up with a few pointers about my natural talents and how I felt more rewarded in such a role. I checked it over and then sent it through to Savage. The last thing I wanted was for him to notice that I had actually changed something. So I just sent it to him instead stating that it was for his records. He hated these forms so much that I was confident that he would save it without looking at it.

I sat back on my chair looking out of the window at the tree. The sky was beginning to brighten and the new shoots were starting to show. I had made one positive action towards making a change and I started to feel a strange contentment. The escape plan had been hatched, and like all escapes, I would now just have to be patient.

Chapter 19

Since getting back from the US, I had been carefully avoiding Emily like the plague. It was the typical man response that I was familiar with. I knew it would feel awkward once we were back on home soil. The breakfast summit in the restaurant of The Sheraton was still part of the same pretence. We were both still trapped in that bubble that floats alongside reality. When you are in that bubble it seems infinitely easier to discuss uncomfortable moments like full frontals (barring the knickers) than if you were in the real world. The bubble popped when the plane landed and good old British air came rushing in to the fuselage. By the time we had ventured as far as the baggage carousel we were almost strangers to each other. The last I saw of her was when she wearily climbed in to her taxi and attempted a smile. I knew then that we were going to follow the normal process that I had been familiar with since I had left school.

I thought that maybe Emily was somehow more cosmopolitan than any of the other girls that I had ever met but obviously not. In the week that had followed she had not been to lunch once and her absence was beginning to raise questions.

'What d'you do with her then?' said Stretch suddenly over the lunch table.

'Who?' I said.

'Emily.'

'Um, what do you mean?'

'Well, let's see. You went to New York with her and since then we haven't seen her.'

'Yeah?'

'What was it? A bit of 'ow's yer father, then she threatened to talk, so you had to kill her?'

'Who says 'ow's yer father' these days?'

'Am I right?'

'No, not really,' I said. 'Close though. I did kill her, but instead of shagging her, she caught me molesting the furry mascot from the New York Yankees. What could I do?'

I started to worry though that they were beginning to sniff a rat. Something had to be done to make the situation normal again. There was nothing else for it than to arrange a peace talk. I had to attempt to be the bigger man and take this head on. Also, I reminded myself that nothing really happened and this made things simpler. In the past, when I had been involved in similar situations before Jane came along, there had usually been plenty that had happened.

The "new me" felt like I was gaining control of my life at last. I thought that the "new me" would choose to be mature and help the poor girl through her moment of embarrassment, welcoming her back to the lunch table with no hard feelings.

The man with the squint had told me that she was Russian. This was not surprising but my continued attraction towards her was. The last Russian girl I knew had tried to kill me with a curtain rail on the back of the Orient Express. I knew that this girl would probably be the same but for some reason I wanted to meet her.

The cocktail bar that I had chosen had a view over the marina and, more specifically, the yacht I had seen her on the day before. My white suit blended in with the whitewashed walls of the hacienda behind and offered me a natural camouflage. I arrived half an hour early to watch the yacht in case I could see any of Goldfeld's men go in or out.

Nothing had moved, and after a while, I began to be distracted by the legs of the lady in the red dress next to me. Standard issue aviator sunglasses offer excellent masking ability and your eye movements are undetectable. I had just managed to manoeuvre into a position where I could make out the inside of the left thigh when all of a sudden, from nowhere, a man with a neck the size of a Ming vase jumped down from the wall behind me.

Having the advantage of surprise, he pulled his forearm around my neck and attempted to thrust a slimline, silver dagger into my kidneys. I was born ready though, and pushed up from my knees whilst simultaneously bending over. The chap flew over my shoulders, over the trellis, and fell approximately thirty feet in to the sea below.

'He fancied a dip,' I said to the lady in the red dress as I sat back down.

She looked over her glasses at me, and just as I was deciding whether I had enough time to acquaint myself with her, the Russian lady entered the balcony. She was tall, with short blonde hair and a look of anxiety about her. She had the gait of a suicide bomber who had just been pushed through the door of a primary school. The diver with the thick neck had obviously been her insurance and now she knew that it was just us two. I sat with my legs casually crossed, waiting for her to join me at the table. All of the cards were in my favour now.

Emily walked into the Miller's Pond and strained to see me hiding in the corner at my usual table. It seemed like I was always here at the moment and Rod, behind the bar, must have wondered what I was up to. She looked terrified as if she was walking out on to the set of Jeremy Kyle. I stood up to say hello and I suddenly became a rabbit in the headlights. I was just about to kiss her on the cheek, but was that too familiar? Maybe I should shake her hand, but that would be weird? I confused myself with the options and ended up just sitting back down and nodding. Good start.

'Em, how are you? I hope you don't mind coming to the pub?'

'No, I can't say that coming to the pub is usually a problem for me. You know that now though, don't you?'

'Um, yeah. Likewise.' We both looked at each other as if that night had connected us in a unique way for evermore. 'I suppose I just wanted to check you were alright and that we were still cool. Are we?'

'Yeah, I'm cool,' she said immediately in a matter of fact way. 'I've got no problems with what happened, it was just one of those stupid things that happens when you're drunk. Why what's wrong?'

'The lads are starting to notice that you're not coming to lunch anymore. I wanted to make sure that you were alright. You know, not embarrassed or anything.'

'Oh, is that it.' She started laughing. 'Jesus Ben, I

thought you were going to say that you wanted to take it further.'

'No, no, no. That's the last thing I want.'

'That bad is it?'

'No, I didn't mean that but... oh, you know... um...'

'It's ok, I'm only joking.' She started laughing again. 'Why are boys so crap at these things? Nothing happened so we've got nothing to feel bad about. Why? Did you think that I was avoiding you?'

'Um, well, I thought that maybe you felt a little shy about what happened?'

'I have to admit it wasn't my finest hour but I'll live. Have you told anyone else?'

'No. Fuck no. This is between us, that's why I asked you to meet me here.'

'Thank you, I appreciate you not telling anyone else. Like I say, it wasn't my finest hour.' There was a silence while we both adjusted our view of the world and realised it was quite a nice place after all.

'Anyway,' she continued, 'I've been away from work for the last four days. I felt so rough when we landed that's why I wasn't talking that much, so I took a few days off. Have you not had anything? It was a really bad head cold.'

'No, I've been tip-top.'

'Just me then. So I had that and then I went for an

interview yesterday.'

'A what?'

'An interview. You know I said I was going to wait and see what turned up, well I'd already applied for it when we left for the states. I didn't want to say, in case nothing came of it.'

'What is it then?'

'Similar to what I'm doing now but for a small company that sells software.'

'You dark horse.'

'I'll be much closer to the board and real decisions for a change. Quite scary really.'

'Blimey, good for you. So, what did they say?'

'A couple of days and then they'll let me know.'

'Fingers crossed then.' Inside it was as if a lead weight had just dropped from my throat into my stomach. I liked Emily and I wanted her to stay, or not leave before me anyway, but also, she made it look so easy. She was fed up so she just went to get another job. Was it that easy? What the fuck have I been doing for all this time? I tried my best to smile through the rest of our drinks but not only had I incorrectly assumed that she was still pining for me, which dented the ego, she had also managed to make my mountain look like a molehill.

After we parted as friends, I dragged my sorry self

back to work and stared out at the misery tree once again. The long game that Wilks had planned for me was all completely logical but I started to doubt whether I had it in me to wait so long. Project Eagle could carry on flying just above the horizon for years. One thing was for sure in the corporate world; if you were under the radar and pretended to be fine then people could forget that you were even there. Projects about the Millennium Bug were still going on for Christ's sake.

The next day threw the world in to the depths of winter once again. It was now mid-March and although the sun had started to lull us into a false sense of security, spring was temporarily over. The phone rang in my office and I answered it with a cloud of breath still visible.

'Are you ready?' asked Dave.

'Yep.'

I had been ready for about three hours unfortunately. Sitting in my office all morning watching the clock on the phone, then watching the clock on the pc, and then watching the watch, and then comparing the watch to the pc, and then comparing the pc to the phone. I was definitely ready.

That day had not even started well. I had been scraping ice off the car at seven when I noticed that I had a flat tyre. After changing to the spare, I finally arrived in the office half an hour later than normal, only to find that the heating had not been turned on. It was so cold in the room that I had to leave my gloves on. But today was also the day of James's funeral and this made everything feel ten times worse. The weather had become the coldest that I had ever experienced. The time had moved slower than it had ever moved before, and finding some work to busy myself in the meantime seemed futile.

I did attempt to look down the to-do list and see if there was anything easy that I could pick off while I was waiting, but it all just seemed pointless. It was not worth setting up some meetings with people I did not like, to discuss something that I did not care about, because of a deadline that did not matter anyway. I was not in the right frame of mind to even pretend to care.

I had used up a few vital minutes going to the café on site to get a coffee. I had even sat in there on my own because it was slightly warmer than my office, obviously not forgetting the piece of paper. I always carried a piece of paper if I was on the skive because of the power that a piece of paper can have. You could instantly transform yourself from a skiver into a person with a purpose. No one would ever go near you if you had a piece of paper. You were either on your way somewhere or sat waiting for someone.

Regardless of this little time stall, the hours and minutes had stretched out all morning. The funeral was due to start just after lunch and it was bound to be a desperately sad event. The nature of the man, and what he was leaving behind, would make sure of that. I had arranged with Dave the week before that we would go together, and the phone had rung to let me know he was on his way down.

Chapter 20

After the phone call, Dave took another five minutes to actually materialise before me. There was no need for words, I could tell that he had been having the same difficult morning. We both finally walked out in to the cold car park together only for Dave to remember his coat, which he had left next to his desk on the third floor. Another five minutes past while I stood outside waiting for a 'not so young' Dave to return, sweating profusely and looking decidedly as though he was about to keel over. He had run all the way there and back, and for someone who was out of shape, he was fortunate that he made it without suffering some sort of attack. I stared at him in disbelief while he attempted to regain his breath. Between gulps of oxygen, coughs and spits he eventually managed to communicate that he was going to drive. I was uncertain as to how I felt about that but still I walked, and Dave limped, over to his Astra.

The funeral was fifteen miles away, in the heart of the Pennines, and the only way to reach it was via a long winding road that weaved around, and up and down, the valleys. As passenger, I was also tasked with the responsibility of navigating the crucial last miles to the church. This gave me the perfect opportunity to try out the new satnav that was included on my phone. Up until then I had only used it on the journey between my house and the RC site. In this controlled environment there was no indication of how first night nerves would make it choke so tragically on the big occasion.

I found the postcode for the church on the internet that morning and after pressing a couple of buttons, the route revealed itself, and there seemed to be no cause for alarm. I was glad that this part of the journey was taken care of because neither Dave or myself were in the mood to be getting lost.

As Dave turned on the ignition the familiar tones of AC/DC came blaring out of the speakers. They were familiar because I had never been in Dave's car when anything else had been played. It was as if Vauxhall had built a car with an engine that made a noise exactly replicating Back in Black.

We had not ventured even as far as the hills when we suffered our first incident. It was the type of road mismanagement that would only be found in a crappy village like that in "Last of the Summer Wine". A truck was offloading some scaffolding in the one and only lane that we could use to get through to the other side. All other cars were sat patiently; full of pensioners and young mums, watching vacantly as the workmen gradually purged their lorry of the last of the metal bars. Dave and I could only sit there and watch in astonishment as the operation unfolded, the same murderous thoughts crossing between us both. I kept an eye on the satnav's expected arrival time as it changed from 12:55 to 12:56, and then 12:57, 12:58, 12:59, and then it was saying that we would be late. The service started at one and the last thing we wanted was to rush. By the time we eventually wheel spun away from the village that time forgot, the expected arrival time was 13:07.

'For fuck's sake, we didn't need that,' said Dave, stating the obvious.

'Come on, we can't be late for this,' I said, still looking at the 13:07. 'We'll be alright, just get your foot down and we'll catch it up.'

'Catch it up? Has it got a time on it?' asked Dave.

'I didn't want to scare you mate, but yeah, it says we're seven minutes late at the moment.'

'Shit on it. Right, well here goes.' It was as if Dave had been born for this very moment. The vocal prowess of Bon Scott ripped through the car as Dave accelerated into the first real bend, the Astra climbed up alongside a dry stonewall exposing a view across half of the Peak District. As the bends kept coming, the view kept changing. I would be looking at fields one-second, then some sheep another, then a gap in a wall, then some more sheep, then another view, then a disused hut.

'How are we doing?' asked Dave after five minutes of silence. He had been concentrating on winning the Nürburgring time trial, but suddenly his mind must have been brought back to the matter at hand.

'We've clawed back two minutes,' I said, looking down at the phone to check. But as if my eyes moving down to the phone were a trigger, a wave of nausea immediately then rose up from my stomach and stopped just before my throat. I looked out of the window in desperation. I had forgotten how to breathe normally and had to consciously think of how my breath was going in and out. I was determined I was going to be fine but just then another wave, bigger than the first, came up in my throat.

I pressed the window button and temporarily enjoyed the icy blast hitting my face.

'You're not gonna woof, are you?' said Dave as he looked across.

'Hope not,' I managed to reply in some strangled voice before returning to my breathing.

'Do you want a bag or something?' he asked but all

talk had escaped me. 'Here, I've got this butty bag if you need something, hold on,' and he emptied his wrapped sandwiches out on to the floor with one hand, 'yep, here you go.' He handed me the old Tesco's carrier bag, and although I was grateful for the receptacle, the smell of ham sandwiches that it brought with it was too much to bear. I dropped it to the floor by my feet registering where it landed but at that moment my body was paralysed. The only thing I could think about was my breathing, as soon as I thought about anything else another wave decided to attack.

The further we went, the more bends we rounded, the more sheep I saw, and the more desolate the scenery became. It was as if we had driven into a wasteland, there were no other cars around, and the only sign of habitation was one cottage far off in the distance with smoke coming from its stone chimney. It was freezing as well.

'Have you had enough air yet?' asked Dave, who by and large had respected the fact that I was feeling peaky, but I guessed that he would probably be turning blue by now and there is only so many lengths a mate is prepared to go to. I put the window back up and noticed that I had become so cold that I was actually shivering.

'Cheers mate,' said Dave, 'are you feeling any better? What time are we on now?' I glanced down and saw that it was still showing 13:02, and as speaking was still beyond my abilities; I showed him the peace sign. 'Shit, we're gonna be late. I can't believe this. Sodding scaffolders. They're going to go apeshit if we're late.' At that specific moment I did not have the ability to care if we made it on time, or not. I am ashamed to say that my mind had become totally preoccupied with the simple task of preventing sickness.

'I - need - get - out,' I managed in my strangled, neanderthal voice. Dave looked at me as if he was going to knock me out but then eventually pulled over. I fell out of the door. All I could do was crawl over to a dry stonewall on all-fours and put my hands on my knees. Dave waited at least thirty-seconds before getting impatient.

'Come on, Ben, for fuck's sake, we're nearly there now. It can only be five minutes or so away,' he said. It was as if we were in a battle and our trench was just beyond the brow. It was a false alarm and I staggered back to the car knowing that I was probably not going to be sick. Feeling marginally better I was able to show Dave the map of where to go before we set off again.

As the road through the wilderness came to an end, I began to point directions to him. I was still unable to speak with any confidence.

'Should've turned there,' I forced out, pointing over

my left shoulder. Dave pulled the car round which brought another wave up within me, and then suddenly the road that we were familiar with turned into a dirt track, which was bumpy due to the mud that had frozen.

'This can't be right mate,' said Dave shaking his head. 'It's not going to be down here,' but then he noticed something which gave him hope. 'Eh, mind you this is where James used to live, I've seen this river before. I reckon your thing's done us a short cut, yeah, this turns into a road down there. Look.' Although I was too weak to contribute anything, I sure hoped he was right because I was having some serious doubts as well.

We could see a church steeple up ahead and it looked like my journey from hell was nearly over. Dave sped towards it but as we drew nearer we noticed there was only one car parked outside.

'I thought he was more popular than this,' I said.

'It's not the right place, Ben,' Dave was staring between me and the padlocked gate that was leading to the front door of the church. The time was 13:06.

'I've got to get out a minute,' I said to him, and before he could say anything I climbed out of the car. 'I can't understand it,' I said, after a minute of pacing backwards and forwards. Leaning in through the window, I said, 'the postcode's right, I know it is. Katie in my department said so, and she lives here. It's not right though, is it? She said it was next to a Sainsbury's. I can't see anything like that anywhere near here.'

'You what?' exclaimed Dave suddenly. 'The Sainsbury's is right in the middle of the village, I know where *that* is. Why the fuck didn't you say that? We could have been there ten minutes ago. I knew we turned left when we should have turned right. Quick get in.'

He started the engine and threw the door open.

'I can't mate,' I closed the door and gestured for him to go. 'Go on without me. Leave me here.' I was so disappointed in myself for getting lost, and more annoyed that I felt sick. I wanted Dave to get there without being held back anymore by me.

'Don't be daft, mate,' said Dave, 'just get back in. Literally it's five minutes away.'

We were late anyway and I suppose he now knew where it was. I started to change my mind and when I noticed that we were literally in the middle of nowhere I jumped back in. 'I'm really sorry, mate. I'm shit with directions.'

Dave started laughing as he drove off, 'where did you get the satnav from? Monkey Harris?' He carried on laughing at his own joke and eventually I started laughing too.

'I am sorry mate.'

'Have you got a load of Russian answering machines as well?'

'What a pair of Charlies,' I said.

As we drove down the hill we saw a much bigger church this time, which was in the middle of a village, and had about a hundred cars parked outside. It had to be right this time. The nausea began to disappear at last. 'I tell you what,' I said to Dave as he found a parking spot about half a mile away, 'if James *was* watching this right now, he'd be pissing himself. It's like something out of an Only Fools and Horses Christmas Special.'

'I think you're right, mate,' agreed Dave, 'if there was something that James liked more than anything else, it was taking the piss.'

We accepted that the church was probably shut by then, and we thought we could wait outside until people started coming back out, but when we arrived one of the huge wooden doors was pulled back. We poked our heads in to see if we could silently sit at the back without disturbing anything. The foyer was separated from the body of the church by a large glass partition. There were speakers in the foyer that were transmitting the service that was already in full flow, so Dave and I thought it best to just sit in the foyer and watch through the window.

This plan would have worked brilliantly but for

James seemingly wanting one more laugh on his big day. Also, it appeared as though he now had the power to be able to do something about it. He was somehow able to send down one of the scrawnier, older angels at his disposal, to get even with us for being late to his send off. The scrawny old angel was sitting on the back row inside the church and for some reason he turned around. He caught sight of Dave and I sitting respectfully in the foyer. If he was not an angel on a righteous mission then he undoubtedly would have just turned back, but because of his orders from one of heaven's new entrants, he stood up and walked to the big double doors in the middle of the glass partition. Our faces dropped and we begged silently with our hands for him to ignore us, but still he continued.

If the opening of the large squeaky doors gave half of the mourners the chance to turn around and see who it was, then as we were ushered towards the only two empty seats that happened to be in the middle of the third row, then this gave everyone else a chance. This walk of shame was accompanied by tuts and slow shakes of the head all the way. By the time we had finally sat down I dared not breathe, twitch a sinew of a muscle or blink until the service was over.

While I sat there I was astounded at what a fuckwit I could be. To everyone else in the congregation I must have looked like a disrespectful, hanger-on that had turned up as an afterthought. It was the furthest thing from the truth but what else could they think. Just like the epiphany that came to me on the plane, another seed planted itself deep inside as I sat there watching his young family going through their grief. I vowed that I would never allow the impact of James's death to be diluted at all from that point onwards.

Chapter 21

Spring was well and truly in the air by the time April came around. The flowers were starting to come out, the sky was becoming more consistently blue and the fields were beginning to look green rather than a murky shade of brown. Colour was beginning to re-enter the universe and people were staggering around wondering how they ever managed to see through the gloom of the winter. With signs of spring everywhere I started to feel slightly more energetic than I had been. The mornings were not so much of a drag anymore and, accompanied by my newly found lust for life, I was actually feeling rather chipper.

Spring holds a magical formula for re-birth. It is not just the birds and the flowers that benefit from this magic either. There were a lot more people at work who seemed to have come out of their period of hibernation and had started to take action. Up until recently it had been rare for many people to ever leave RC. Once you were in you tended to stay in until they told you to leave. But now there were more cases of people taking their lives into their own hands and this was changing the corporate world that everyone knew. New blood was coming in with new ideas and mixing with the old blood. Old blood was leaving and making way for more new blood. New blood was leaving because it was rejected by the old blood. There was blood everywhere and it was beginning to resemble a Tarantino film.

There used to be a tried and tested process that was followed whenever anyone would leave. The manager of the leaver would know exactly what rules to follow. It was written in the sands of time and everyone knew where they stood, but now managers were forced to adapt the process depending on the leaver. If a leaver had been there for long enough then it was customary to receive a collection, a team lunch in a local hostelry and some kind sentiments bestowed upon them. If, on the other hand, the leaver had only been there for two months, then being asked to hand back their ID badge was about the extent of it. This left a grey area the size of Russia in between the two. Managers would struggle to find what was expected of them and Savage was no exception. In fact, the personal touch that Savage was blessed with stood him in a better position than some. Other managers would err on the side of caution and offer too much to leavers that had only worked there for less than a month, whereas Savage approached it from the other angle.

Fifteen of us were crowded in to an office at the end of a corridor. The leaver on this spring morning happened to be a contractor which usually left the manager in an even bigger quandary, but not Savage. False smiles were etched on to all of our faces as we eagerly awaited the entrance of Savage. The leaver was called Katrina and the entire Project Eagle team had argued with her at some point during her stay. She was not the most popular of people and this is what made the turnout for her send off so impressive. We all knew what Savage was like and I actually started to pity poor Katrina, who had no idea what was to come, but then the door flew open.

Savage looked more ferocious than usual. He was actually grunting as he took his position at the front of the expectant crowd.

'Whose leaving?' he shouted. 'Katrina, is it? Bloody hell, how long have you even been here? Well, we're all busy so let's get this over with. Did we have a collection or something?'

'Yes Rupert, I don't think we asked you,' said his long suffering PA.

'Where is it then?' he said not visibly affected by this subtle slight on his character. He was passed an envelope with Katrina's name on the front. 'Right then.

Well, I can't say that you've been here for very long because you haven't. In the old days you wouldn't have even registered for any of this, you must have someone here that likes you. Heaven knows how. Anyway, let's think about what you've left us with. You were brought in to the team to sort out the hopeless way that some of you present your progress and, I suppose, that it has marginally improved.'

'I was actually brought in to support the senior management team,' said Katrina.

'Ah, well if you weren't clear on what you were meant to be doing then that's probably why you're leaving us.'

'No, I'm actually leaving because you didn't renew my contract.'

'I beg to differ,' continued Savage. 'We asked you if you wanted to stay but you didn't reply.'

'Um, well,' Katrina was caught between setting the argument straight, and the awareness that the argument was being held in front of a crowd. 'Let's just say that I obviously wasn't asked clearly enough, and leave it at that for now.' She was referring to the nature of the contract extension that was mentioned to her by Savage one day in the middle of something else. At the time he had asked, *'Think about whether you want to stay or not?'* and had left it at that, and with nothing else uttered afterwards the contract then gradually came to an end.

'I think you've probably said enough already so I agree with you at last. Who would have thought that we would finally see eye to eye with each other on your last day. It is normal protocol to give you the floor to say a few brief words but please remember that we're all busy.' With this he took a step backwards and invited Katrina to stand where he had been stood.

'I just want to say thank you to all of you that have helped me try to fit in. It's been difficult for me to help you display progress because actually none of you are making any, this is something that...'

'Woah, woah, woah, that's enough of that,' interrupted Savage.

'I'm just explaining how it was,' said Katrina.

'Very good but I don't think anyone wants to hear it. Here's the envelope and thank you for your efforts. Don't forget to hand in any of RC's property that you have, on your way out.' Savage turned around and immediately walked out of the room.

All of us that were still in the room were looking at each other, smirking and commenting that it may have been the best one yet. Katrina was left in the middle feeling relieved that she could finally put an end to this nightmare in her life. A few people nearer the door started to leave when Savage bounded back in the room.

'Ben, I want you in my office, now.'

Everyone turned to face me curiously, but unfortunately I had no idea what it was going to be about. Someone was running their finger across their throat and I started to panic. I always felt guilty when Savage wanted to speak to me and that, in turn, would make me feel guilty about feeling guilty. I left the room at the end of the corridor and, with my heart pumping through my open-necked shirt, I put my hand on the handle of Savage's door.

'Yes Rupert, you wanted to see me?'

'Come in and close the door,' he said. I racked my brain about what this could be about. 'Sit down and listen. I want to know what you want to do when this project ends?' He studied my face for any kind of reaction.

'Well, it's like this Savage. This project is never, ever going to end. If you're asking me what I want to do when I retire then I don't know. I should be asking you what you're going to do when they sack you for being so hopelessly out of your depth. I want to leave immediately, today if possible, I would like Katrina to stay and take my place and I want to leave. I don't need a presentation from you, or a special collection, just a package and I'll be fine. I want to be free from all of this

bullshit. I want to break out from this crappy existence and do something that might be interesting for a change. I want to feel that I'm actually making a difference to something rather than just turning up and going through the motions. Do you know what I mean, you horrible excuse for a human being? Did you once have hopes and dreams too, or have you always been like this?'

'Right, well,' I started thinking quickly on the spot, 'I obviously know what the landscape's like at the moment in finance, it doesn't seem to be getting better either.' I felt like a politician. Slowly though the plan started coming back to me. 'I would like to get back in to the real business facing side of finance if I could, where I was, but I know that this may be easier said than done, so I'm resigned to the fact that I may have to be forced to look elsewhere. In my situation though I can't afford to just leave and risk everything, so if I can't be redeployed in to an area that suits, then... I'd rather look at redundancy.' My heart was beating fast, and his eyes seemed to be fixated on a spot right next to the iris of my right eye.

'Stop beating around the bush. What would your preference be?' he asked eventually.

'What do you mean?' I asked.

'Do you want to stay or go? It's very simple.'

'It's difficult to say because knowing what I know, I would rather take redundancy, but I'm not able to leave otherwise,' I was trying really hard to not start speaking in a high-pitched voice.

'Ok,' he said, 'it's just that you sent me that development plan and you've changed it. I want to know whether we need to waste energy trying to find you a suitable position, or not.'

'I've realised that this type of work isn't for me, that's all.'

'I won't argue with that,' he said. 'But if you want another position after this project then I need to try and find you one. I don't really want to do that, especially if you don't really want one.'

'I would like one but if there isn't one available then that's alright as well.'

'Right, ok, that'll be all then. Another waste of time, close the door on your way out.'

I am sure that Wilks had told me not to mention anything at this stage but it was too tempting. I was hopeless at playing the corporate games and now Savage knew that I was looking to leave. I had no idea what position I was in and I might have just committed the cardinal sin but I felt as though a weight had been lifted. As I began to smile Emily poked her head around my office door.

'Hello, Ben, are you busy?' I gave her my best "highly unlikely" look so she came in and closed the door. 'How are you?'

'You know,' I said, 'my usual state of disarray. Not quite sure what to do and when to do it. How about yourself, I didn't think you even knew where my office was.'

'I've had some news and I'm itching to tell somebody straight away. Unfortunately you're my only option.'

'Sorry.'

'You know the interview I went for a few weeks ago? They've only gone and given it to me. I need to hand my notice in tomorrow and in a month I'll be gone.'

'Brilliant,' I said trying my best not to show my bitterness. 'That'll be so good for you. Well done. I mean it, well done. Obviously I'd love to be in your shoes right now, but still, good for you. You'll have to leave a trail of breadcrumbs so I can find my way out.'

'I can't wait, it'll be so nice to have a change. It's for more money as well.'

'Great, it just gets better and better. Are you going to do anything before you leave? You know, in terms of a leaving do or anything?'

'I don't think so. What would be the point? I don't know, maybe *we* could go out for a drink or something.'

'Yeah because that always ends well,' I smiled and luckily she could tell I was joking. 'We'll have to go for a few drinks just as an excuse more than anything else. I'll let Dave, Wilks, and Stretch know. Dave doesn't get out much these days, it'll make him happy.'

'Ok, if you want, but don't tell anyone for a few days at least. I need to make sure that it's all sorted first.'

'Very good, your secret's safe with me.'

'What's that?' she asked changing the subject and looking at the corner of the room. There was a trophy that had been sat on the windowsill for so long that I had forgotten it was there. It was about twelve inches high and made from a single block of glass stuck into a wooden plinth. On it was etched the words, 'Project Eagle - Team of the Year'.

'Oh that, just some naff award that was given to us about a year ago. I'd only been on the project for about a month. Don't think for one minute that it's an actual award that we won for anything. It's an award that was made up by the team to give to itself. I think they wanted to motivate us at the time but unsurprisingly it didn't work.'

'It looks lovely,' she said. 'I'm going to miss this place and it's little ways.'

'Hmmm. We got that award at the same time as the dreaded eagle.'

'The what?'

'A soft, cuddly eagle called Eddie. They keep it in the temporary offices at the back of the car park.'

Chapter 22

'How big's this eagle?' said Emily after she had stopped laughing.

'About twelve inches high,' I said. 'It's got a baseball cap on and a yellow t-shirt. It's horrible. Someone brought it with them as a bit of fun to that team building day and it's still here. Every now and again it makes an appearance.'

'Wow, that's really sad,' said Emily. 'I might take it as a souvenir.'

'You can't do that. For one, it wouldn't be worth it, but two, you'd never get your hands on it. It'll be under lock and key. There would be more chance of getting your hands on the crown jewels.'

'Why don't you take it?'

'And do what with it?' I said.

'You know… stuff.'

'Right, ok.'

'Ah, I know,' she said excitedly. 'How about you kidnap it? Take loads of photos and write ransom notes. Oh, you could go to town on it.'

I looked at her strangely at first but then the idea started to capture my imagination too.

'You're only suggesting it because you're leaving,' I said.

'Go on, it'll be funny. You could even set up a special email address for Eddie the Eagle.'

'That's a bit technical.'

'Not really. You can do it in seconds.'

I thought about it for a moment. 'I suppose it would be a laugh, and these things need to be addressed. I could even decapitate it and send it's headless, lifeless corpse back to them in a jiffy envelope.' Emily looked at me concerned. 'Yeah, ok... probably a bit too far.'

Emily eventually left and the doubt that I was having, about telling Savage that I wanted to leave, was replaced by a new mission. The days had been beginning to drag ever since I had made the decision to get out so a distraction would be good. I started to think through a plan and realised that to take the Eagle properly, it would be a two-man job.

'Alright Dave,' I said as he picked up the phone.

'Ben,' he said with about as much enthusiasm as a geriatric sloth.

'Cheer up mate. I've got a favour to ask.' I talked him through the plan to kidnap Eddie the Eagle.

'What are you going to do with it once you've got

it?' he asked.

'Take photos of it and then send ransom notes via email.'

'They'll be able to tell it's you by your email address,' he said.

'No, I'm going to set up a special one. It'll be completely anonymous.'

'How are you going to do that?'

'On the internet.'

'Oh, that's clever then,' said Dave sounding even slower than me. 'Be careful though. If I were you I wouldn't be rocking any boats given what you're trying to do. They won't give you redundancy if you start taking the piss.'

'It's only having a laugh,' I said.

'I'm sure Savage will see it that way as well.'

'I'll make it funny, it'll be team building. It'll be good for camaraderie.'

'You'll have to show me the pictures when you're done,' he said.

'I'll need more than that mate. I need you to help. I want you to be look out for me when I pinch it.'

'Where's it kept?' he asked. 'I'm not going to break the law or anything.'

'You won't have to. Blimey, what do you think I'm talking about? It's in the offices at the back of the car park. Listen, tomorrow's Friday and they all work from home in those offices on a Friday. Are you around at, say, five-ish? I just need you to stand at the door, is that alright?'

'Yeah, if you want, just bell me when you're ready.'

The temporary distraction of the Eagle had already begun to subside by the time I arrived home that evening. I was in no mood to talk to Jane about any part of work, even my made up distractions. I had been used to this general apathy about work for years but recently I had begun to revel in telling Jane how terrible the project was because I knew it was connected to my freedom. That night however, I sat quietly and watched the television, deep in my own thoughts. I was still unsure about the harm I had caused by confessing too much to Savage but more upsetting was knowing that Emily was leaving. I still felt guilty about that night in New York so there was no way I could talk to Jane about Emily. I would only go red, feel uncomfortable, and Jane knew me too well. Over the past few months I had grown to like Emily as a friend, it obviously helped knowing that she fancied me, and the thought of her leaving made me sad. It also made me insanely jealous and, as I was caught in the crossfire of both of these emotions, it was hardly surprising that my dreams were affected that night.

'Private Sanderson.'

'Yes Sir.'

'Is it true that you have found a way out of the compound?'

'Yes Sir. There's some loose ground behind the temporary offices at the back of the car park.'

'What do you propose to do about it, Private?'

'Dig a hole and slip underneath.'

'Do you need any assistance?'

'I don't think so, Sir. The digging won't take too long and once I'm under the fence I'll be free.'

'What about those that you leave behind, Private?'

'Sir?'

'Do you think it's fair to do a bunk on your own?'

'Anyone else can join me if they want to, Sir.'

'What are you going to do once you're on the other side? You can't expect to just run.'

'I'm going to travel to the coast and board a ship that travels to Europe. It's all arranged. Quite straightforward actually.'

'Is there room for anyone else on that boat?'

'I don't think so, Sir, I believe it will be easier to hide just one body. The ship is called The Eagle, a small fishing trawler that has been used in smuggling

operations for years. The captain is a friend of my uncle Eddie's and he sent word last week.'

'Do you need any lookouts?'

'Not really, Sir.'

'So, you're all set then Private.'

'I think so, Sir. I leave tomorrow night after darkness.'

'Excellent work. Please inform the war office on your return that we are all still alive.'

'I will, Sir. But may I ask a question?'

'You may, Private.'

'Why don't you come as well? The hole will be filled up after I leave and the undoubtedly increased security is bound to make escape almost impossible in the future. You could travel with me to the port.'

'That's very kind of you, Private, but I won't be able to do that. You see, one's duty is to look after one's men. I would very much like to follow you through the trees but I'm afraid that I will not be able to do such a thing. I wish you all the best and pray that you will send help eventually.'

'If you say so, Sir.'

'I do and besides, I told the German Officer that my preference was to escape. That is why you are now talking to me through a hole in the side of my lodging. I fear that I will not be permitted to leave this room until

Fritz has moved his sentry point from my door.'
'I understand, Sir. Goodbye and farewell.'
'Goodbye Private Sanderson. God speed.'

The next day, it was five thirty before I could be bothered to ring Dave about the eagle kidnap. We crossed the car park to reach the "temporary" office space, which had been there for fifteen years incidentally, noticing that most of the cars had already left. I remember thinking that this should be relatively straight forward as we approached the door.

'You stay out here Dave, and if you see anybody coming then give us a ring on my mobile. Ok, let's sync our watches men,' I was playing on the idea of a secret mission, and was deliberately making it more complicated than it needed to be. Dave just stood there. I knew that all I had to do was walk in and grab it, and walk out again, but where would the fun be in that? I considered that even if I did get caught it would only mean that the kidnap idea would have to be cancelled. I had brought Dave along for a bit of company really.

'Oh,' exclaimed Dave, as I had just placed my hand on the door handle, 'what's your number?'

'You've got my number,' I said. 'It's the one that you've rung me on for about five years.'

'Is it this one..., 'Ben Mobile'?' he said showing me

his phone display.

'Hmmm... What d'you think? Might be,' with a gentle shake of my head, and a little smile to let him know that I was only joking, I turned and headed back for the door.

When I entered the quiet confines my senses suddenly became alive; I noticed pictures on the wall that I would have ignored in the past, the floor that was ever so noisy as you walked on it, and the corridor which I thought was quite short was actually filled with a load of office doorways.

As I walked along the main corridor, to the very end, I kept watching and listening for any evidence that someone was still in there. I checked the offices as I walked past, by peering through the head height windows, and only as I reached the end was I satisfied that it was empty. I allowed myself the first smirk as I set off to find where they had displayed the cap-wearing eagle.

'I'm sure they used to keep it up there,' I thought to myself as I looked on the top shelf, but it was empty. I scanned the whole office like the Terminator, checking on every possible surface, but there was still no eagle.

'For God's sake,' I muttered under my breath, *'where can it be?'* It was definitely not in this room, even though I had not explored the drawers and cupboards -

why would you put a soft toy in a cupboard if he was a mascot? I considered the possibility that someone had actually taken the eagle with them on holiday, or worse still, perhaps someone else had beaten me to the kidnap, maybe Emily. But then again, why on earth would Emily kidnap an eagle from a project team that she was not a member of, unless she had some bizarrely deviant attraction to cuddly toys. I ruled it out and moved to the office next door.

I looked around this room and nothing obvious jumped out at me; no fabric wings peeping out over a lever arch file. What if this was a trap? Maybe Emily, or even Dave, had double-crossed me and someone was watching me at this very moment, desperately trying to find an eagle that had already been removed? Perhaps I was just being paranoid, but then there was a noise. It sounded like a rustling coming from down the corridor. As I heard it again, I realised that it was the sound of a toilet flushing and this was suddenly followed by the toilet door opening. Although initially I had been relaxed about the whole affair, I soon began to realise that I had a really flimsy excuse if anyone did catch me.

I heard the steps move closer and closer. There I was, stood like a scared rabbit, all alone in someone else's office. *'Surely they would not be coming in to this office,'* I thought to myself, as the footsteps came nearer still. *'What would be the chances of them coming in here?'* The time seemed to move in slow motion, my heart was thumping through my ribcage, and I felt like a burglar just about to be rumbled. Suddenly the fear took over and I weighed up that I had two choices; firstly, I could just walk out of the office confidently, say hello to the mystery stranger and act as if nothing was out of the ordinary; or secondly, I could hide.

I had been in this situation once before when growing up and, instead of choosing to hide, I had come out of my hiding place and confidently walked past some policemen. That particular experience had left a large impression on me as at that time it was very much the wrong decision to take. I am uncertain whether that situation was influencing me now but, as I was stuck in the office having to make a split second decision, I chose on this occasion to hide. I ducked down into a crouching position and shuffled sideways under the nearest desk. I was hidden from the door and covered on the other side by a chair. The footsteps kept coming and I waited.

Chapter 23

The whole world had disappeared and my entire focus was now on the sound of ever nearing footsteps. *'How long was this corridor?'* But just then the silence in the room was penetrated by the noise of the door handle turning. My heart was in my mouth, possibly all of my other organs as well, as the anonymous footsteps stopped about five feet away. *'Why on earth am I under a table?'* I thought to myself, *'surely it would have been simple enough to have explained my reasons for being in someone else's office, but now I'll have to explain crouching under a table. That looks a hundred times dodgier. This is ridiculous. What is this person doing? They're not moving. I wonder if they can hear something. No, that's writing. They must be writing a note. That'll be it, they'll finish the note and then leave.'*

Sure enough they did finish the note. After putting it down on someone's keyboard, they walked across to the door, I heard the handle turn again, the door opened, and then the pneumatic door closer made it take forever to click shut.

It was nearly there. Six more inches. Four more inches. *'How long did this bloody door take?'* Two more inches and then, just as the click could be heard from the door, my phone started ringing.

'What?' I whispered, after my breathing had recovered and I had finally wrestled the phone out of my pocket.

'Alright mate,' shouted Dave, 'just to let you…'

'Ssssshhhhhh,' I whispered again.

'What?' shouted Dave. 'I can't hear ...'

I turned the phone off and sat listening for the footsteps. There were none to be heard. I had somehow escaped detection and so, like a happy Ann Frank, I quickly jumped to my feet, to urgently continue the search for Eddie the Eagle.

Eventually, I found it in the far corner, partially hidden by a pile of papers and a nest of teacups, its stupid head arrogantly looking at me. I reached up and grabbed it, a filthy layer of dust covering its furry wings, but just as I was opening my bag I heard the footsteps rushing back.

Shit!

I dived to the floor and scurried as quickly as I could to my hiding place under the desk. If the feet saw me materialise from within an office that was empty not a minute ago then it would look strange. However, I suddenly realised that it would not quite be as strange as the position I now found myself in. Predictably the door flew open and the footsteps stomped across the office to the note that was written previously. They snatched it up, turned around and said, in a man's deep voice, 'I'll get the right office next time.'

I recognised the voice immediately. Instead of the feet walking back towards the door though after they had grabbed the note, they stopped after a step and stayed where they were. I noticed that the chair which had covered me before was now pushed back against the wall. The feet started walking over to the chair and then, without any warning, I was face to face with Darren Heavyside.

'You?' he said with a disgusted look across his face. 'What the fuck is wrong with you?'

Just like the time with the lasagne incident, I was unable to speak and yet my eyes were working perfectly. I glanced down and imagined what this must look like to a bulldozer security guard. I was hunched over with my knees bent up to my chin, both my hands were around the twelve-inch eagle between my legs and I was breathing heavily. I watched his expression changed from disgust to anger as he came to his own conclusion for what I was doing.

'No, no, please it's not like that,' I said pulling

myself out of the cubby hole.

'You sick fuck.'

'Honest, I was… I was… looking for something.'

'Yeah, course you were, sonny.'

'Ah, here it is,' I said picking up the first thing I could see, which was a stapler.

'Right, you were going to clip his wings were you?' he said shaking his head in disbelief.

I stood next to the desk, in Heavyside's shadow, wondering what he was going to do. Self-preservation was at the forefront of my mind but the desk was between us and the door. Slowly I began to sidle around the edge, hoping that the big guy would be stunned into paralysis by his own revulsion. It seemed to be working and I made it to within three feet of the door before he spoke.

'I don't know what to do with you,' he said. 'In all my years I've never come across anything like this before.' I guess cuddly toy perverts are off the syllabus at the disused volcano headquarters. 'You were lucky that day in the canteen. You were lucky there were that many people around. There isn't no one here now though, is there? Who would ever know what happened? I can still smell lasagne on my collar even though it's been washed. Every time I smell it I think of your horrible face. But now this… I don't know what to make of it.'

'It's not what you think,' I said nearly crying. 'One of my mates is outside waiting for me so if you do anything he'll know.' Then a thought struck me. 'Look, I'm ringing him now.' I pulled the phone out of my pocket and held it in front of me. I could sense his disappointment and, mixed with my relief, a strange smell materialised in the room. 'Alright mate, could you come in here, I'm in a spot of trouble at the minute. End office on the left. Cheers.'

Heavyside looked at me with murderous eyes, 'I'll get you next time. Sickos like you should be locked up. Watch out for me because I'll be watching you. Sorry.' He shoulder barged me as he made his way to the door and I fell off balance, slamming into a filing cabinet. He stormed out of the room and thumped his way down the corridor. I could hear Dave walking up and after they passed, I heard Dave say, 'oh eck,' and quicken his pace.

I was perched on the edge of the desk when Dave rushed in.

'What happened?' he asked.

'Well, the good news is that I got the eagle, the bad news is that Heavyside now thinks I'm a perv that fiddles with cuddly eagles, under a desk, in a temporary fucking office. It could've gone better.'

'Ah.'

'I'm glad you were here though mate. I think he would have killed me if not.'

'No problem, I tried to tell you but the phone cut out.'

I took a deep breath and thrust the stupid eagle into my bag.

'Pint then?' suggested Dave and we both walked out.

'Guess what this is?' I said as I put the eagle, still with a bag over it, down on the kitchen work surface. Jane was washing up.

'What?' she asked.

This game could have gone on all night with Jane guessing again and again, I am sure that with every guess it would have become funnier. But we were never that sort of couple so I changed tact and showed her instead.

'Ta-da,' I said lifting up the bag.

'It's an eagle,' she said.

'Not just any eagle. This is Eddie.'

'Where did you get it from?'

'Work, it's a mascot.'

'Are you sure you go to proper work?' she said.

'I know, it's hard to believe, isn't it?' I picked it up. 'But this little puppy is mine now.'

'It's an eagle.'

'Thanks. So, what shall we do with it?'

'What do you mean?'

'Oh yeah, I forgot the good bit... I've kidnapped him.' I stood nodding at her with an insane smile.

'What, so you mean you've nicked him?' I nodded. 'Unbelievable. Are you that bored at work?'

'Um, yeah, I guess I am. I wish I hadn't taken the thing now but as I have I might as well make the most of it.'

'What are you going to do with it?'

'I thought I'd take some photos of it, you know, in compromising positions and stuff.'

'Has anyone ever told you that you're sick?'

'Quite recently actually.'

'Have you got any ideas?' she asked with a smile creeping on to her face.

'I've got one idea,' I said and I hurried into the lounge. Truthfully it was the only idea that I had come up with, but a real corker. I took our fireguard, which looked like a cage, away from the fire and put it against the plain white wall. I then grabbed some clamps from a baby toy and proceeded to chain the eagle to the cage. I also put a note at the front of the cage stating simply, 'Help Me!' The photo came out much better than expected with the lighting giving it a darker, sinister edge. 'Here look at this,' I said rushing back into the kitchen. 'What d'you think?'

'I think you definitely are sick,' she said, 'let's have another look.' She grabbed the phone and looked closer at the picture. 'Leave me in the kitchen for a minute,' she said and then went to work.

Jane came up with a nice shot of the eagle in a baking tray, stuck in the middle of a mass of Aluminium Foil and surrounded by vegetables.

'Very good,' I said, commending her for her efforts, 'that's why I love you. We could be like Bonnie and Clyde. My turn again,' I grabbed the toy and headed off.

This time I placed the eagle in one of the kid's chairs and made it look like an electric chair with foil in various places.

'Here you go,' I said excitedly, running back into the kitchen and thrusting the phone under Jane's face. She did not even comment this time. Instead she grabbed the moose and walked out of the room with it, like a cold-blooded killer about to do something really nasty.

She returned with an image of a poor defenceless eagle getting buggered in our shower by a soft, fluffy, pink poodle that was much too big for him. Behind the scene, on the bathroom tiles in lipstick, was scrawled the message, 'HURT.'

'That really is sick,' I said after I eventually stopped laughing.

'I think we should probably stop now,' she said, 'before Social Services hear about us.'

'Yeah, I think you're probably right,' I agreed.

'Are you sure you're not going to get into serious trouble for this?' Jane asked showing concern for the first time.

'Dave asked that as well... he still helped me mind... I reckon I'll be alright. The worst that can happen is that they find the pictures, without knowing the context, and someone e*lse*'ll think I'm just a sad, sick, depraved loser. I can't imagine anything's going to happen in an official sense. It's only mucking around. Besides, I wouldn't mind betting that Savage has done a bit of kidnapping before anyway. He's probably a dab hand at it.'

'Well, just make sure that you don't lose your job because you're bored.' Jane walked off upstairs leaving me with second thoughts about how funny it would actually be.

Chapter 24

Friday night came and went and passed into Saturday, the way it tends to do no matter what is going on in your life, but by Saturday night I was beginning to drive myself crazy. The eagle kidnap had made things worse. It was only meant to be a laugh but now I had Heavyside on my case thinking I was some kind of fruit as well. I had not told Jane because it was too embarrassing and I was frustrated about letting myself down. It did seem funny when Emily and I were talking about it initially and this was another thing that was frustrating me. She was younger than me and yet she knew exactly what it was that she wanted. She was more in control than I had ever been and she was going to be leaving in a few weeks. With everything that I promised myself when James died, I had still managed to let the weeks slip by without anything changing.

By the time the kids went to bed on Saturday night I had reached fever pitch.

'Jane, I'm going out to the pub,' I said grabbing my coat.

'Are you alright?' she asked.

'Yeah, I just need a drink.'

I walked out of the house and called Dave. Within twenty minutes we were both sitting at the corner table of The Barleycorn, the pub that was almost halfway between us. Its "olde world" charm was mixed with a genuine seventies retro look and was enough to put most people off but we had been going there for years. As soon as Dave arrived my head exploded and for about ten minutes I spoke endlessly. Dave nodded and sympathised, letting me get it out of my system but then I became aware of what I must have sounded like.

'Sorry mate,' I said and finally paused to take a sip from my pint. 'You must be getting fed up with this?' He shook his head adamantly but I could tell. 'Every time we go for a pint I bang on about the same subject. Just tell me to shut up, please, I'm boring myself.' I sat up straight and shook my head. 'Let's start again. How's you? Do you have anything that you'd like to share with the group today?'

'Oh, mate, I'm with you, I really am. It's all a load of shit nowadays,' he stared into his glass. 'You're trying to do the right thing. I wish I could do the same. Get out while you can, Ben. It's the same wherever you look now. People are getting squeezed and it's starting to take its toll. You know Cheryl?' I frowned. 'Cheryl the Peril?'

I remembered. 'Well, she was telling me the other day that she hasn't been for lunch for about two years. She always used to go to lunch, she used to sit with the woman who looked like Darth Vader. Remember? But not anymore. She hates it. She was saying exactly the same thing that we say. She's just sitting it out now, waiting to get to fifty-five and then good riddance. The problem's all of these stupid ideas. We just get through one change and then we all change again. It's relentless. You see it time and time again, some wanker comes in and thinks up another way of skinning the same fucking cat. I tell you what, the bloody cat has been skinned that many times it wouldn't surprise me if it charged RC with war crimes.' He stopped and had a big gulp from his drink. 'Ha, sorry bud, seems like it's my turn to download. While I'm on it though, this new project that you're on is going to be a headache by the sounds of it. It's another example of a change which is only going to give us more to do. It's bad enough as it is and this'll just make it worse. Did you know that loads of us met last week?' I shook my head. 'Yeah, we all met to talk about the fucking mess it's going to put us in. No offence mate, it's not your fault. It's Savage, he hasn't got a clue. I bet he doesn't even care, he'll be out in a year or two. Why should he?'

'I agree with you mate. I've been saying the same

thing for ages but no-one wants to listen. It's going to be shit, I know that, you know that, but trying to make other people realise is impossible.'

'That may change soon.'

'Why?'

'None of the business are going to accept it.'

'Who was at this meeting then?'

'All the usual suspects,' Dave continued. 'Everyone that's going to use it. So you had Joyce, Sid, Steve, Rebecca, Mark N, all of that lot. There were even some of the managers there as well, so we had Brian, Mike, Anders, about fifteen of us in total.'

'Who set it up?'

'Don't know, I think it was Anders.'

'What about anyone from the project?'

'No. I don't think any of your lot knew anything about it.'

'This is what I've been waiting for. I knew something would happen eventually. What came out of it?'

'Simply that no-one wants it. Some of them were really slating it.'

'Why hasn't anyone told the top dogs? I've been trying to tell them for ages.'

'Yeah, but the only reason it's happening now is because of the timing. A year ago nobody was bothered, but now people are actually getting asked to do work for it and that's when they start taking it seriously. No-one's going to rock the boat given how much hope is riding on it. It would take some bottle to stand up in front of these guys and say they've just spent twenty million quid on a load of rubbish. No way. They'll all wait for someone else to go first. That's the game, isn't it? Keep your head down and hope it dies of natural causes.'

'So in the meantime, RC spend twenty million quid while somebody sits on their hands.'

'Yep. There's no point being surprised mate, it's just the way it is,' said Dave. 'Anyway, the good news for you is that people are starting to talk about it.'

'Brilliant,' I said sarcastically. 'So as long as one of them grows a set of bollocks at some point, I may be able to leave before the kids leave for university. What are we going to do about it all, mate?'

'Nothing, as usual.'

'Come on, for fuck's sake, you were meant to be cheering me up. Let's think.' I paused for a second. 'How about a killing spree in the boardroom?'

'Too messy, and we'd get caught.'

'Ok then, what if we just didn't turn up on Monday.'

'We'd get sacked and then we'd be left with nothing. I haven't worked there for nearly twenty years just so that I can kiss goodbye to that package.'

'I'm stumped then, I guess you're right… nothing.'

'You could start by stopping this stupid project of yours?' said Dave.

'Yeah, if only. There's nothing I'd like more, believe me. If only someone would listen.'

'They don't have to now, do they? Get someone else to say it.'

'Like who?'

'There's enough people that want it stopped, mate. All you've got to do is get one of them to say it.'

'Oh right, that sounds like a piece of piss then.'

'Yeah,' Dave laughed. 'Fair enough. It was an idea anyway. Oh, I just remembered something that Savage did on the phone the other day. It was on one of those Pension calls.'

'The big group pension calls? I thought that was all done and dusted ages ago.'

'Yeah, yeah, they had their way and all of the contracts are going to be changed,' he replied. 'But this call was to just end it all basically. Apparently we've now gone through the "consultation period", so that's that. Never any doubt was there? But your boss, Savage, came on at the end of the call and started ranting and raving about "being let down" and "everything's changed". There must have been a hundred odd people on the call. No-one usually says anything especially after that dog debacle.'

'You're kidding,' I said. 'Why was he so bothered?'

'It's all about the money, I guess. He's probably at the wrong age if you think about it. He's been here for years, his kids have probably grown up and he was settling in to a future of early retirement where he'd never have to worry about money ever again.'

'I doubt he will anyway.'

'But that's not the point. If you're promised something for twenty years and then they take the rug away, that's going to piss you off.'

'True.'

'Oh well,' said Dave. 'There's no point complaining about any of it, it won't make any difference. They own us and, although I've been a bit slow to realise that, I'm under no illusions anymore about where I stand. Any so called loyalty that they expect from me can be shoved right up their arse.' He picked his drink up quickly and as he put it to his mouth it splashed all over his chin.

I had never seen Dave this angry before. He was one of the most consistently placid men I had ever met. Since I had known him people had always taken advantage of his better nature. He was one of the nicest guys there was and to hear him talk like this was a revelation. He did what he did very well. He was the classic safe pair of hands that companies used to rely upon. People like Dave used to be looked after because it was obvious how important they were. Dave never asked for much, too little in fact, but one thing which was important to him was that feeling of loyalty and this was the first time I had ever heard him really question the value of it.

All day Sunday though, the idea of doing something about it kept going around in my head. I suppose I could do something about it, but what? What could I do that would be able to make any difference whatsoever? Savage hated me and was incapable of listening, plus I still had a hunch that he wanted it to carry on for as long as possible so that he could retire. Apart from Savage, the only other person that could push the red button was his boss. Hamish McTaggart was a man few trifled with. He was the CFO of RC and he was a pretty big deal. I had only ever met him once in person and even then I was only in the audience when he was delivering some year-end speech to his minions. He was unaware that I even worked for the company, so why would he listen to me telling him of twenty million pounds that had been wasted.

I was feeling nervous when I turned up at work on Monday morning. It had rained heavily overnight, leaving huge puddles everywhere and the air felt heavy.

I had decided that I would try and talk to a couple of the managers that Dave had mentioned at the weekend. I thought if I could get some of them on my side, and start chipping away at their reasons for not saying anything, then maybe something would happen. It had to be worth a try.

Chapter 25

Meetings make the corporate world go round. No-one worth their salt could turn down a meeting request. It was seen as a sign of strength to have your schedule completely filled with pointless conversations with people. The strongest people of all were those who would print off their schedule and leave it on full display when they were in another meeting. It was the only appropriate outlet that these people had to publicly display their egos and, accompanied by a comment about how busy they were, left everybody clear about how important they must be.

The managers who I wanted to stir up were all slightly more senior than middle-management, but definitely more junior than senior management, and I knew it would be easy to get a meeting with them. I fired off three emails asking if I could talk to them about Project Eagle and the preparations, if any, they had made. I had to make sure that they were unaware of what I was up to because they all met Savage a lot more frequently than I ever did. I had decided over the weekend that I would ask them about their preparations and hopefully tease out their opinion at the same time. It was a dangerous game and one that was a bit more serious than putting up posters or stealing toys.

All three had accepted to meet me during the course of the week and so, after doing as much as I could, I relaxed a little. My thoughts came back to the eagle that I had forgotten about since Friday night and I reluctantly looked at the photos on my phone. In the cold light of day they looked about as funny as a hangover but I had nothing to do until the afternoon so I set about creating an email address.

The name I used summed up my enthusiasm for the prank. I surprisingly managed to create badeagleman@hotmail.com in about five minutes. How easy is it to be a kidnapper these days? Once upon a time you would have been ringing from pay phones all across a city, making sure you hung up before a minute was out because there was always some guy in a hotel room with an eight-track recorder and tracker. It took the romance away knowing that you could just send an email.

For this exercise I chose the photo that I considered to be the funniest rather than the sickest, which was the shot of the eagle behind bars, and attached it to an email. I then realised that I had to choose who to send it to. I could hardly send it to the whole team, after all, what would Savage think if he received a photo like that? Savage had not seen the funny side of a joke since 1973 and even that must have been at someone else's expense. I decided to include a few of the team who were a good laugh and also the person whose desk I had hunched under on Friday night, as I thought they deserved to be involved.

The phone suddenly rang just as I was about to send it. It was Dave asking if I was going to lunch, so I stood up and took one last look at the incriminating evidence before pressing send. I thought nothing more of it for the rest of the day because of the eventful meeting that I was to attend after lunch. The entire Eagle-gate affair was finished in my mind.

Rannheiser Components had several office spaces in offsite business parks. Business Parks were always bland, with their conveniently landscaped gardens gently caressing the shiny glass and metal structures; a convenient road always meandered through the park like a canal, providing convenient access to each destination. There was always a man-made lake somewhere nearby that could provide a convenient place to eat lunch; a lunch that was conveniently bought from a convenience store situated in the park.

Two people who were involved in the project team wanted to meet with me to discuss a critical point. It made sense that we met where they were based, which was a business park on the outskirts of town. I always accepted these meetings because it meant that I had to drive to the meeting and then drive back, easily killing an hour out of the working day.

I had no idea what the meeting was about though. The two people worked on the technical side of the project and spoke in a weird gamer language. I was on the side that spoke to business people mainly and did my best to avoid this strange group as much as possible. Every company has people like this. They work in jeans and black t-shirts, have code names like Dragon-Wizard and laugh condescendingly when you mention Star Wars. Organisations need these people to write computer programmes which can then be used in the real world but they prefer to keep them out of sight, which is why they are always located away from the main offices.

No-one understands them, they have their own culture, they have their own dress-code, they are vital for the future productivity of the company and yet nobody wants to see them. They call themselves the slaves because of the similarities.

RC hide these freaks in a business park, away from

everybody else, and usually deal with a liaison that can translate. These translators are sad enough to have watched every single Star Trek episode but not quite sad enough to have ventured into the Deep Space Nine series too.

I would occasionally have to talk with them, through an interpreter, and usually I just nodded. They always seemed to be reassured by the nodding and the more meetings we had the more reliant on the power of the nod I became.

I sat down in the empty meeting room and went through my usual routine of placing a pad, with a pen on it, in front of me. In the few moments I enjoyed of staring vacantly at the wall I started to think about what the subject could be about. I had not read the covering email because I never understood them anyway. I concluded that I had no idea so instead I sat happily daydreaming.

As the door opened, a serious-faced man with greasy black hair walked in. He was wearing a black South Park t-shirt that said, 'Kill' on it, as well as grubby black jeans and Dr Martens. He was about six foot two and weighed twenty stone at least but, unlike Darren Heavyside, this was all fat. His mother had probably kept feeding him, when he was a child, to make him forget that he was inside all day on his own playing

Mega-Drive games.

He never even glanced at me as he trudged in and sat down at the opposite end of the table. I continued to look at him waiting for a response but in the end I gave up and noticed the second of the two had walked in. This one seemed a bit more accustomed to modern day, social interaction and greeted me in the appropriate manner. He was also wearing a shirt and trousers, which must have meant that he was my go-between.

'Ok then,' I said. 'Let's get started shall we? How about you begin?'

'Don't tempt me, you cretin,' mumbled the gamer at the end making me suddenly sit upright in my chair.

'Excuse me?' I asked.

'Don't worry,' said the liaison, 'don't mind him, he's in a bad mood today because someone's deleted a load of his files.'

'I couldn't think why anyone would do anything like that,' I said, immediately regretting the sarcasm.

'We just want to talk to you about the project and what exactly we're supposed to be doing,' said the liaison.

'Oh, um,' I said, 'well it's probably best if you keep, you know, *ploughing on* for the time being and keep doing what you're doing.'

'That's the problem though,' said the liaison. 'We

don't know what we're meant to be doing. The project seems to have come to a standstill because there's no information coming back to us, telling us what we need to know.'

'This is typical,' blurted out the caveman at the end still not making eye contact. 'You lot are all the same. You swan around, go to meetings, talk bollocks, and never get anything done.' I had to agree. 'We're here and unless we start getting some proper information about what it is that you actually want, then we can't do anything.'

'Ah, well,' I said. 'You see, that's the problem. There are people who still don't know what that actually is. I think it's hard to be explicit about exactly what it is that we want. Details are going to be hard at this stage. Would you not be able to just write what it is you think we want and perhaps other people could take a look at it?'

'Fuck off,' he said.

'Oh,' I said.

'Come on, Troy,' said the liaison, 'I know you're wound up at the moment but we have to keep this professional.'

'This is a joke,' the missing-link said getting to his feet, 'a fucking joke. I sent him an email telling him all of the things that we needed to know or we wouldn't be able to get any further. That was a month ago.' He was talking to the other guy but occasionally pointing viciously in my direction. 'All I want to know is what to build. If I was a fucking builder I wouldn't get this shit. I've never heard anything so ridiculous in all my life.

'Forget about it,' said the other. 'We'll talk about it another time.'

'No,' said the lump. 'This always happens and I've had enough of it.'

'Um,' I said, 'perhaps we can work out what it is immediately that you need and start with that?'

He shook his head and that condescending laugh came out of his face. My patience was starting to wear thin and I was just thinking of walking out when he carried on.

'Do you even know what this project is meant to provide?' he asked, presumably of me, but still looking at his friend. In all fairness he had hit the nail on the head. I was uncertain that anyone knew the answer to that question.

'Why don't you look at me if you're going to start flying off accusations,' I said.

'What did you say?' he shouted, becoming more and more animated. By that point he was jumping on the spot and wobbling everywhere. I was still sitting down and was completely taken aback when suddenly he hopped around the table towards me. I rested my hand on the table to stand up as quickly as possible but it was too late. He hit me, square in the face, with a weighty jab. I rolled over the back of the chair and ended up as a heap on the floor with the chair on top of me.

Thankfully, big Troy looked about as shocked as I did and went back to his seat at the end of the table to sit down. I tasted something metallic and put my hand to my mouth, only for it to be covered in blood. My lip was split and it was bleeding profusely. The only other time this had happened was when Paul Reeves took offence at me snatching his G.I.Joe action toy at primary school. I stood up and quickly collected my things before walking out towards the toilet.

The liaison had no idea how to handle the situation and just sat staring at the table. I was glad about this because the last thing I needed was someone following me into the bathroom to check if I was alright. It was humiliating enough to have been knocked off my chair by a man who spends every night watching porn on his super-charged pc. I looked at myself in the mirror and weighed up that it was fortunately not that bad. It was a small cut that would heal pretty quickly and then I would just be left with a fat lip. I leant on the basin, looking at my reflection and wondered if this was possibly a new all-time low at work.

I decided to go straight home after this because getting punched at work was probably enough of a reason to leave early. On the way I received a text from the liaison who had been in the room. He explained that he was sorry and had had no idea that Troy the Tempest would do that sort of thing *again*. Apparently he had hit someone two years ago while on another project and since then he had been taking medication and receiving counselling. This was a step backwards in his treatment and proved that he was not up to the pressure of work. He was dismissed immediately, as soon as I had left, and I was asked if I wanted to press charges.

I considered the whole process which would result if I did. I would have to talk to the Police, I would have to tell Savage, I would have to own up to lots of people that I had just been smacked in the face by a blancmange. I did not want to cause myself anymore aggravation. The grubby, nerd, role-playing balloon had been sacked and that was all I cared about. Besides, although I disagreed with his methods, I could understand his frustrations completely. This was the condition that Project Eagle was reducing people to. Something had to be done about it and now I was ready for the fight. When I had assumed that I was only saving myself it was easy to let things drift but now it was clear that other people needed my help too. I needed to become a double agent who would bring the house down from the inside.

Chapter 26

Over the next week I met with each of the three managers I had arranged to see. Although the conversations went well and my motives went undetected, each meeting became more frustrating than the last. The two women and one man that I knew from previous encounters were all perfectly friendly and completely in agreement with my concerns over the doomed project. They all knew that it would not work and they admitted that all of their teams would suffer because of it. I tried to suggest to each of them that perhaps if someone spoke up then it would prevent a great deal of unnecessary time and money being wasted. They all looked at me in their own way, and gave me three different reasons why that would not be them, but between the lines I knew the real reason.

They were scared; firstly of Savage and then, more importantly, they were scared of Hamish McTaggart. He owned them. He had the power to crush their lives. I could see in all of their eyes what I had known all along. Project Eagle was too high profile to throw stones at.

There were always initiatives, or projects, or strategies, that came along and carried the weight of improvement on their shoulders. Savage was managing the thing but it was Hamish McTaggart whose head was on the block.

McTaggart had been lied to since day one. He was too far away from the operational, day-to-day happenings to know the truth. He had recruited Savage because he trusted him and expected him to deliver what he had promised, but Savage had lost all sense of reality. I had access to the financial systems and could tell what the accurate spend of the project was but this was not being communicated accurately. Rupert Savage had been covering up costs for the duration of the project, I doubted that McTaggart knew even half of the real cost of the project so far, or worse still, how much would have to be spent to complete it. But he listened to Savage and it was this good information that he would pass on to the board - costs were being kept low and delivery was on track.

Each of the managers knew that if they were to explain to McTaggart that the project was a write-off then they would be accused of being a trouble-maker. The golden rule in corporate life is not to rock the boat and Project Eagle was not even their boat. If only McTaggart were to discover the truth of the project then his judgement could be swayed. It would be difficult for him to explain to the board, but twenty million was not the end of RC's world and Savage's head on a platter would help to rectify matters.

I was demoralised after the meetings but I was not surprised. Common sense seldom prevailed and chain of command was usually stronger. Unless there was a serious change to his personality and Savage decided to confess everything to McTaggart then I would have to think of another way of getting to the top man.

The more I thought about it, the more I became uncertain about my own escape if the project failed. So far, my discussion on redundancy had lasted for all of a minute with Savage back in January. If I took riskier approaches from now on, then I wanted to be certain that I would definitely leave at the end of it.

I could hear Savage, through the wall, banging on his keyboard with his sausage fingers. Time was of the essence I thought to myself. Every minute I spent in this place from now on, which was not going towards the ultimate demise of Project Eagle, was time that I would rather spend chewing off my own arm. I walked out in to the corridor and was just about to knock assertively on the door next to mine when I was interrupted.

'Here he is,' said the one attractive lady who remained on the project. She happened to come out of her office at exactly the same time. 'I know what you're up to.'

Normally I would have been delighted to have spent the next five minutes flirting with her, but right now my mind was focussed on Savage.

'What do you mean?' I asked carefully.

'Oh, it's like that, is it? You don't want anyone else involved in your little game?'

'Um, what?'

'Come on, give it up,' she said smiling, 'everyone knows you've got him.'

The penny finally dropped, 'oh, you mean Eddie?'

'We all know you've got it, we're just wondering how many more of those dodgy pictures you've taken. That photo was sick. Did you let your kids play with that toy afterwards.'

'I don't know what you mean,' I said.

'Very funny,' she looked at me in the way that people look when they are trying to work out if the other person is lying. 'I don't believe you. You can't fool us. Anyway, Melanie forwarded it to Savage. See ya.' She skipped off down the corridor leaving me with my heart in my mouth.

I stood there for a moment, uncertain if I should continue forwards or retreat. Why send it to Savage? Why did I send it in the first place? What a mess, but I only had a brief time to mull it over before suddenly the door, I was stood in front of, opened.

'What are you doing?' barked Savage.

'Um, I was… um… going to see if you were free.'

'Why? Do you want to play golf?'

'I'm sorry but I don't play golf, Rupert.'

'Good, I wasn't asking.' He walked back in to his room. 'Are you coming in then, or what?'

I sat down on the other side of his desk and smiled, but he became rather impatient and ushered me with his hand to begin.

'Sorry, um, sorry to disturb you. I just wanted to talk to you about the project and how it was going.'

'You should know, you're on it.'

'Um, yeah, yeah, that's true, that's definitely true but I only really see a few small parts of it. I just wanted to get a feel from you about, you know, how it's going overall.'

'Can't you read the communications that go out?'

'Yes, I've read them but you only sit next door and I thought it would be good to discuss it. Listen, if this is a bad time then don't worry about it. I'll come back at some other time. When are you free? How about tomorrow?'

'Get on with it now if you must. What do you want to know?'

'I just wanted to know where I stand in it all,

particularly, what I mean by that, is where my future stands. In other words, how are my future and the project linked? Or, better than that, what will happen to my future at the end of the project?' I stopped there and hoped he had understood more of that than I had.

'What do you want me to say?' he said after frowning. 'It's up to you, but in previous discussions you've made it perfectly clear that you don't want to stay. If you've changed your mind then by all means tell me, but otherwise I assume that you're looking for redundancy at the end of this. Right?' The words sounded like a Shakespearean Sonnet but they were being delivered out of an AK47.

'Yes, that's right,' I smiled. 'I would still prefer that, but I suppose what I want to clarify a bit further, is when will you know if that's definitely going to happen?'

'It's going to happen, ok?' He stood up and turned to look out of the window, at the same tree that I had studied so closely. 'You were right,' he said still looking out of the window. 'Finance is going to be laying off people, left, right and bloody centre, and you're probably best out of it all. This place isn't the same as it used to be. You used to know where you stood, it used to be somewhere that meant something, but not now. Now it's just a machine and we're just the ones that turn the handle. Yeah, you're better off out of it.'

'I heard about the pension change,' I said, not really sure what to say.

'Yeah, the good old pension change. Yep, well, what can you do?' He turned back round to face me. 'How old are you, Ben?'

'Thirty-four.'

'Thirty-four,' he sighed and shook his head. 'If I was thirty-four again I don't know what I would do nowadays. You're doing it right, I think. Get out while you can and find something else. It's too late for old farts like me.' He turned around again and returned his focus to the tree. 'There's one promise I'm going to make to you Ben. I know how shitty it feels to be let down by your managers, so I promise that you'll have written confirmation that you *will* be made redundant when this project ends. Is that good enough?' He turned back again and returned to his seat.

'Thank you Rupert, I appreciate that.'

'But there's still something else I need to talk to you about.' He grabbed his mouse and looked for something on the computer. I knew what was coming but after seeing Savage behave like this I was unsure of which way he would go. 'I assume that you'll be looking for a different type of career after this project?'

'I'm not sure yet. I'm not sure what I'll be doing *if* I

leave.'

'Because Jenkins, you are an idiot. This bloody email thing has been a right pain in the arse. Why do you do things like this? What's wrong with you? Do you have any idea of the amount of hassle this has caused me.'

'No, Sir.'

'A shit load, that's how much. I suppose you think it's funny, don't you? Well, you're thirty-four, Ben, and you have to start growing up. You can't ever send offensive photos around again. Melanie complained and so I had to follow the bloody thing up.'

'I'm sorry, I didn't mean for it to cause any problems. I just sort of did it for team morale, I suppose. I didn't think that it would cause an issue.'

'You didn't think, full stop. So, anyway, because someone's complained I've had to take it further. I had no choice. There's policy for this sort of thing and I couldn't ignore it. I like you Ben. Not every day and definitely not working with you, but on some level I understand you. But then you do a thing like this which I can't understand at all. Look at it, just look at it.' He turned his monitor around and facing me was Jane's photo of the eagle being buggered, in my bathroom at home, with the word 'HURT' scrawled in lipstick. I thought I had sent the photo in the cage but I could hardly use that as a defence now.

'I'm really sorry, Rupert, it was just a joke that was obviously in bad taste and got out of hand.'

'It just so happens that Melanie's brother has experienced something similar to this at Her Majesty's pleasure and she was very upset when she saw it. You can't do anything about it now but I had to send it to Darren Heavyside, the Head of Security, because that's what I have to do in these situations. We had a chat about it and he wanted to throw the book at you, in fact he was very determined to do that indeed, but in the end we have agreed that you will receive a stern talking to, on the promise that you won't do anything like this ever again. Understand?'

'Yes, Sir.'

'So, now we both have a promise, don't we? If you don't let me down then I won't let you down. Got it?'

I nodded solemnly.

'Now piss off and do some work.'

I walked back into my office, shut the door and let out such a sigh of relief that I nearly fainted.

Chapter 27

The next couple of weeks zipped by and I started to feel a lot better about it all. At least the redundancy was definitely in the bag. All I had to do was wait for the inevitable car crash and the fat lady would begin singing.

The month of May brought with it the usual British preview of summer. Lovely blue skies were juxtaposed with lush green fields. The stream that ran through the site was littered with dragonflies meandering along its course. Each morning I would drive through the blossoming countryside and, more often than not, I started to stop off on the way.

I began to spend less time at work and more time in friendlier places. I obviously made sure that I answered emails promptly and, turned up for unavoidable meetings, but the rest of the time was free. As long as I kept my head down and stayed out of trouble, I would be alright. Since I had all of this time on my hands, I began to clarify everything I knew about Project Eagle. All of the reasons why the project was doomed. I only did this so that I could cheer myself up and gauge how long I thought it would limp on for.

I prepared a document which stated all of the failures that the project had. It stemmed from the fact that nobody actually wanted it, right up to the point where delivery would be impossible, and covered every reason in between. It resulted in quite a large document. I also pulled together an up-to-date financial statement that showed how much had actually been spent up to that point and a forecast for the foreseeable future. The size of the difference between the published and the actual figures surprised even me. I knew there would be a discrepancy but this report showed that it would cost four times more to complete it, which meant one-hundred million pounds.

The early summer, the time outside of work and the hard facts of doom all worked together to leave me feeling positive. I was so happy that when I went into work at the end of May to hear of a planned Project Eagle Conference, I eagerly made my way to the Conference Centre without a second thought. I had been unaware of one being organised but then I was hardly there to pick these things up anymore.

The Conference Centre was on the same site as my office but was a new building that had only been finished for about a year. I had never been invited to it before and part me was actually excited. It looked very shiny and new from the outside, so shiny that it would blind me with sunlight as I drove past it every morning. It was a huge, monolithic structure which dwarfed everything else in its shadow.

I walked in to the auditorium which resembled a proper theatre. The stage was down below, lit up by a rainbow of professional stage lights, and everywhere else was in darkness but for the dimmed houselights. The stage was as empty as Project Eagle's delivery record; there was a lectern on the right hand side, a couple of chairs on the far left, and a screen in the middle which must have been as big as the side of a house.

I sat down and noticed there were only fifty other people in the audience. I had read somewhere that there was meant to be a buffet and cocktail reception afterwards but with only this few people in attendance I decided that I would give that a miss.

There were large banners emblazoned with Project Eagle hanging either side of the large screen, very similar to the Nazi swastikas at a Nuremberg rally. The project branding had been disappointing though. Departments usually spend a lot of effort designing their own logos, so that they can communicate their blandness to other areas, but my project had plumped for 'Project Eagle', written in arial font and simply enlarged. There was something incredibly depressing about it and it reflected the mood of the audience perfectly. Not one person in the room could be proud of their association with this project and the banner accidentally symbolised this desperation.

Once the conference itself was due to start, a surprising guest walked up on to the stage. Alongside Rupert Savage was, an incredibly bored looking, Hamish McTaggart. This was only the second time I had ever seen him but it looked to me as if he had endured a bad few years. McTaggart was the type of man that you would usually only see in photos and now I knew why. He was a bloated, sweaty, unhealthy looking man in his early fifties who looked about as interested in Project Eagle as the rest of us. He had the air of a man that relied on his old Etonian network to get him to where he was, and now he was there, he was going to do everything in his power to remain there.

He was too busy looking at his phone to engage with the audience but this was in direct contrast to Savage, who seemed to become angrier the bigger the stage he was on. Nerves usually affect people in the opposite way but Savage began pacing the stage like a tiger. He welcomed everyone to the event by leaning on the lectern with both hands as if he were just about to launch it into the first few rows.

I had no idea what the purpose of the conference was, but all through Savage's slides, nothing was communicated that was not already known by any of the spectators. He bullied and spat and raged for about forty minutes before finally coming to an end. The auditorium descended into silence and without any applause, or musical accompaniment, he made his way back to his seat. Hamish McTaggart was still looking at his phone during all of this but after being prompted by Savage's physical presence next to him, he stood up and shuffled across to the lectern.

He began with some highly polished openers and then launched into the strategic importance of Project Eagle. 'We, as a company,' he said in a rich, public school accent, 'have never been prouder of a programme of work that will deliver so much internal benefit. The improvements that are forecasted are immeasurable. You should all feel incredibly excited about what you're involved with and remember to keep your eye on the prize. I speak for the rest of the board when I tell you that we are relying on this project to deliver and I know, with all of your input, that it will become a reality. The next few years will be challenging in the industry as a whole and more importance will be put upon the way we run our business. The bottom line will be under the microscope of the market and thanks to Project Eagle, and other lesser initiatives, we will be able to achieve double digit growth. The strategic importance of this project is greater now than it has ever been. This is why I am pledging my unerring belief in the delivery of this project and expecting the employees of RC to bring it home. I have heard rumours that it may be scrapped, thrown on to the pile, you have heard these rumours too. But I am here, in person in front of you, to declare that this project will never be scrapped. I believe that eagles, like phoenix, will rise from the ashes and be victorious. Thank you.'

This time a round of applause started near the front and spread across the thread-bare crowd, growing into cheers and shouts of euphoria. All except one person, that is. I sat near the back, on the side, with my head in my hands. The noise started swirling around, my eyes would not focus and the stage appeared to be a dangerous distance below. I grabbed for the side of the seat and pulled myself up. After staggering across to the door, I opened it and the cool rush of air across my face felt good. I stumbled and tripped all the way downstairs and found the sanctuary of the men's toilet refreshing.

I sat in a locked cubicle trying to rationalise the startling information. All I could remember was McTaggart saying that it would never end and at that point a black hole seemed to appear before me. How could he possibly say that? Was he that blind? Had no-one told him anything? The small cubicle felt like it was flying through space.

I had to do something about it. I had to find McTaggart and tell him. He was such a difficult man to reach but perhaps that moment was my opportunity. He was at the Conference Centre, he was within touching distance, and all I would need is five minutes with the man.

I burst out of the cubicle and began my search for McTaggart. I could smell the buffet nearby and followed the direction that people were heading. The smell became stronger and the number of people grew until I was in the middle of a crowd of at least a hundred people. Most of them must have turned up at the end for the free food.

I frantically looked around, over the tops of people's heads and around the corners of pillars in the vast concourse. All I could see were the faces of the people I had worked with for the last two years. Faces that I never wanted to see again.

'Hello Ben,' greeted the same girl who had told me about the eagle photo a couple of weeks before.

I nodded without saying anything. I turned away, still searching across the room, and attempted to walk off.

'So, did Savage say anything about the photo? You pervert,' she smiled.

'Um, yeah, yeah he did. It's all sorted now. See you later.' I walked off but she followed me.

'What did he say? Did you get in to trouble?'

'Um, yeah, yeah, a bit. I've got to go.' I carried on walking but still she followed.

'Melanie was really upset by it. I don't know why she took it so bad, perhaps she really liked that eagle. She might have thought it was cruelty to animals. I think she's one of those Friends of the Earth, or whatever they're called. So, anyway, what did he say? Was he really annoyed? I bet he was. Rupert's annoyed by life itself, let alone anything else that happens. Go on, tell me, what happened? Go on Ben, what did he say?'

'Sorry... whatever your name is... but... fuck off.' I ran through the rest of the crowd until I reached the far side of the room. Still McTaggart was nowhere to be found. I caught sight of the girl walking back into the crowd and I felt bad for a second. I realised that I should probably get control of myself otherwise if I did manage to catch up with Hamish McTaggart, he would be more likely to think that I was some kind of a lunatic.

I walked outside to get some fresh air and by pure

coincidence I saw McTaggart and Savage talking to each other by the edge of a conifer. This had to be my chance. I stood still and waited for Savage to finish whatever it was that he was saying. They were both smiling and laughing with each other. I started to feel uncomfortable and moved further away, around a corner, so that I would not be seen.

There were huge concrete pillars outside the main entrance to the Conference Centre. They ran from ground level all the way up to the overhang which was four storeys high. I was positioned behind the second pillar, my hands resting on it and my head peering around the edge so that I could keep an eye on the conversation. They were both stood far enough away for me not to be able to hear what they were talking about but still I waited, poised to move as soon as Savage disappeared.

Suddenly, I felt a hand thud down on my right shoulder and I spun around in shock, only to see Darren Heavyside leering at me with a vicious smile stretched across his face.

Chapter 28

'Yes,' whispered Heavyside as his breath melted my face. 'I've got you now, Jenkins.'

'Uh,' I stuttered.

'No need for words now, sweetheart. You're mine. This way.' He dragged me by the left arm in the opposite direction to Savage and McTaggart. 'I've been waiting for this moment for a long time. Get in the car.' His security jeep was parked on the pavement opposite the Conference Centre. The smell which came out when he opened the door was a mixture of smoke and sweat. It made me gag and I considered making a run for it, but he would only catch me up at some point. I climbed in to the passenger seat and off he drove.

The site road weaved in and out of the trees. We came up to the building where I worked and then we kept on going. We then passed another two office buildings that I was familiar with but still we kept driving. I had not realised before how long the site road was from one end to the other. Eventually we reached a small single-storey building hidden behind some trees.

He pulled up outside and ordered me to get out.

When I walked in through the front door it was obvious that this was Security headquarters. There was a man behind a counter wearing a security uniform and aviator sunglasses. In front of him was a large book opened in the middle and surrounding him were small black and white monitors showing CCTV footage.

'Who's this then Daz?' the man behind the counter said reaching for a pen.

'This is the freak I was telling you about,' said Heavyside.

'Which one?'

'You know the one with the cuddly toy?'

'Oh yeah,' he turned his nose up, 'that one. Horrible little pervert. Eagle Knievel we called you.' He started laughing at his own joke and it sounded like he was having an attack of some sort. 'It makes me sick. Did you catch him fiddling again? What's your name?' he said looking at me. 'I suppose you've got one?'

Up until this point I had been silent. I felt as if I had just been teleported into Deliverance country.

'His name is Jenkins, Ben Jenkins,' said Heavyside. 'Write him in the holding column. I've finally got this one banged to rights. He's going down. Come with me,' said Heavyside as he grabbed hold of my arm and pulled.

'Stop pulling me about,' I said.

'Oh yeah, Doris, what are you going to do about it?' said Heavyside turning around and measuring up to me.

'Nothing but I'd like it if you stopped pushing me around.'

'I bet you would but I've got to make sure that you don't get away, haven't I?'

He led me behind the counter where there was space enough for three desks and then at the back was a makeshift prison cell. It had floor to ceiling white bars and was only big enough to accommodate one chair. 'Get in there and stop your moaning,' he ordered, 'oh and give me your phone too.' He shut the door and locked it with a key that was on his belt.

'What is this?' I said. 'Are you even allowed to do this?'

'We are issued with a holding cell in order to protect the safety of the employees that work on this site. In my opinion you're a danger. You're also a freak, a pervert, probably a kiddy fiddler and fucking irritating too. So, to answer your question, yes we are allowed to do this.'

'Terrific,' I said and reluctantly sat down. 'I'm hardly a danger.'

'You could've fooled me,' he said. 'I've just found you spying on the CFO of the company. To my trained eye it looked as though you were preparing something that could have caused a threat to a key member of personnel.'

'No I wasn't.'

'That's what I saw.'

'I was just stood there.'

'You were spying.'

'Are you not allowed to stand in certain places now?'

'You were spying with intent.'

'Well, I wasn't, but whatever. Anyway, how long do I have to sit in here?'

'That depends.'

'On what?'

'On how much your manager likes you.'

'Go on then, give him a ring. Hurry it up, I haven't got all day.'

'No, but I have,' smiled Heavyside putting my phone down on his desk. I knew that Savage would get me out of here as soon as he found out. He might have his problems but at least he was not unhinged. Heavyside on the other hand was beginning to worry me.

'Barry,' said Heavyside to the buffoon at the counter. 'What do you reckon we do?'

Barry was small and scrawny. He had little eyes like a pig and an unfortunate twitch in his top lip. 'I'd leave him in there, Daz. There's no telling who's safe when you've got someone like him running around.'

'What do you mean?' I shouted. 'I'm not a pervert. I was just hiding under a desk.'

'With a soft toy, wasn't it?' said the idiot. 'Sounds bloody normal to me,' he said laughing once again at his own joke. His laugh sounded like a cross between a pig and a chicken. It was unbearable.

Heavyside sat down and put his feet up on the desk next to him. He contentedly picked up the latest copy of Guns and Ammo and began whistling. I had no choice but to sit still and think of how I could get out of it.

'You're not going to be able to prove any of this,' I tried.

'I'm probably not going to have to,' he looked up and smiled. 'You're on your last legs now. One more cock up and you're gone. You know that as well as I do.'

'But I'll just say that you picked me up for no reason.'

'And you think that'll work, do you? Do you see all of those CCTV monitors that we've got there? Well, they're plugged in all around the site. It's amazing. They record things all day long. That brand new Conference Centre of ours is one of the most modern bits of the site. We've got all kinds of paraphernalia protecting it from any potential break-ins. One of the best bits of kit we invested in was an automatic detection recording system. So you see, Mr Ben Jenkins, you were on candid camera. If anyone decides to question my word then I'll just show you hiding behind a pillar like a peeping tom. I wouldn't mind betting that you've probably done that sort of thing before.'

'He probably looks at little girls getting changed, or even better, little boys,' added the village idiot from the counter before breaking into another laugh that even made Heavyside wince.

'It's all over for you, my friend,' said Heavyside, then he leant closer to me and whispered, 'you're going to regret the day that you ever threw a lasagne at the back of my head.'

'I didn't throw it at you,' I protested. 'It was an accident. It was a fucking accident. My arm shook and it just so happened…'

'It just so happened that a lasagne travelled six feet through the air and landed directly on the back of my head. Is that what you were going to say?'

'Yes.'

'I don't believe you. You office lot are always taking the piss out of us at security. Saying we're not important and all that. Well, take the piss out of this, I dare you. You contravened a serious breach of IT rules when you sent that photo around work computers.'

'It wasn't from me.'

'Stop lying. We've got records that show which

computer it was sent from and guess what? You're screwed. All it's going to take is one call from me and your manager, Rupert Savage, is going to be left with no choice. Start saying your prayers.'

I sat still again, desperately thinking of ways to get out of it. Heavyside picked up his magazine again and then put it down straight away.

'La-de-da-de-da,' he sang. 'I think I'm going to take a piss, Barry. Can you watch our young pervert here?'

'Not too close though, eh?' Barry started laughing again and Heavyside walked off.

As soon as he disappeared I remembered something. It was a few months ago and it had been overtaken by other events but finally my memory came to the rescue. Barry had been constantly staring at me with his little eyes and his twitchy lip. He was the type of man that you always found hanging around bigger men. Thankfully he said nothing while we were alone and I was able to think about how to make my move. Once it was clear in my mind I happily waited until Heavyside returned.

'La-de-da-doo-doo,' sang Heavyside on his return. 'Have I missed anything?'

'He's been brickin' it, Daz,' said Barry.

'I bet he has,' said Heavyside with a smile.

'You've well and truly got me,' I said.

'Thank you for agreeing at last,' said Heavyside. 'Not that it's going to help you though.'

'I didn't think it would,' I said. 'I guess I'll just have to get used to finding a new job. I've been here twelve years, do you know that?'

'Not my problem,' shrugged Heavyside.

'No, I realise it's not. It's mine, all mine.' I paused. 'I won't be able to travel away anymore. Those far off places I used to go. Sydney, Mumbai, Moscow... New York. I don't suppose you two get to travel much in your job.'

'We do actually,' said Barry. 'You go all over the world, don't you Daz?'

'Oh is that right?' I asked.

'Yes it is, as a matter of fact,' said Heavyside. 'It's not just you fancy-dans that go gallivanting.'

'Have you ever been to Sydney?' I asked.

'No.'

'What about any disused volcanos?'

'Eh, what are you talking about?'

'It doesn't matter. How about New York?'

'Yes, I have been there actually.'

'With work?'

'Yeah, I had to go there only a few months ago.'

'Why?'

'Making sure everything was safe for a conference.

My security role doesn't just cover this site you know. I'm responsible for the people on this site when they are in work hours, wherever that might be.'

'Well, I never knew that. I guess you learn something new every day. So, do you have to check the facilities?'

'Yeah, that's one of the things I do. I also have to go wherever most of the delegates go and make sure they're kept safe.'

'How do you do that then?' I asked.

'I keep an eye on them,' he said angrily. 'Stop asking so many questions.'

'I'm just curious because I was in New York a few months ago,' I said and watched as Heavyside suddenly became very interested. 'Yeah, we stayed in this place just south of Central Park, even went to the Waldorf Astoria one night.'

'So what, we don't want to be touched up by you,' said Barry who started up his horrible laugh.

'Shut up, Barry,' said Heavyside. 'What are you getting at, you horrible little fuckwit?'

'I'm just saying,' I carried on, 'that I didn't feel very safe on the night I went to the Waldorf Astoria.' His face began to drop. 'No, it felt very much like a whole party of us had to walk several blocks home without anybody really watching out for us at all. I don't suppose that's strictly true though. New York is such a nice place, I'm sure we were perfectly safe.'

'What do you know?' said Heavyside so quietly that only I could hear.

'I know about you drinking,' I whispered back to him. 'I know about the Police, I know about the indecent exposure and I know that you weren't doing your job that night. Is that enough?'

It stopped Darren Heavyside in his tracks and his face froze.

'Oh good,' I said. 'Maybe now we can come to a new understanding?' I had rendered him completely speechless and it was at that point that I knew I had him. 'How about you let me out of here? There's probably no need to call Savage and no need to mention any of this ever again, wouldn't you agree?'

I waited for a moment because I could see the anger filtering through his system but eventually Heavyside knew he was beaten. He reached on to his belt and grabbed the key.

'What are you doing, Daz?' asked Barry suddenly realising that the door to the cell was open. 'I'd let him piss in a bucket if that's what he wants. Dirty toe-rag.'

'Shut up, Barry,' said Heavyside.

I stood up and walked as casually as I could out of the cell. I then had to reach over Heavyside, to grab my phone, before coming out from behind the counter towards the door. Barry looked on incredulously, checking back with Heavyside in case he wanted him to act.

'Don't worry, *Daz*,' I said when I opened the front door. 'I'll find my own way back. Ta ta.' Heavyside's face had turned bright red and he began to get out of his chair. I quickly stepped outside and shut the door behind me.

As soon as I reached the site road I started to run. Even though I was about a mile away from my car, I kept running. That was as close as I had ever been to losing anything in my entire life and the nervous energy was shaking all around my body. By the time I reached the car, I fell in to the driver's seat and started to laugh uncontrollably.

Most people would have been deterred by what had just happened but I had come face-to-face with the worst case scenario and lived to tell the tale. The plan was already forming in my mind by the time I arrived home. McTaggart had said that the project would never end and I knew that it was only me now that could change his mind.

Chapter 29

'What are you doing?' asked Jane later that evening as she walked in to the spare bedroom. 'I thought you were still putting the kids to bed.' She noticed all of the paper I had around me. 'What happened at work today?'

'I've had enough,' I said. 'I was bloody close to losing my job today.'

'What do you mean?'

'Let's just say that it was really, really close, but it's ok because I now know what I've got to do to end it all.'

'Right?' she looked concerned. 'So, what are you going to do then? Kill them all?' The thought did seem appealing and I have to admit that I had considered it.

'No, that won't work. It'll take too long. But I'm going to take things into my own hands. I can't keep sitting by and waiting for someone else to do something about it. I've got all of the information that others have, and if they're not prepared to use it, then I will.'

'Good, I've always said that, what's the point of having all of these people if none of them actually do anything. With what you've told me, I can't believe that someone somewhere is spending this much money on something that nobody wants.'

'Exactly. What I've got to do is get to McTaggart and tell him how much money it *is* costing, and prove to him at the same time that no one wants it.'

'Who's McTaggart?'

'Yeah, good question. He's the chap at the top of the tree, the one right at the top, the one that holds his fingers on the big red button, and the fella who has been spun various stories since the project's conception, and wait for it but he's none other than the CFO of RC himself.' I stared at Jane expecting her to look aghast and bring her hands to her face in shock, but instead she just shrugged slightly as if to say, *'So?'*

'Well, okay,' I carried on. 'Maybe that doesn't sound so hard, but I've never met this guy before. He doesn't know me from Adam. The problem I have, the real problem, the beauty of a problem that I now have, now that I've decided to do something about it, is ... how on earth do I get to talk to this man, without him knowing who I am, because I'm pretty sure that if someone found out what I was doing then I would probably, no - definitely get fired.'

'Just go up to him and talk to him, I can't see why you can't just do that. He's only a man after all. Your company doesn't make any sense, they're all just...'

'... because if I do that,' I interrupted, 'then I'll be seen to be doing the wrong thing, and you can't do that.'

'But it's not the wrong thing,' said Jane starting to get angry. 'If you're telling someone that they're wasting their money on a load of rubbish, then surely that's the right thing.'

'It's just not the way it's done, Jane, honestly I'm going to have to be cleverer than that.'

'I don't see why not, but...' she turned and walked out of the room. 'Just make sure you don't blow it all,' she added as she walked down the stairs.

'Obviously, I'm not going try and do that. I'm doing this for us,' I shouted after her but by then she had gone.

After a moment of looking around me for something to throw I realised that she was talking absolute sense. It was the senseless situation that was making me angry. I should be able to simply talk to a person, present them with several facts, and convince them to pull the plug on a project that was hopelessly going nowhere. But I knew it was more complicated than that, even if I did have trouble explaining why.

The plan, which had come to me as I was driving home that evening, was to collect together all of the evidence that I had and simply email it to McTaggart. It was such an overwhelming case against the project that the decision would be a foregone conclusion. It had to work even if all I could hope for was to open his eyes to the truth.

I stayed up late collating all of the evidence into one zip file. I included the minutes of the meeting that Dave had gone to a month before. I had asked for them because I wanted to know how bad it actually was, and even I was surprised when I first read them. Every single manager was quoted in the minutes as totally rejecting the project.

I gathered together all of the financial information which I had calculated and even screen prints from the accounting system to back it up. This conclusively showed the extent to which the finances that had been presented to McTaggart had been fabricated. I knew that even the numbers on their own would cause the reaction I needed.

The presentation that I had prepared just for my own benefit was also attached. After looking at it again I hoped that it would clearly highlight the flaws in the design, which would prevent it from ever working in the first place.

For good measure, I also included any emails that I had received which questioned the validity of the project, reports that had fallen by the way side over the last year, and I drew up a timeline which showed how many missed deadlines and false promises there had been.

I finally completed it in the early hours of the morning. I looked over it all and was satisfied by the amount of evidence that I had managed to collate. I closed the zip file and saved it all on to a pen drive that was marked with a red X.

Bond concealed the microfilm in the secret compartment in the base of his shoe, which had been supplied by Q department. The killing of four Russians, three Croatian fishermen, a whole army of Chinese Triads and a Welsh school teacher were necessary in order to secure the information. The capturing of the plans for the underwater nuclear reactor would ensure that it never saw the light of day, and millions of lives would be saved. He leant back on the sun bed and allowed himself a smile while the sun warmed his cut face. Two beeps interrupted the silence and then suddenly a voice came from the watch on his wrist.

'Hello 007,' it said in an Old Etonian accent.

'Good morning, Sir.'

'Well done, James. You've saved the world once again. Return back to England and get the bird back in it's house.'

'I will, Sir, but first I'm going to stay here for a few more days.'

'James, this is a direct order. Return immediately.'

'Sorry Sir, there seems to be a... problem with the connection.' He took the watch from his wrist and threw it into the swimming pool. A lady then walked up to him wearing a white bikini with matching stilettos. 'He was getting rather hot. Now, where were we?'

I was more nervous going into work the next morning than I had ever been before. I had hardly slept due to all of the possible outcomes which had been swimming around in my head for most of the night. I was weary but I knew I had to keep going. The trees, the wildlife, and even the wind seemed to stand still. Other employees were walking into work in the usual way but I was the only one who knew something big was going to go down. That day was Judgement Day and by the end everything would be different.

Initially though I had to avoid Heavyside. I knew he would be out to get me from now on. I kept my head down and walked as quickly as I could into the relative safety of my office. When I shut the door behind me though something seemed different. It was as if it already belonged to someone else. I stood for a moment and looked out at the familiar tree. The sun was beginning to reach the top leaves and the shadows were dancing upon the grass. If I ignored the ugly office building that surrounded it on all sides, it actually looked beautiful. A snapshot of nature encapsulated within a corporate world. The tree never touched the buildings and the buildings never touched the tree, and yet still both were able to exist in harmony.

During the night I had remembered the close shave that sending an email from a bogus account had caused. I needed to find a way to get the file to McTaggart without him knowing who it was from. I spent the rest of the morning thinking up clever technical solutions which I then rejected for one reason or another. By lunchtime I had exhausted every single possibility that I could think of. The only thing for it was to fall back on to the lo-tech solution. The only way that I could be absolutely sure that McTaggart read this information was to somehow put it directly in front of him.

McTaggart was rarely in his office at the site, in fact he was rarely in the country, but after checking his online diary I could tell that the first bit of luck had gone my way. It looked as though he was busy all day but at least he was around. All I had to do was find a way of getting the paperwork on to his desk.

I walked up to the top floor and wandered the corridors of power looking for his office. I had only ever been up there once before and that was by accident. It was as if I had walked inadvertently into another company. The carpets were thicker, the doors were made of a different wood and even the smell was different. There was no beige being transmitted from here. Small coffee tables were placed in the alcoves with vases full of floral displays, original canvassed artwork was hung on the walls instead of the corporate prints that were everywhere else, and there was a hush that I had never experienced before at RC.

I was intimidated but pressed on regardless. All I had to do was find his office and, wait for it to be empty, before placing the folder that I had printed out that morning on his desk. The whole operation was straightforward.

It was not long before I was stood outside a heavy oak door with a brass plaque on the outside reading, 'Hamish McTaggart - CFO'. I knocked but, due to the door being so heavy and the carpet absorbing any level of sound, it was unclear whether there had been an answer or not. I turned the handle and slowly pushed the door open. There was no sound of anyone talking so I opened the door further and put my head through the gap.

'Hello?' said a female voice suddenly.

'Oh, um, hello,' I said as I fell through the remaining gap out of surprise. 'You made me jump.'

'Can I help you?' she asked. The lady was in her

mid-forties, immaculately dressed in a red suit, and a wonderfully kind face.

'Um,' I had no idea what to say. She was smiling at me and I was tempted to give her the file. 'Where am I?' I asked stupidly, given that I had just seen a great big plaque on the outside of the door.

'This is Hamish McTaggart's office, I am Hamish McTaggart's personal assistant and through there is Hamish McTaggart's private office.'

'Ah.' I suppose I could have given her the file to leave on his desk and at least he would never have seen me, but that would have been too easy. 'So, this isn't HR then?'

'No, this is definitely not HR. Would you like me to help you find somewhere if you're lost?'

'Ha, no. Bye.' I quickly turned around and almost sprinted out of the office. I rushed back along the corridor and descended the stairs at the end as if all of the oxygen had been sucked out of the air. As my feet landed on the floor below I breathed in as deeply as I could. Still panting, and ashamed of my cowardice, I walked all the way back to my office on the ground floor to collapse in a heap.

It would have been easier to have left the file with his PA but I definitely could not see myself ever meeting her voluntarily ever again. I would have to think of another plan and I went back in to his online diary to see where else McTaggart would be that day. Luckily it showed that I had one more chance to deliver the file. The Long-Service Awards dinner was at five o'clock in the Restaurant and I knew that McTaggart was definitely going to be there because he was down to be presenting the awards.

Chapter 30

The long-service awards dinner was a memorable moment in the life of an employee of RC. If you had worked at the company for twenty years then you were invited to share a five-star evening of entertainment, with a board member of RC being present. Each member of the board would take it in turns to do their duty and represent RC.

The employee would receive a small token of appreciation from RC to recognise their service and made to feel special for at least one night. The employees would come from various different departments and would rarely know each other but they all had their loyalty in common. Fewer of these evenings took place at RC in the modern day as experience was replaced with cost effectiveness. It was another indicator of the changing corporate world but one that the likes of Hamish McTaggart would be oblivious to.

That afternoon I had dug out an executive looking black folder and placed my printed evidence within it. I would simply wait for McTaggart to turn up and then slide the folder into his bag. It was completely foolproof and for the rest of the afternoon I went for a long walk in the sunshine before getting ready for the main event.

The Restaurant was connected to the main staff canteen but as an employee you were rarely given the opportunity to eat in there. It was a lot smaller and the food was of a much higher quality. The long-service awards were usually held somewhere larger but there were only thirty-five people being honoured that evening. The tables had to be pushed around the side to accommodate as much standing room as possible for the pre-meal canapés and the room unfortunately ended up resembling a British Legion Social Club.

I had arrived ten minutes earlier than the start time so that I could be sure to notice when McTaggart entered. I hid myself behind an outside staircase with a clear view of the entrance. This time I stood with my back to a wall to prevent any unwelcome interruptions from Heavyside and his gang. I dared not move although my heart was pumping viciously and sending vibrations through my entire body. Gradually the people began to arrive and I was glad to see nobody there that I knew. I needed to be anonymous so that I could be in and out as quickly as possible.

McTaggart finally walked up to the restaurant about

ten minutes late. He had the walk of a man who was in control even if his body looked like a giant swelling. I made a mental note of the bag he was carrying (an executive flight case), as he sauntered past my hiding place unaware of the danger that lurked behind. After waiting a couple more minutes to make sure that he was comfortably settled inside, I summoned up some courage from a reserve that I was previously unaware of, and followed him.

Once inside the restaurant, I could see that people were beginning to talk to each other and it was already quite crowded. I smiled politely to a few people who caught my eye but made sure that I kept moving, the last thing I needed was a conversation. There were not that many people crowded in to the small place but I could not see McTaggart anywhere. He was a large man and one that would definitely have stood out. I started to panic and wondered if he had somehow left already; perhaps he had just turned up to send his apologies. I had just decided to walk around the room once more when suddenly he appeared from the toilets at the far end of the room. He walked confidently through the crowds, nodding politely, and every person stopped what they were doing as soon as he drew level with them. He had a fantastic presence and I suddenly wondered, only half-jokingly, whether he had ever ordered anyone to be killed.

He finally stopped moving after approaching a bald man in his late forties. They seemed to know each other because they shook hands and began to laugh almost immediately. The temperature was rising because there were so many people squeezed into such a small room and McTaggart removed his coat. Folding it over his arm, he moved to his left and placed it on top of the case that I had seen him come in with. After a further exchange with "mystery bald man", he laughed once again, and gracefully turned to join another conversation behind him.

During all of this activity I had been moving around the edge of the crowd like a shark waiting for its prey. I now moved nearer to where his bag and coat sat unattended, and waited to see whom he would talk to next. This time he chose a lady in her sixties who was wearing glasses and had her hair tied up on the top of her head in a bun. He had his back to the case and this was my moment to strike. I reached inside my jacket and pulled out the folder that I had secretly been carrying all along. I bent down, hidden by the crowd, and as quickly as I could, I unzipped the front pocket and poked the folder inside. It was too big to be zipped up again and part of it stuck out the top a little, but it was definitely in there, and at least it would be even more noticeable when he picked up his bag.

I stood up with relief and allowed myself a smile of satisfaction before looking to see if anyone was watching. For once I was thankful for my non-existent charisma and not a soul had noticed anything. As I headed back towards the door a wave of doubt past over me. In those situations the best course of action is always to keep going forward but on this occasion I stopped and looked backwards.

One of the table service staff was making last minute checks to the tables. He was only a young man, maybe eighteen, and the very last candle at the end of the table had gone out. He was eager to please and so reached into his pocket to pull out a lighter, hoping to spark the candle back up before his superiors could see. Just as the candle jumped back into life the young man was nudged by a particularly heavy-set woman with a blonde perm. He lunged forward, knocking the candle out of its base. It rolled over and over towards the edge of the table and then, as if in slow motion, it fell directly on to McTaggart's flight case. The case was made of sterner stuff though and there seemed to be no damage. The boy picked up the still lit candle and, as he was returning it to the table, it brushed past the edge of the folder poking out of the front pocket. The young man was unaware of this development and continued to return the candle securely to its base.

I was stood by the door unable to decide what to do for the best. I was the only one that could see the fire emitting from the front pocket of the case but if I intervened then McTaggart would know who had left him the folder. I stood there watching as the flames grew higher, they began to lick the edges of the tablecloth and soon they began to climb up to the table. I watched it rapidly worsen and desperately resisted the urge to sound the alarm.

Thankfully the lady with the perm noticed that her legs were getting warmer and happened to glance down. She shrieked, which made everyone else look around and then a gentleman with a monocle grabbed a fire extinguisher from next to him and began spraying indiscriminately. After about a minute and, a gallon of foam being shot out of the canister, the man was satisfied that he had smothered the fire. The room went silent and McTaggart walked up to his case to inspect the damage.

Only one side of the black case was visible through the mountain of foam. The silk-lined Armani coat, which had been so carefully draped over the top, was now completely ruined. McTaggart stared at the devastation and coolly decided on the best course of action.

'I'm very sorry, Sir,' said the waiter who had suddenly become ashen-faced.

'Someone clear this mess up and rescue what you can from the debris,' ordered McTaggart with a flick of the wrist.

Three members of the restaurant staff jumped in to help and within another couple of minutes the foam had been cleared up. The coat was ruined but the contents of the bag had remained surprisingly intact, all except for the folder obviously that had been sticking out of the front pocket. The folder was so badly burnt, and then water damaged, that McTaggart could not even recognise what it was. He ordered for it to be thrown in the bin and the rest of the stuff to be put somewhere for safe-keeping, his PA would collect them at some point.

I stormed out of the door I had been stood next to throughout the drama. All of that work, all of that time and all of those dreams, wasted in a few minutes of madness. I stood outside for a moment kicking stones as hard as I could when suddenly the door opened again and McTaggart came flying furiously down the steps.

'What a bunch of fucking idiots,' I heard him say as a black Mercedes approached. The chauffeur's window slid down and the back door automatically opened as McTaggart fell into the comfortable black leather. The driver's window gently slid up again and the car silently pulled away.

I had to think quickly. I pushed my hand deep into my pocket and felt the smooth surface of the pen-drive nestled at the bottom. Without considering all of the consequences, I jumped out from the shadows and ran as quickly as I could to my car. It was thankfully not parked too far away so by the time I had started the engine and driven out to the main site road, I could still see the Mercedes's lights in the distance.

I cornered the last bend on the site road and saw the barriers lift up for McTaggart. I squeezed my foot down on the accelerator and the needle shot forward. I was approaching sixty miles per hour when the gate started on its downward motion. I knew that James Bond would not let up now and nor would I. He would end up taking the top of his Aston Martin clean off and leaving the remains of the gate spinning on the road. In reality it was not as exciting. My car carried on speeding towards the exit and I held my breath as I drew level with the gate, but nothing happened, I easily slid under the gate and then bounced on to the country road that led away from the site.

I had no idea what I was doing anymore and worst of all I had started acting on my instincts. If I was a trained killer then those instincts would have served me well but I had been an office worker. All of the sane voices in my head were telling me to stop but an obsessive maniac was currently telling them all to sit down, shut up, and if one of them even dared to breathe then he would cut their arms off. I was under the complete control of this man and as my eyes focussed on the car in front I felt the adrenaline enhancing all of my senses. The rest of the world disappeared into a blur and the only thing that mattered to me at that point was McTaggart.

Chapter 31

I had seen enough spy films, probably too many, to know that I had to keep a safe distance behind and be careful not to make it look too obvious. This is exactly what I did. The longer I followed McTaggart and, his shiny black car, the more I was able to calm down and think about what I was doing. I began the arduous challenge of convincing myself that this was still the right thing to do. Why does self-doubt always creep in just at the very last point before no return?

I reasoned to myself that it was perfectly normal to be following the CFO of RC to wherever he was going. On the balance of probabilities he was probably just going home and, although I had no idea of exactly where that was, I knew it had to be relatively close. Once he had gone inside, and the driver had left, I would simply deliver the pen drive through the letterbox with a small note attached.

To make myself feel better I compared it to any other work errand, the only difference being that I was doing it away from work. I continued to follow the

Mercedes as it passed effortlessly through the country lanes. Gradually the countryside began to be replaced by more concrete and eventually we had driven into the depths of the city.

Our route took us through the industrial warehouses and disused mills that stood guard over the urban heartland within, the poorer districts that were full of poverty and decay, the newly fashionable Bohemian section with its fancy bars and galleries, and eventually the business district loomed high in front of us. The mirrored walls reflecting the black Mercedes like a car advert. The better restaurants were beginning to attract the city workers in their suits meeting to discuss the events of the day.

The black car continued past all of this and then, all of a sudden, it turned surprisingly in to a quiet side street. The road, that was only just wide enough for two cars to pass each other, had been forgotten by the urban regeneration surrounding it.

McTaggart's car temporarily lit the street and, in this brief time, it was clear to see that it was empty. I knew that if I followed, it would be obvious, so I parked just past the turning and quickly continued the hunt on foot. McTaggart's car was parked on the left hand side but the black windows made it impossible to see if he was still in there when I walked back to the corner. I crossed to the other side of the main road so that I could still spy on the car but make it look as if I were waiting for someone else.

After about five minutes, and also a moment when I thought I was going to be mugged, I finally saw the backdoor open. McTaggart appeared in the darkened street and, after scanning both directions carefully, he walked towards an uninviting doorway immediately beside the car. He walked in and a few moments later the Mercedes reversed back down the street to join the steady flow of traffic on the main road.

I crossed the street from where I had been stood and walked towards the point where McTaggart had disappeared. On the right hand-side there was a conveniently disused doorway that offered me some cover. I could hear the faint sound of the city in the background, as the cars rushed by and the occasional shout, but in the midst of all of this noise, the alley was almost silent except for a crisp packet being pushed along the gutter by the wind.

Somehow there were a few businesses which still stood proudly along its ancient edges, baring testament to the endurance of their owners and to better days gone by. The fronts looked as though they had not been changed for fifty years and the combination of dirt, and deteriorating paintwork, made it hard to imagine any of them having any customers that were still alive.

There was "Isaac Stein & Sons, Jeweller and Purveyor of Rare Gems", who had three watches, four rings and a brooch displayed haphazardly on crème silk in a grubby little window. "B.J. Martin's Collectibles and Miscellany" was painted in gold writing on black wood above another doorway; and a sex shop simply called "XXX" was flashing in red neon towards the corner of the main street. The only other establishment to be found on Little Hilton Street was the most joyless looking florist in the entire world.

The forest green paintwork had been transformed through the years of dirt and smog until it was now nearly black, and the white writing was more of a dark shade of grey, as it whispered its name to passers by - "Lily's to Die For". It was hard to picture anyone wanting to buy flowers at the place, but there appeared to be a dim light coming from behind the window. I was fascinated by the glow this emitted and was staring at it like a transfixed moth when, out of the gloom, the florist's door opened. A rectangle of light shone on to the uneven stone pavement and a man in a suit carrying a briefcase walked out towards the main road. The door closed just as quickly and I watched as the man rounded the corner and joined the city tides.

I waited, hidden in the doorway, for about half an

hour and saw two more men leaving from the florist's darkened doorway, and another man entering. They were all of a similar age, somewhere between forty-five and sixty, dressed in tailored dark suits, and looking suspiciously about them.

I started to become restless and my nerve was disappearing fast. I wrote a note on the back of a flyer that had been blown into the doorway where I stood. It simply read, "The truth that you need to know about Eagle".

I was going to wait until McTaggart emerged and follow him again because it would be too obvious if I approached him on the pavement. But as I stood watching the Florists, the curiosity eventually became too much and I decided to come out from my hiding place.

I walked slowly towards the mysterious shop, carefully looking around to see if I was being watched, and then I was standing in the doorway. The door itself was wooden panelled, in the same dark, dingy green colour, with a small brass plate next to the handle. A Greek symbol for Omega was stamped into the plate. I tried the handle and to my surprise it opened.

There were buckets of flowers situated around the floor, and a long wooden counter, with a large panel of wrapping paper at its centre. The interior looked exactly as I would expect a Florists to look, and yet, this was the last thing I had expected to see. I was unclear of exactly what I *had* been expecting but as I was walking around the floor, looking at the items for sale, there was nothing that looked out of the ordinary. There was even an aroma in the air that could only have been caused by fresh flowers. I peered in to one particular bucket of red carnations when suddenly a noise from the back of the shop scared the living daylights out of me.

It was a whirring, mechanical noise and after a few seconds I realised that it was an elevator. I hid between the counter and some ready-made bouquets, just in time for the shop to be illuminated in an orange light. From where I was crouched I could see the source of the light coming from one of those old lifts with a caged, metal gate at the opening. A man appeared in the shop casting a shadow that stretched all the way on to the inside of the front window. Once again he was in his fifties carrying a briefcase and, after quickly running a comb through his hair, he left through the front door.

I jumped out from my hiding place and ran towards the lift noticing that the gate had not been closed properly. There were three buttons in the lift; G, 1, and Ω, and I instinctively pressed the Omega button knowing that this had to be the floor I needed.

The elevator erupted in a cacophony of cogs and

pulleys, and rattled itself up the antique shaft. I immediately regretted it and was sure that someone was going to be waiting for me at the top. I had no idea what I was getting in to and it suddenly dawned on me how stupid I was. Why was I even here? I was definitely past the point of no return. Anything could be at the top of this lift, but I had no time to think of an escape route because just as my anxiety levels threatened to cause a heart attack, the lift jolted to a stop.

The good news, on looking through a yellowy window at head height, was that no one was waiting for me. I opened the gate and then peeked through the crack in the door. I had never seen a place like this in my life. It had incredibly high ceilings, probably fifteen feet at least, and was decorated to the highest quality. There were gilt framed paintings lining a thickly carpeted corridor and the lift, that I was in, was one of only two doors along it.

I tiptoed about forty yards to the large white, Georgian door at the far end. I stood there and listened for a while, my heartbeat thumping in my chest. I waited until I was sure that it was quiet and then I slowly turned the handle. Through the inch, that I dared to open it, I could see a small room and from there I could see another much larger room beyond. The first room seemed to be a cloakroom and the larger room, from what I could tell, appeared to be a bar. I realised that I was either in a brothel or a secret club.

I pushed the door open a bit wider and satisfied myself that the first room was empty. I looked for another hiding place while I was still at the door and an antique desk offered the perfect shelter. I leapt behind it like a puma and crouched down out of sight. The adrenaline-fuelled madman was back in control of my actions and my senses had become almost feral.

The new vantage point offered a fantastic view of the next room. There were seven or eight small round tables that I could see, but there were probably more in the other direction, and each of them was accompanied by two leather chesterfields. Of the tables that I could see; there were five men sitting on their own, four of whom were reading newspapers, and one using an iPad. They sat in silence, except for the occasional, gentle rustling of paper and for a moment I was mesmerised by the scene of calmness in front of me. It was the complete opposite of how I was feeling at the time.

Unfortunately, McTaggart was not one of the five men that I could see but I had no doubt that he would be beyond the door somewhere. I was wondering how I would be able to get a better view of the next room when suddenly, a steward came into view and walked up to the man sitting at the table nearest to the door.

'Excuse me, Sir,' the steward whispered, 'Mr McTaggart has requested an audience with you.'

'Yes, very good,' uttered the man sat in the chair. I noticed as he spoke that he was slightly older than some of the others there, and his immaculately groomed grey hair was combed in a side parting. He folded his newspaper neatly in half, then in half again, and placed it carefully on the table in front of him. He wore heavy-framed, black glasses that made it hard for me to see his eyes.

'Hello, David,' said McTaggart respectfully as he approached the table.

'Good evening, Hamish,' said the grey haired gentleman in a softly spoken accent with a hint of Irish. 'Please take a seat. How are we?'

'Very well,' said McTaggart as he sat down and straightened out his trouser legs, 'we have had some excellent news from Beijing.'

'Splendid, splendid Hamish.' He continued to look directly at McTaggart and spoke with an even tone that was devoid of emotion.

'And you'll be glad to hear that the message that was leaked has now been dealt with,' said McTaggart looking around the room nervously, his eyes only momentarily glancing at the other man before darting away again.

'Come now, Hamish. You have not sat with me just so that you can talk of these trivialities. You would like to ask me for something. No? If I required a progress update then I would have come and asked you, but instead your presence here is proof that you require something of me. Please dear boy, get it off your chest.'

'Yes, of course, Sir. I would like to explain where I'm up to with our agreement.' The man's face did not move. 'Yes, well, I actually believe that it's going to start delivering soon. I was with them today and that chap I put in charge seems to have actually done something.'

'We have been through this Hamish,' said the man softly. 'The project must fail. The market expects a success and I have some very persuasive business partners that have invested in a failure. Is this all you have to tell me?'

'Sir, with all respect I don't think you understand the gravity of what I'm saying. The project looks to be on track despite my best efforts to impair it. I don't know what else I can do.'

'Hamish, it is you that is having trouble understanding. My business partners are not in the habit of being disappointed. You must make sure that this project fails.'

'How can I? It's too late to divert.'

'Sometimes a runaway train cannot be diverted,

sometimes a runaway train must be exploded.'

'How?'

'I meet with my associates in a week. Good news must have been delivered to me by then. I am sorry Hamish but sometimes it's better to put an animal out of its misery than to keep it performing tricks.' The man kept his eyes focussed on the RC CFO until McTaggart looked away. 'I think that is all then, yes?' Hamish nodded reluctantly. 'Good Evening,' and with this he picked up his newspaper, glanced over at the steward and began to read again.

The steward appeared at the elbow of McTaggart implying that the meeting was over. He rose from his chair and walked elegantly away from the table, directly towards the cloakroom.

I stayed hidden behind the desk. McTaggart was obviously angry as he entered the anteroom; he was shaking his head and his lips were moving as if the anger inside was too much to constrain. He stopped and looked distractedly at the floor just in front of the desk I was crouched behind. I held my breath and my skin began to tingle. Suddenly, he turned around and reached for his coat which had been hung on a rail along with several other identical black coats. He was just about to put it on, when he had second thoughts and decided to hang it back up again. He turned around and it looked as though he was going to make a scene, but instead he walked briskly to the only other door in the chamber. It was obvious, when he opened it, that it was the bathroom.

This was the chance I had been waiting for. I sprang from my hiding place and charged over to the coat that I had just seen him pick up. I put the pen drive and, the note that I had written before, into one of the side pockets. I then immediately left through the same door I came in by and ran down the corridor to the elevator. I pulled the metal door open and thankfully it was still on my floor. It surged into action and took me back down to the florists below. In the orange glow, I could see that the Mercedes was waiting outside the door.

I dived down behind the counter again and waited for the elevator to go back up and collect McTaggart. The time seemed to last forever but eventually I could hear him coming. The elevator opened and he walked through the store in four long strides before yanking the front door open. Through the dirty window I could just make out the shape of McTaggart on the pavement. He paused before he climbed in to his car and was clearly turning something over in his hand. He took one last glance at the florists before disappearing from view.

After about five minutes, I mustered enough courage to come out from my hiding place and walked as casually as possible out of the shop. The Mercedes had long gone and the street reverted back to its quiet decay. I felt as though I had definitely been through enough to change the mind of one man and now, finally, I was satisfied.

Chapter 32

The room was dark, I had been sitting in an armchair all night and staring at a blank wall. The events of the last week were spinning around and around in my head making me feel dizzy and it was impossible to rest. I started to think that perhaps I had taken it a bit too far, maybe I had lost it. It was hard to know if I was in control or not, although I definitely began to feel more positive after emptying the first bottle of merlot. It was the fifth glass, however, which finally sent me over the line.

I started to feel proud of what I had achieved. I had saved the people on the project team, whether they wanted to be saved or not. Sitting in the dark was my moment of calm before the expectant storm. I was finally the people's champion, the working-class hero and tomorrow would be the day where I would be lifted aloft by the crowds. I was the saviour of the corporate world.

'You're an idiot,' said Jane as she walked into the room and immediately turned the light on. I had explained the sequence of events to her earlier and, at the time she had looked at me in disbelief, but obviously now she had had time to think about it. 'Why are you sitting in the dark? You're not getting carried away again, are you?'

'No,' I lied, 'just thinking.'

'Why did you do it, Ben? Did you not think that it was mental?'

'Well, yeah, I did but I just kept going anyway.'

I thought she would have been proud of me.

'You always say I should take things into my own hands more,' I said.

'Yeah, not like this though. I meant for you to maybe have a meeting with someone, not follow them and break in to their private club.'

'You should have seen it, Jane. It was really nice. There were these pictures that looked original and...'

'I don't care if it was the Sistine Chapel, you shouldn't have been in there. What if you had been caught?'

'How could I?' I said scoffing at the very idea. 'I wasn't even seen by anyone. I was hiding in the shadows, invisible to the human eye.'

'Ok then, Bruce Lee, what if you've been caught on CCTV at the club. A place like that is bound to have cameras especially if it's as nice as you say it is. God, even bingo halls have security cameras. What about your handwriting on the note? It's obvious that it's come from someone on the team. What about the pen drive? Is that traceable? Fingerprints? Did you have your name on it? At least you've not been in trouble recently, I guess they won't suspect you straight away.'

'Well, ah, actually I did get into a bit of trouble with that eagle.'

'Fantastic. Do you realise that you could be actually arrested for this? What's going on in your head?'

'I just want to get out, Jane. I had to follow him so that I could tell him.'

'No, you didn't *have* to follow him. You followed him because you're a nutter. You're obsessed with it. You followed him because you're deranged. You followed him because you're deluded in your own fantasy world. You've been like this since you got back from New York. I don't know what's happened to you. You've got to let it go, Ben. I mean it. Just let it go. What will be, will be. This is ridiculous.'

She stopped talking and started looking at the floor, slowly shaking her head. 'I was completely behind you telling someone about all the corporate crap that was going on, but this is stupid Ben. There are so many things that could go wrong and you don't even know if he's going to see it.'

'He will,' I said. 'I'm sure he will. How's he going to miss it?'

'And if he does? Will he understand it?'

'Ah, come on, Jane, you're just looking at the shit side. Oh, by the way, there's something else that happened. I didn't tell you. I overheard him being told by someone else that he had to end an agreement, or something. It was hard to hear, but this other guy seemed to be threatening him.'

'What if you've got mixed up in something big? I saw a film the other day where Tom Cruise got involved with the mafia without realising it.'

'Bloody hell, Jane. Listen, I did my best and it's done now. We'll just have to wait and see.'

'Ok then. But you're still an idiot, and when our kids have to visit you in prison you can tell them yourself what an idiot you've been.' She kissed me on the forehead and walked out, leaving me alone again.

Even when I finally went to bed, I could not sleep and instead I stayed awake all night, staring at the ceiling and the reflection of the street lamp as it shone on to the top of the wardrobe. At the time it had felt like I was being thorough and professional but I had not seen any of the dangers which had been there all along. If this was an episode of Columbo, he would only be able to get through half a cigar before he had wrapped it all up.

They say that the darkest hour is just before dawn but a good while after dawn my mood was still dark. I was dreading the journey into work, and especially the long, slow walk up the corridor to my office. I could imagine the voices whispering as I walked past the other offices, and finally, when I arrived at my door I would see the committee waiting for me with their judging eyes. Savage would be at the front with a muzzle on, being held back with a lead around his neck by McTaggart.

The worry was too much to bear and, before I arrived at work, I went to sit in a cafe for half an hour just to delay the inevitable. When I finally reached the office though there were no hate mobs, no whispers, no welcome committee and no hangman's noose swinging from the tree in the courtyard. It was disappointingly normal. The only thing I noticed was that Savage was missing.

The next two hours were spent nervously biting my nails, looking out of the window and listening out for any noises coming from the corridor. It went on forever. I paced up and down like an expectant father, which in my office meant that I walked two steps one way and two steps back.

As the time went by I had to assume that the lack of fireworks perhaps meant that nothing had happened. Jane might have been right, McTaggart had probably not seen it, or instead he had thrown it straight in the bin. After about an hour the phone rang and I jumped so high that I clattered my knee against the underside of the desk, but the call turned out to be a false alarm, just a work call from someone that assumed I cared.

It was about half eleven when suddenly I heard someone running up the corridor towards my office. I held my breath, praying that it was something else but as the door flung open I knew that this was it - it was on. I had only ever heard one other person run along a corridor before at RC and at the time they were going to be sick. The girl standing in my doorway was definitely not going to be sick but she did look as though she might pass out.

She was panting and trying to get her words out as quickly as possible. 'Savage… wants us… to… meet in the… big meeting room… oh god… as soon as… we can. Go. I'm telling… people.'

'What's it about?'

'Don't know… but… he said it's urgent.' She left just as quickly and I could hear her bursting into another office not far away.

This was it then. I took a deep breath and made my

way as calmly as possible towards the big meeting room. It was warm outside and I was sweating from everywhere, it was even running into my eyes. Trying to keep that much sweat under control was a challenge, especially in a way that would not make me look like the guiltiest man in the line-up.

I was one of the last to arrive, probably because my office was one of the furthest away. Savage was stood up at the front already and was obviously just about to speak. I slid in towards the back and tried not to look anybody in the eye.

'Right,' started Savage, 'you inept bunch of tossers. I'll keep this short and sweet. Most of you will probably agree that this project has been the worst part of your entire life. It's not been a bed of fucking roses for me either but we've given it a go. Now, something's happened between yesterday afternoon and this morning which has made us go from the great white hope to no fucking hope. If any of you were at the conference yesterday then just assume that it was all a pack of lies.'

He paused to take a swig of coffee and sniff loudly.

'I've just come from a meeting with Hamish McTaggart where he explained a number of things that not even I fucking knew. We've been sabotaged by some other fucker who hasn't had the balls to do it to our face. Hamish has declared that the project is out of control and has no chance of ever delivering even a fucking letter. So, that's it, the project's over and we've all got to go home.'

'What about our jobs?' said a plumpish lady at the front, clearly shocked..

'If you've got a permanent contract then you're ok. That was the one thing I got Hamish to agree to. You'll be looked after. If you're a contractor then you're on your own.'

'What do we do with all our stuff?' asked the same woman.

'I don't fucking know. I've just come from the meeting. I've had four cups of double shot americanos so far and to be honest, I'm feeling a little wired. Go home for the day and we'll sort everything out later. That's all I've got to say right now.' He pushed past the people that were in his way and stormed out in to the corridor. Someone came out of their office about ten yards in front of his path and must have felt like they were in Pamplona.

Everyone in the meeting room was still in a state of shock as I looked around at them all. For the first time I realised that the imagined, grateful faces of the villagers who I had saved from the evil Sheriff of Nottingham, were nothing like the distraught faces in this meeting room. The uncertainty had led to panic and Savage's gentle approach had not helped to stem the tears. Some of the women were crying, even one of the men, and the room had fallen into a state of abject misery. I was unable to look upon what I had created for a moment longer.

I trudged back to my office and could hear Savage thumping something next door. I went to check, just in case it was a person, and through the small window in the door I could see Savage methodically lifting his head up, then slamming it back down on the top of his desk repeatedly. I walked in thinking that this would be a good moment.

'Are you alright, Rupert?'

'Of course. Never better. How can you tell?'

'Was Hamish McTaggart annoyed?'

'No, do you know what, not really. He almost seemed happy. In fact the bloated, fat, sweaty fucker was even smiling when he told me. Can you believe that? Said something about getting someone off his back. They talk in riddles, that lot. He made no sense to me all morning. He had all of this paper with him, and on every page there was something else that was a nail in the coffin.'

'Did he say where it came from?'

'You're joking, aren't you? Like he's going to tell me who's just shot me in the back. He knows I'd kill them.

No, he said that he didn't know anyway, some gibberish about pennies from heaven. Like I told you, he wasn't making any sense.'

'You know when you said that we'd be looked after, what does that mean? In a mafia way, or…?'

'I wish. No, I mean that we can all choose what we want to do. You're going to get what you want and I'll get what I want. Not that it's really what I want. Do you know, I've worked for this fucking company for thirty-two years and I'm not even being afforded the dignity to leave quietly out of the back door? I'm being marched up on to the roof and being thrown off the fucking thing for all to see.'

'Oh well, at least you'll be alright, that's something.'

'I might be once this coffee's gone through my fucking system. Aaarrgghhh,' he said as he banged his head back down on the desk. I left him to it and went back into my own office.

'Jane?' I said as she picked up the phone.

'Hello?'

'Well, it's happened. It's all over.'

'Just like that? How did it happen?'

'Not sure really. We've just been told.'

'How did everyone else take it?'

'Could be better really, most of the team are crying and Savage is self-harming.'

'What about you?'

'Well, yeah. I think it's all over. I'll know more tomorrow I guess. To be honest it all feels kind of weird. Anyway, I'll be home soon, I'm not hanging around, it could be like Lord of the Flies in a minute, plus I don't want to be a witness to whatever Savage is just about to do to himself.' I put the phone down and grabbed my jacket.

I looked around at the office and I finally began to smile. I may have caused a little damage, perhaps affected the lives of people who thought they were happy, but how was I to make an omelette without breaking some eggs? I looked out upon the tree and at last it seemed to be smiling too, after all, we had been through a lot together.

Chapter 33

A mass of casualties were propped up against the edges of the path as I stumbled along, anguish and disappointment burnt into their eyes. Clothes were ripped, cuts were bleeding, and injured limbs were being cradled. These people had used all of the energy they could muster to drag themselves as far as the path. They waited there to be rescued by the clean up operation that would eventually arrive to make sense of this madness.

The fact that it was all over had been announced via loudspeakers about thirty minutes before. A collective sigh could be heard coming from the whole site when it finally came. The desperation turned immediately to disappointment and the pain began to take hold. I saw grown men dropping to their knees with exhaustion, unable to carry their bodies a single step further.

We were warned that gangs had started patrolling the remote areas of the site, looking for employees who had already captured a golden envelope. Innocent people were being attacked and searched on the spot.

On my way back through the desolation I came across three such cases, one of whom was a lady in her sixties who had tried to run for it but had been hit with a rock fired from a makeshift slingshot. Blood was covering her face but worse still was the look of helplessness that she had in her eyes. I decided to lift her up and support her back towards the path where it was deemed safe. Halfway there she turned on me with the shard of a broken Lucozade bottle. It took me by surprise and as I instinctively stepped back so she fell to the ground and began to sob. The tragedy was unbearable, but after that, I tried to block out the cries of the wounded.

The path that ran through the woods was full of people trying to find their way home. The ones who were unable to go on could only fall back on to the edges and wait. The announcement had said that help would eventually be deployed and this was what they were waiting for. Those who could walk though, were struggling to get out of the woods and to the relative safety of the main site road. This was where I was headed too.

I had been fortunate enough to have found my golden envelope after an hour, but for everyone else, the search continued for at least another hour and a half after that. I had decided not to risk swimming back across the lake in case a group were waiting for me on the other side, so I remained on my island with the tree and the upturned boat.

The boat, after careful inspection, proved to have a hole in the bottom and was useless as a lake-faring vessel. Instead I used it to hide under, the hole being a perfect height to spy upon any potential intruders. I was just about able to hear each of the announcements as they were read out across the site. The gap between 700 being found and 800, took about twenty minutes, but the last 200 took over an hour. In the time I spent under the boat, the only distraction I had was the golden envelope in my hand. I must have looked at it a hundred times to check that it was real and I began to memorise the words written on the golden ticket inside.

Congratulations. You are being made redundant.

You will receive the full package of terms and conditions that you are entitled to, as per your contract of work. Deliver this ticket, with your ID card, to the most convenient security lodge. We recognise the value you have given to Rannheiser Components and wish you the very best for the future.

Clever sparks don't litter

Rannheiser Components are an Employer of Choice

After the last of the envelopes had been found I could sense, by the urgency of the announcements, that the intensity of the violence had increased to unacceptable levels. I knew that I would have to be careful to get out of the site in one piece. I lifted the boat up and rolled out from my hiding place. All around the lake I could see people limping towards the main site road. There was no other way that you could get out and so they began the exodus.

I realised that I would have to do something with the envelope. There was no way that I could hold it in my hand and expect to avoid attention. I remembered some wise advice that my Grandad had once given me about pickpockets. 'Put it in your pants, son.' So, that was what I did.

I slid quietly into the water again, the temperature was much colder the second time around, and I gently made my way to the other side looking out for anyone that could be waiting. I was lucky and the only people who saw me were not strong enough to do anything about it.

Once I made it as far as the main site road, I knew that the worst of the danger was probably behind me and I started to relax more. I still pretended that I was one of the wounded though because I had seen a few smiley people being punched in the face just for smiling.

I joined in with the slow march back from the front, avoiding eye contact and remaining as miserable as I could, even though the closer I reached to the perimeter fence the happier inside I became.

The main site road travelled right up to the perimeter fence and then ran parallel alongside it until it reached the security lodge. On the other side of the fence you could see violent outbreaks occurring as the golden envelopes polarised people's emotions. Speaker announcements kept reminding people to move away from the site as soon as they were cleared through security.

Finally, the gates appeared in front of us and the security lodge resembled a General's tent on a battlefield. There were armed guards at the sentry point and papers were being checked for admission. All of the people I was walking with were heading straight out of the open gates knowing that they would have to return on Monday. The majority of these were older and most of them were women, and for the first time it crossed my mind that the system may not be that fair.

I walked up to one of the armed guards at the door of the security lodge.

'Envelope?' he said loud enough so that everyone nearby looked around at me.

I thrust my hand into my wet pants and pulled out a

damp, but perfectly valid, golden envelope. He stood aside and I was allowed in.

There was a calmness within the lodge that was not present outside and the registration process was running like clockwork. Firstly, you had to show your envelope again, then you joined a queue to show your ID card. There were four people on computers typing in your ID number and printing out the terms of your contract. You were then passed down the line where a senior manager signed your redundancy papers and confirmed that you were free. You left through a side door which led directly out on to the other side of the fence.

I stood for a moment, watching the various emotions on display and an overwhelming surge of relief knocked me to the floor. The tears came to my eyes and I could feel the weight of the redundancy contract pressing against my flesh.

'Ben, Ben,' shouted Dave who was running through the debris towards me. 'Are you alright, Ben? I guess you didn't find one either.' Dave had no shirt on and his nose looked broken but apart from that he seemed cheerful enough. 'That was crazy. Did you get the impression that people wanted to leave? Wow, who would've thought? Look at everyone.'

'I got one, Dave,' I said quietly.

'What?'

'I said I've got one.'

'No,' he looked gutted initially. *'No way, oh well, well done. Brilliant. Good for you. I knew you would. Where was it?'*

'On that island in the middle of the lake.'

'Good one. I couldn't find one anywhere.'

'What happened to your nose?'

'Oh, someone was beating up a guy in a wheelchair so I stepped in.'

'Good for you, mate. What did he do, turn on you?'

'No, it was the twat in the wheelchair who swung at me. He thought I had one of the envelopes. Crazy, the whole thing was madness.'

I looked at him in disbelief. Only Dave, I thought to myself, could get his nose broken by someone in a wheelchair.

'Eh up, lads,' shouted Stretch as he jogged over to us, smiling.

'Oh, here we go, you look happy,' said Dave.

'Cor, that was something else, wasn't it?' he said. *'I'm right up for it now. I haven't had a ruck like that for years. Brilliant.'*

'Where did you find yours?' asked Dave.

'Oh, there was one poking out of a drain cover. I found it right at the beginning but I ended up giving it to

that girl who works on the third floor. Fit. Then I found one just floating around in the middle of the playing field, that was a good one, I picked it up in one fluid motion while I was running. Anyway, I had that one for quite a while but someone knocked me over the head and tried to take it. We had a scrap by the farm and in the end I left him counting his teeth, but for some reason I felt guilty so I went back and gave it to him. Then I found the last one right near the end. It was stuck in a bramble bush in the woods.'

'So, you've got one then?' asked Dave shaking his head at him.

'No, I ended up giving that one to a girl, I think she works in the operations department, anyway it was right near the end and she was desperate. She offered to show me her tits, so I thought that was fair enough.'

'So, you haven't got one then?' I asked.

'No. What's the point? I've been here long enough and I've only got a few years left. It wouldn't seem right, would it? What would I do instead?'

Dave nodded, seemingly understanding Stretch's sentiment.

'Oh well,' I said. 'I guess we're all happy then. I got one by the way.'

'Nice one,' said Stretch smiling.

The three of us stood where we were for a while

longer until we noticed that the grassy area where everyone had collected together was beginning to empty. We started off on the long walk in to town, a pub would be our eventual target. Sadly, there were still some people dotted around who had more than just superficial injuries. St.John's Ambulance were tending to them and making sure they kept their spirits up. We weaved in and out, not wanting to unwittingly trip over one of them.

'Hang on,' said Stretch suddenly. 'Is that Wilks?'

He was pointing to a man that was lying down on the grass, about twenty yards in front of us with a bloodied bandage wrapped around his head.

'I think it is,' said Dave and we jogged over.

'Mate?' said Dave. 'You alright?'

'Urrghhh,' groaned Wilks.

'Come on, we're going to the pub,' said Stretch. 'What's wrong with you?'

'The, er, what do you call it, the, um, ambulance fella told me that I've got concussion.'

'How?' asked Dave.

'I think I fell out of a tree. How many stitches have I got in my head?'

'Don't know, you've got a great bandage wrapped round it.'

'Oh, well I think I've got stitches somewhere up

there. Luckily these blokes that I knew helped me out. I was carried through the security lodge on the back of a bench, they used it as a stretcher.'

'So, you got a ticket then?' I asked.

'Yeah, somehow,' he replied and a smile came to his face.

'Come on,' said Stretch. 'Come with us to the pub. As the eldest here, I say that we all deserve a pint. Up we go.' Stretch grabbed him under one armpit and Dave supported him under the other. Between the two of them, they pulled Wilks to his feet and eventually managed to get him to move forward. I squelched along next to them, my clothes were beginning to mildly chafe but in the circumstances I considered it would be better to keep such a minor inconvenience to myself. The four of us then walked off into the setting sun, each smiling for our own reasons.

I looked behind at the gates. The same gates that I had driven through every day for twelve years. The remnants of a gold envelope blew against the bars and there was no need for me to wake up this time. I turned back and continued walking away, I had no idea where I was going but it had to be better than where I had been.

Epilogue

This summer has gone on forever, apparently it has been one of the longest since records began. It started way back in May and now September has come, yet still we sit outside long into the evening. The fields roll away in all directions meaning that Jane and I can see the kids playing somewhere, usually near the bottom of the dip, right by the blackberry bushes that line the edge of our little kingdom of paradise.

I never used to know what I wanted to do, what the purpose of my life was, but over the last two years I think I have realised something important - there is no overriding purpose to life. The sequence of events that have led me to this place all happened in their own way, and I would never have thought them possible when I was staring at that one tree outside my office window. A single idea has the power to grow into another idea and, if you follow their path, then more ideas will follow after that. The ability to trust in yourself and, to simply go along with the ideas as they come, can change everything. I have no idea where they will take me in five years time, or ten years time, and retirement already seems irrelevant.

Jane and I had an idea once that we would go on holiday, shortly after I left RC. The end had come quite quickly after that last farewell from Savage and the rest of the team had realised, after the shock, that it was probably a good thing that the eagle had not landed. They never did find out that it was me who planted the information on McTaggart, and I never found out why McTaggart wanted it to fail, but sometimes acting on an idea simply makes everything turn out for the best.

Dave and Stretch stayed on and a year later Stretch was able to take his early retirement. Dave is still there although RC have now reduced the redundancy package which means that he now feels trapped for the next ten years, at which point he will be old enough to retire too. Wilks left and apparently now works with Emily, as her boss, although nobody has heard from either of them since.

So, anyway, I had some spare time on my hands after I left and it was the summer after all. We had wanted to go to Cornwall because of the beaches, but everywhere was booked and we ended up going to a farmhouse in Devon instead. I remember that we drove down slightly disappointed because we knew nothing of the place and assumed that boredom would hit us quite quickly.

Instead, after a couple of days, I met the old farmer, called Seth, who lived on the farm next to ours and he invited us over to his farm for a ploughman's lunch. I had trouble understanding him, he was a real countryman, and I was not keen on going to a stranger's house for lunch either. So, I politely declined the offer making up an excuse that we had to go somewhere else instead. Unfortunately the kind, but slightly forgetful, farmer had mentioned it to Jane as well who thought it was a lovely offer and accepted it straight away.

We all trooped down the lane, for about half a mile, until we came to Seth's house. It had a thatched roof, stone walls and looked as though it would have been the perfect country house, about a hundred years before. However, the old windows that showed the ragged yellow curtains behind gave me the impression that his dead wife was probably still sitting in one of the armchairs. Without mentioning this to Jane we carried on following him around the side of the house until we reached a wooden table out the back with all of the lunch laid out upon it. The plot of land that old Seth owned was clear to see. There were a couple of acres of overgrown grass leading down a dip to a blackberry bush and beyond this were orderly, ploughed fields in all directions. As long as you looked out at the fields the view was extraordinary but the poor old farmer's immediate garden was an eyesore.

The lunch looked fantastic and I decided that I may as well make the most of it. The food was all fresh and there was a jug of his homemade apple juice on the table. The kids turned their noses up at the juice so I had to drink both of theirs to save any awkwardness.

By the time Jane practically carried me home the sun had started to go down. I knew the apple juice was a particularly potent scrumpy more or less straightaway but the actual strength of it still came as a surprise. The next day I went for a walk on my own to clear the hangover and started talking to Seth again. This time he showed me the orchard that he had around the other side of the house. Like the rest of the property, the grass was over knee high but there were at least thirty apple trees still standing there. We sat on a wall at the far end and he told me how, years ago, he used to make different types of cider for the village. When his wife died it became too much for him and now he was just drinking through his stock. He also mentioned that he had buried her in the churchyard, which put my mind at rest about the armchair. I went home, after saying my goodbyes, chomping on an apple that I found on the ground where we had sat.

It was two days later when he mentioned that he was going to have to sell the house because it was all beginning to get too much for him to maintain. I sympathised with him and we shared another jug of cider, but by the end of that evening the seeds of a new idea had been sown.

Three months later we were driving down to Devon, behind a removals lorry, with two fighting kids in the backseat and two adults smiling like children in the front.

Since then, we have had to make a few changes to the place. We sorted out the windows and cleaned the house up a lot, but most of the work was done to the outside. The land has been cleared and sown with a number of different vegetables. Jane has become the head gardener and our produce has thrived over the last year. We started to sell what we grew at the market but then decided to build a wooden hut at the side of the house where we now have a farm shop.

I work in the shop most of the day. We have a few tables so that people can come to have a drink and something to eat while they buy their vegetables. It ticks over nicely and allows me to think up new schemes all of the time. One of the early ideas was to learn how to make cider again like the old farmer did. We had all of the materials necessary to start it up again and we were even lucky enough to inherit the old cider press.

The orchard is my main focus now. The ancient

apple trees are now cared for once again and are producing the top quality apples that go in to making the very best cider. One of the brands that we have is called "James' Dream Juice" and is named after my dearly departed friend that inspired it all. It surprisingly won a few awards this year and I often sit out at night to drink a glass to James' memory. We sell it by the barrel, and the bottle, from our little shop but we still have too much to know what to do with. So, I had another idea one day to buy a small catering van and to go around festivals selling the stuff. This new venture is keeping me busy most weekends and, like all of the other business ideas, it is doing far better than I ever expected.

I often sit on the wall, at the back of the orchard, and think about the corporate world where I used to live. I wonder if the anxiety that comes from following the rules, and processes, of that world is so much different to that which is caused by the weather and the earth in this. Of course, in the corporate world you are led to believe that you can control these external forces and the frustration comes from realising the truth.

The trap which threatened to destroy my soul was always in the mind. I had forced myself to stop listening to the ideas which continue to come. Ideas are a natural part of life but, if you stop trusting those ideas or, if you talk yourself out of them before they even have a chance to germinate, let alone fail, then the bars will begin to close down upon you.

So, what I am trying to say, what I have been trying to tell you since the very beginning, is…

… freedom can only come from trusting in your ideas, and…

… believing that they *will* come true.

'Twenty years from now you will be more disappointed by the things that you didn't do than by the ones you did do. So throw off the bowlines. Sail away from the safe harbour. Catch the trade winds in your sails.

Explore. Dream. Discover.' – Mark Twain

Acknowledgments

I'd like to thank the following people for their intelligence, sensitivity, talent, friendship and time; without which this book would not have seen the light of day.

Simon Raine
Lian Trowers
Des Howlett
Amanda Murphy
Phil Roe
Kathy LaViolette
And Maggie Mansfield

Also, a big thanks to Chris, Sid and Jarvo for being there during the writing.

About the Author

Michael J Holley is the author of the comedy novel, The Great Corporate Escape.

He was born in Southampton, England in 1977, and then moved up to Liverpool in the mid-90's to go to university. He started a band and moved across to Manchester where he tried to be a Rock n' Roll Star for quite a while. He now lives in Cowes, on the Isle of Wight, looking out to sea.

His second novel, Plaster Scene, is due out later in 2013.

Please visit his website www.michaeljholley.com

Contact him by email writer@michaeljholley.com

Or follow him on:

Twitter - @mjholleywriter
Facebook - MJHolleyWriter

Thank You

The Great Corporate Escape

by Michael J Holley

Printed in Great Britain
by Amazon.co.uk, Ltd.,
Marston Gate.